THE SPEED OF
SLOW CHANGES

Praise for Sander Santiago

Best of the Wrong Reasons

"I absolutely adored this book, I couldn't put it down. The best friends to strangers to rekindled lovers trope is one of my favorites, and Santiago did it so well…This book will make you laugh and cry and feel so many emotions."
—*QueerBookstagram*

One Verse Multi

"*One Verse Multi* is my favourite kind of sci-fi. It was clever, it was witty, it was insightful…just a glorious time all round!…I LOVED this book from the absolute get-go. I was instantly drawn into the story, and every time I put the book down I was counting down until I could next pick it up again. It was genuinely funny without shying away from big topics and themes, and despite being fantastical felt down-to-earth and grounded…This book is a hidden gem, showcasing science fiction at its best."—*Elementary My Dear*

"Let's talk about representation! One reason I wanted to love this book more than I did is because of how cleverly Santiago works in diverse representation. Santiago himself is a queer, trans BIPOC writer, and so he writes Martin's character with a very authentic voice: Martin is a Black, gay trans man, and a significant part of the book is his self-discovery of polyamorous attraction as well. To be clear, I'm not praising *One Verse Multi* for the way it checks a lot of boxes—that's not what matters to me when it comes to representation. It's the quality that matters here."—*Kara Reviews*

By the Author

Best of the Wrong Reasons

One Verse Multi

The Speed of Slow Changes

THE SPEED OF SLOW CHANGES

by

Sander Santiago

2023

THE SPEED OF SLOW CHANGES

ISBN 13: 978-1-63679-329-0

This Trade Paperback Original Is Published By
Bold Strokes Books, Inc.
P.O. Box 249
Valley Falls, NY 12185

First Edition: February 2023

Credits
Editors: Jerry Wheeler and Stacia Seaman
Production Design: Stacia Seaman
Cover Design by Tammy Seidick

Acknowledgments

Thank you to my family. I have a lot of great people encouraging me to put my stories out there and I am grateful. I also owe so much to Bold Strokes Books. Thank you.

For:
John
Robert
Stephen

CHAPTER ONE

Alexander

I went to sip my drink and, of course, it was empty. It was a sign, a bad omen. I was at this party with no one to talk to and an empty Coke in my hand. I crushed the can a little, barely able to hear it crinkle over the music. I dropped it into the mesh pocket on the camping chair I was sitting in. *Thanks for tuning in, friends and neighbors, but our MVP, Al "the Gunner" Jefferson, just doesn't seem to have it in him, folks.* I resorted to the classic "try not to look boring or bored" tactic: my phone. I had plenty of Snapchats waiting for me. My daughters must have gotten hold of my sister's phone. I opened the app and watched scenes of my girls playing with their cousins.

"Good Lord, Al," Dani cried, coming from the living room into the sun porch where I was sitting. The blue Christmas lights along the screened-in room made it feel like the cold night air was visible, icy, and she looked festive with the blue stars shining down on her.

"Hey, love," I said, welcoming her onto my lap.

"What's up? You look sadder than a toothless dog in a steak factory."

I groaned. "I don't think that's a sayin'."

"Don't change the subject. What's wrong?"

I sighed. "Nothin', just no one really to talk to."

She gestured skeptically to the whole party. "No one?"

I looked around. The room was full of great people, and it was nice to be in a crowd of likeminded folk. While not our first polyamory party, this was the first that was color coordinated. Red meant present and accounted for but not lookin', yellow meant lookin' to hook up but nothin' serious, and green meant lookin' for more. That's at least what the invitation explained. There were also gender preference colors. If you were into men, it was blue, women pink, and if it didn't matter and nonbinary was purple. The whole scheme could have been a clashing nightmare, except the group was clever, the colors worn so only those who knew the system would notice anything. I had on an Incredible Hulk shirt and Dani had on Wolverine. Some people displayed their preferences in assorted plaids or with accessories or makeup. I still wasn't interested in anyone, though.

"I don't know, I guess…I don't know." I stumbled, trying to place my mood.

"Wanna go home?" she asked.

I pulled her closer and shook my head. I liked being out and surrounded, for once, by adults. "I ain't havin' a *bad* time, just not…"

"Not the time you expected?"

"I mean, I didn't really expect anythin'." I tried snuggling into her neck.

She squirmed so I had no choice but to look at her. "Like hell you didn't."

"What's that supposed to mean?"

"It means I don't need Painted Waters PD to solve the case of why you're poutin'. It's been so long since we've been in a place where we could do this. I bet you expected to show up tonight and meet the man of your dreams—"

"Nuh-uh." But she was probably righter than I realized.

She just giggled and kissed my mouth. "I fall for this romantic drama king at least once a day. You might not always act on it, but I can see your heart."

I rolled my eyes and tried to look less like a marshmallow. "Well, either way, are you havin' fun?"

She shrugged, but her expression was smug. "There's potential."

I laughed. That meant she had been approached by enough people that she was willing to play the field awhile. *Forever the huntress.* It also wasn't surprising. She was beautiful. Her shiny brown hair was pulled up in a high ponytail, her features square but not necessarily sharp. She was fit, a gym owner by profession. She looked like an athletic wear catalogue model, but whenever anyone mentioned how pretty she was, she'd just tell them what her last deadlift was.

"You want me to stay with you for a minute?" she asked, finally returning my nuzzles. I let my face be engulfed by her chest and arms.

"This is the most action I've seen all night, so I wouldn't say no. But I guess you didn't come here to meet me."

"I could. We could role-play a—oh my Lord…is that…?" She turned in my arms to track someone moving across the party. I looked up at her. She was staring into the crowd.

"What're you lookin' at?" I asked. I turned and could only see the same people I'd been staring at for an hour.

"Good Lord, it is him. How can you miss him?" She was almost giggling.

I blinked a few times trying to clear some of the blur caused by her body pressed against my face and by the dim, warm lights decorating the living room. Finally, I spotted him.

"Oh, shit. Is that Lucas?"

She cackled. "Well, I think your night just got more exciting."

I huffed but couldn't argue. I also couldn't pull my eyes away from Lucas. He had been the in-home nurse to my best friend's mother. I had met him a few times. Every time, I couldn't help thinking how handsome he was. And funny. And smart.

"I'll be damned," Dani said, her voice small.

I shared her surprise. Seeing Lucas Laverty at the party was extraordinary. He was married and hadn't given any indication they were open. So, the green T-shirt he had on was a shock. However, the bigger surprise was the purple bar of makeup around his eyes, creating a sort of abstract mask. He must have gotten the idea from the party's host, a dark-skinned woman with similarly applied yellow and pink makeup. He was talking to her and another woman. The purple was dynamic on his light brown skin and looked perfect with his fully tattooed arms. Even without the makeup, it would have been hard to miss his purple ball cap, purple nails, and purple gauges.

"Wow," Dani said, pinching my arm.

"Kelley Danielle, that hurt."

"Don't you full name me, Alexander Hamilton. I've been talking to you. What happened to the sad guy, huh? Lucas shows up and suddenly you're ready to party?" She pinched me a second time to emphasize her point.

"I…well…"

She kissed my cheek. She knew how it was. We had been honest about our preferences from day one. I hadn't hidden how attractive I found Lucas over the few years we had known him.

"You gonna talk to him?"

"Uh…I'm gonna…get another drink."

She giggled and hopped off my lap. "Chicken."

I pinched her ass as she walked back into the crowd. I wandered into the kitchen through the sunroom, avoiding the main part of the party. Was I going to talk to him? It seemed a little too real, even though it was nothing at all. The guy just showed up to a party. Looking good. Really good. *This is it. Will our MVP pull out a game-winning play?* I sighed and shoved my head into the fridge. It had been emptied of all the ordinary house fixin's for the party and was now full of every kind of drink a person could want. I considered getting another Coke. Orange soda maybe?

Just because I was into him in no way meant he would be into me. We had seen each other, what? Four times in the last two years? He probably didn't even remember my name. I hadn't seen him for a long time because my friend's mom, Rose, was almost a year officially cancer-free and it had been about that long—

"Hey."

I jumped at the voice and the sudden tap on my shoulder that accompanied it. My head was still in the stupid fridge, and I banged it against the freezer door on my way to standing.

"Oh shit," I said, turning and putting a hand on my head. I didn't know what else to say after that because Lucas, his brown eyes framed in a wide purple cloud, was looking at me.

"Shit, man, are you okay?" he asked, taking a step toward me.

I chuckled, trying to back up. I just ended up colliding with the open fridge door, and since I was no small guy, I practically took it off the hinges. "Yeah, I'm fine, just surprised."

"I didn't mean to scare you, Alexander." He grinned.

So, he *did* remember me. My mouth took over without consulting my brain. "Hey, Lucas. Call me Al. Everyone does. I saw you come in, not that I wasn't gonna say hi or nothin'…you just looked…but I'm… you're here at this. Right."

We've never seen the Gunner fumble this badly. I stepped out of the way, and he reached into the fridge for some sort of beer lemonade thing. I was probably coming off super weird, but his grin remained. Why was I nervous? When he closed the fridge, he turned to me.

"I mean, yeah, I'm surprised to see you too. I saw Kelley. She said you were in here."

I laughed awkwardly and tried to take a breath. "Yeah…she, uh, prefers Dani, by the way. We only introduce her as Kelley at first. So… and you know Etta, I saw you talkin' to her."

"Yeah, she's a nurse at the hospital in Valdosta," he said, looking at me with concern. "I…are you okay? Are you bleeding?"

I blinked. I hadn't noticed I was still rubbing my head. "No, yeah, I'm fine. I wouldn't've survived sports for as long as I did if I couldn't take banging my head a few times."

He grinned and tried to hide it by clearing his throat. "How do you know Etta?"

The question, the gentle way he asked it, and the casual shape of his body as he leaned against the fridge went a long way toward easing my nerves. "I…we're on the poly group site. We only know her through there."

"You've been to a party like this before?"

I leaned against the counter and happened to find myself near the bottle opener. I picked it up and held it out to him. Instead of taking the opener, he just held out his bottle. I braced one hand against his and opened the bottle with the other. He smiled wider, all bright teeth and full lips. I felt my guts turn over like a pancake. *This is flirting, right?* Almost too slowly, I answered the question.

"We've been to a few. How about you?"

"This is my first."

"Oh, well, welcome. Is it just you?" I asked, remembering his wife.

He hummed and took a sip. "Yeah, Kyoko is working."

I nodded. I half expected him to make a run for it and go find someone else to talk to. Instead, he took a step closer. And spoke again.

"Since Kel—Dani's here, you must both be poly. But given your colors, you're here for different reasons?"

The sound that came out of my mouth would have passed for a laugh if I'd been some sort of cartoon. Instead, it was just embarrassing. I faked a cough to regroup. "To say the least. She's…let's just say she never planned on gettin' married, but since we did, it could only be non-traditional. We've been open pretty much our whole marriage."

He squinted at me.

I squinted back.

"Don't you have a bunch of kids?" he asked slowly.

"Yeah, seven."

He blinked. "And…this works with all that going on? Seven—how do you end up with seven kids?"

"It's a long story. My dad and siblings help a lot, but there's fifteen kids between the four of us—well, my little brother doesn't have any. And Dani's family helps in the summers. And the rest is just being super great in the bedroom."

I had to hate myself because I actually shot a few finger guns at him. He had a kid too, a little girl in the same preschool as one of mine. Not that I really wanted to talk about my kids. I love them to death, but I really wanted to focus on Lucas's arms and chest—*why's his shirt so tight?*

I could see the scrutiny in his eyes, but he laughed, so it must not have been for the worse. He said, "Okay, fair enough. So, what do people *do* at these parties?"

"Oh, God. There's dancing out there and games in the den. We could make out—" And there it was: my big-ass foot in my awkward-ass mouth. *No chance on that one, folks—it's like Al Jefferson has never played the game.* I stood up straighter, as if preparing to run away. Lucas's eyebrows rose, and he paused with his beer halfway to his mouth.

"I—wow…um, I didn't mean *we* per se. Not that I wouldn't. It's just it was—"

"Now, hold up."

I held up. His tone was neutral. He took another sip of beer and squared up with me. I wasn't scared, at least not in a threatened way. Both of us were big as houses. His muscle definition was out of this world, but we were damn near the same size, both of us in the range of six feet. Plus, the party had strict rules of engagement, and if he was offended…but he didn't look offended. No, I wasn't scared of him, but I was afraid of being rejected.

"When you say *make out*, what do you mean?"

"Wh-what?"

The smile that broke on his face was frighteningly beautiful. "There's different ways of making out. Wondered which one *you* meant."

His magnetic brown eyes were steady on my face.

"Not sure I could say…" I tried to swallow the lump in my throat.

"I could demonstrate if you want," he said. His actions were sensual, biting his lip and watching my mouth.

I sensed my own goofy grin and tried to sound casual. "By all means."

He nodded and took a step toward me. "Well, there's this."

He surprised me with his mouth on mine, even though I saw him coming. It was a kiss, plain and simple. Our lips pressed together but not much more than that. He smelled amazing, and his warmth was almost tangible. I was one neuron firing away from pulling him closer. He stepped back, not far but enough so we could look at each other. That was an appetizer. It was the sight and sound and smell of the meal to come.

I pretended to grimace, which was hard given my light-headedness. "Naw, that's not quite it."

He nodded, doing a better job than I was of seeming unfazed. "Right, so option two."

He stepped into my space and brought his hand to my face. I tried not to anticipate his moves, wanting to see where he would go with it. He kissed me again, this time with an intensity that made me feel like someone had lit a fire around me. His fingers were firm on my neck and he pressed his thumb slightly on my jaw. My response was to open my mouth. That must have been what he wanted because he pushed his tongue in.

I may or may not have moaned. I needed to steady myself against something. I put my hands out, reaching for anything to hold me up under the sexual electricity crossing from his mouth to mine. One hand found the counter, the other his waist.

Touching him back must have reassured him because he intensified the kiss, adding the rest of his body. He pressed his hips against mine. The hand on my face circled to the back of my neck and into my hair and his other hand came up to meet it. Suddenly I was surrounded by him, and it felt amazing. *This is it, folks—our first points of the night, and the crowd goes wild.*

I could sense the rest of the people at the party. I wanted to focus on his lips and skin and hands with every ounce of attention I could muster. But that required a bit more privacy than we had. I put my hands on his forearms and pulled gently. He understood and backed up, maybe too quickly, probably thinking it was too much or I was over it. I was far from over it.

Before he could second-guess what just happened, I said, "Yup, that's about right. Only what I was thinking involves a little more privacy."

He grinned and looked around the room. I followed his gaze. We were alone in the kitchen but in sight of everyone else, should anyone have wanted to look over.

"Is there a space for that?" he asked. He stepped back again, almost stepping out of view of the rest of the party, wiping his mouth in a way that was affirming rather than discouraging, like when someone ate something they liked and were drooling for more.

I nodded. I started toward the hall, looking back only to make sure he was following. The house had several rooms Etta had converted from whatever their ordinary use was into "private" rooms. Each had a chalkboard and a piece of chalk on a cord hanging on the door. There was a code for the doors too, but I couldn't remember them all. The only word I needed was "occupied." Most of the rooms were available. It was early enough in the night. I chose one and opened it for Lucas. He stepped in, and I wrote on the board before closing the door.

"This is an office?" Lucas asked, looking around.

Most of the furniture was pushed out of the center of the room. A blanket had been laid out on the floor with pillows piled on top, and there was a lantern in the center of the blanket. Another chalkboard designating the room as "the campsite" was hanging off a draped piece of fabric that gave the impression of a tent.

"Rustic."

"All right, welp, let's hear it," Lucas said, practically throwing himself on the pillows.

"Hear what?" I asked, settling myself down near him with the lantern between us.

"Your best line. I gave you mine, now let's see what you got." His voice was teasing, but his eyes gave away a hint of nerves.

"That was your best, huh? I mean, it was good. I...well, I don't have any lines."

"Oh no? You just expected 'Sorry I accidentally blurted out my horny desires—unless...' to work?"

"It did, though."

"Naw, I took pity."

"To-may-to, to-mah-to. Anyway, I don't need lines. I've got looks. I just stand there and people...flock."

"Flock?"

"Flock," I repeated.

"All right," he said, "let's see that, then. Give me your best look."

I made some fuck-boi face I had seen on the internet. He laughed. Then he nodded appraisingly. He even went so far as to pick up the lantern and hold it closer to my face. I honored him with a second, equally horrendous pose.

"Needs work," he said before laughing again. His laugh was so light, so airy. It was surprisingly gentle for as large a guy as he was.

"Needs work? *Needs* work? Those are A-class poses."

He pointed at me. "Looks goofy with a cartoon character on your shirt."

"You literally have the same guy tattooed on your arm."

I pointed to the Marvel tattoo he had as if he didn't know it was there. It was a cool tattoo—down one side Marvel heroes were seated at a table just like in *The Last Supper*. That was matched on the other side of his arm by a table of villains.

He made a noncommittal sound. "I don't know. Maybe you should just take it off."

He gave me a sheepish look I recognized as part show, part real. I knew he could be more direct than some people liked, so part of me wondered if he was teasing to make me comfortable.

"You're a dingus. You can just ask if you want me out of my clothes," I said.

He pointed a finger gun at me and made a face that said *noted*. He gestured with his hand for me to carry on. I shook my head and pulled my shirt off.

"Yours," I managed, trying to ignore the appraising look in his eyes.

"Come and get it," he challenged.

I accepted by moving the lantern to somewhere behind me and practically crawled to him. He sat up and let me slip my hands under his shirt. His skin was hot, and I could feel the details of his muscles before I could see them. Neither of us said anything, and it was hard to wait for his face to be free of his shirt before I kissed him. In a sort of hazy shuffle, his lips occupying most of my attention, I found myself between his legs, and even though he was the one beneath me, I felt held down by him, *to* him. Yet, aside from our mouths and where our hands landed, we were barely touching. I had one hand bracing me up; the other was on his jaw. His hands were on my back. I lost all stability when his hands came around to my front. I jerked away, half laughing and half gasping.

"Sorry. What happened?" he asked.

"Nothing. That just tickles," I said.

He smiled. "You're that ticklish?"

"Yes, and unless you want this to turn into the WWE, don't try it."

His eyes narrowed, considering it. He shrugged. "Fair enough. Anywhere else?"

"Yeah, everywhere, but if you keep it hard enough, it won't be a problem."

"Keep it hard—got it," he said, and of course, he winked at me.

I rolled my eyes. Looking at the purple on his face, I remembered we were both wearing green. *Looking for more.* Was being on top of him too fast for that? "Lucas—"

"Call me Luke. Lou if you want."

"Okay…um…how far'd you want this to go? I didn't…well, neither of us have on yellow." I hoped I was clear enough. I couldn't get my brain fully involved since there was a distinct lack of blood heading in its direction.

He thought a minute and ran his hands up my arms. He looked up at me, his expression so invested that I almost lost my balance again. He said, "Hadn't really thought I'd get anywhere, so I hadn't thought that hard about it. You?"

"Same. I guess we keep goin' as we are till the plan changes?"

"Well, according to the internet and a survey of high school students I taught sex-ed to over the summer, most people spend five to ten minutes making out, so you have time."

I chuckled. "That doesn't seem scientifically sound. How big was your sample?"

"Big enough," he said, bucking his hips against me.

"That's not what I meant."

"Wow," he snorted, "do you want to make out or debate my methodology?"

I made a show of looking at my watch. "In five to ten minutes, if this doesn't go any further, we debate."

"In five to ten minutes, it's going to be a cage match—"

I didn't let him finish. Instead, I kissed him, this time letting my body press against his. He made a sound of slight annoyance but kissed me back. He kept his grip on me firm, his hands on my back and hips. I braced my elbows against the floor so I didn't put my whole weight on him, not that I thought it would matter. Maybe it was habit because Dani was so much smaller, maybe it was unconscious self-consciousness because of his fitness level compared to mine. I didn't think about it that hard, focusing on enjoying his mouth instead.

It didn't take much to pin down a few things he liked. He seemed to like things slower, small moans escaping him when I backed off to a graze of lips. He didn't chase me; he let me come to him, let me explore his mouth. Hearing him was sending all the right signals south. It didn't help that his lower half was starting to get more involved. His responsive mouth was starting to generate equal responsiveness in his hips and in my—

A confusing sound caused us both to pause. It sounded like someone knocking on the door. We looked at each other with the same question of *Did you hear that?*

Then it happened again. I sighed and called, "Occupied."

"Al, it's me," Dani called back.

I didn't have enough blood flow to my brain to understand her. My instinct, however, was enough to get me to my feet and to the door. I opened it a crack.

"What's up, love?" I asked, surprised by my own breathlessness. I was even more surprised by her panicked face.

"There's an emergency. We have to go," she said.

The panic in her sentence sobered me. I went back and grabbed the nearest shirt. "The girls?"

"No," she said, "it's Coach."

My head whipped around to look at her so fast you would have thought I was an owl. "Dad?"

"Is there another Coach? Yeah, come on. Sorry, Lucas," she apologized for me. "Gage is taking him to the hospital."

I looked at Lucas. He wasn't on the floor anymore. He was standing and looking just as worried and ready for action as you would expect from a person in the medical field.

"Don't look at me," he insisted. "Go."

I couldn't help but smile at him. I pulled on the shirt as I followed Dani down the hall and out of the party.

CHAPTER TWO

Lucas

I drove home with the windows open, letting the cold winter air take care of any leftover horniness. Painted Waters was dark save for the Christmas lights some people had already put up and a few lonely, lit windows. Big trees blocked the shine of the stars and the moon, creating eerie patches on the roads, lawns, and houses. It wasn't creepy, though. I never felt unsafe. It was just old and rural.

The drive and the cold weren't distracting enough. I was thinking about Al again as I climbed the stairs to the apartment. I took a deep breath. It didn't seem fair to Kyoko to walk into the house thinking about someone else. I knew I wouldn't be able to control my thoughts all the time, especially if I started dating someone. And it wasn't like Ky minded. She said she thought about soil samples sometimes when I was trying to talk to her. I took another breath. I wanted to be intentional for anyone I had a relationship with, though, and not just let it happen and hope for the best.

I unlocked the door, surprised the lights were still on. I took my shoes off and tossed my keys in the bowl before going to the living room. My home was a three-bedroom apartment over an insurance company in downtown Painted Waters. It had looked like something one of the design couples on HGTV would put together when we moved in; now it was chaotic, tacky, and homey.

"Ky?" I asked. She was sitting on our peach-colored, thrift store couch we were pretty sure was haunted.

She seemed just as surprised to see me. She had a plastic bag on her head, which meant fresh color on her hair. She was a stunning, tall, thin, half Japanese, half white, American woman. Her hair was straight and had been green for the last few years even though it was naturally black. Her clothes were always black. She put her phone down and turned to look at me.

"What are you doing to your head?" I asked.

"What are you doing home?" she countered.

"I thought I'd come home early." I had given the party another hour after Al left. No one else caught my attention.

"I thought I'd touch up the green."

I nodded and climbed over her, doing my best to try to cuddle. She resisted, trying to keep the dye off the couch, not that our couch didn't already have dye on it. Both of us had dyed our hair green when our daughter Lila was born to troll coworkers who wanted a gender reveal. We had been saying for months we didn't know, and we didn't, then Lila was born, and we decided to go with the convention of she/her until Lila told us otherwise. My hair wasn't green anymore. On a whim, I'd shaved the mohawk and let my hair do whatever it wanted. Right now, it was a light brown, curly fluff, flattened by my hat.

"I'd ask how it was, but since you're wearing someone else's shirt, it must've been a good time." She giggled, rubbing my back as I settled with my head in her lap.

"It's not exactly what it looks like." She made a curious sound. I laughed and explained. "It started out as what it looks like, but the guy had an emergency come up and had to leave. Something about his dad going to the hospital."

"Baw, that sucks. Who's the guy?" she asked.

I propped myself up to look at her. I wanted to see her expression when I told her. "Alexander Jefferson."

Her eyes went wide, and surprise and pride paraded across her face. She had called his queerness when she first met him at my former client's birthday party. I thought it was just wishful thinking. Turns out she'd been right.

"Khaki Daddy himself?"

"Yikes, you have to stop calling him that." I thought it was funny, though. While Ky looked like you would expect a goth scientist to look, Al regularly looked like he was about to sell you insurance.

"How...what...tell me." She tried shaking me, but it wasn't effective since I was twice her size. I was about to explain when the alarm on her phone went off. She climbed over me, grabbed her phone, and ran to the bathroom. "Shit, I have to rinse. Give me twenty and come shower with me? You can tell me about your new bae."

He wasn't my bae. We hadn't even gotten to talk about that. I looked down at the Incredible Hulk on the shirt he had left behind. It fit, which was no surprise since we were built basically the same. I grinned and tried to picture him in my shirt, the one he had grabbed by mistake. I liked shirts that were a little small when I went out in order to tempt people. I bet it fit him tight.

I opened my phone. I could just message him. *Slide into his DMs.* He wasn't hard to find. Six degrees of separation became more like three in a town as small as Painted Waters. He had been suggested as a friend more than once. I wondered if that would work. My heart started to race as I thought about it. My mom, Silvy, would say, "Why bait the hook if you aren't going to cast the line?"

For starters, Al had a wife, siblings, seven daughters, a job, a house, and about a thousand other things that made dating him impossible. Not that I didn't have those things—well, I didn't have siblings. Or a father, for that matter. But he seemed to have it all at twice the volume. How did he keep any of that in order? How would he find a place for me? Then again, under him was a place. *Cart before the horse?*

I pulled up Snapchat and searched for him. I sent him a friend request and a snap of me lying on the couch in his shirt. I captioned it *made a new friend.* I thought about standing with him in the kitchen. The last few times I had seen him he was wearing a hat. He hadn't been tonight, so the brightness of his blond hair was surprising. The goofy way he looked at me was everything, though, big brown eyes even bigger in surprise. There had been what? Butterflies? Sparks? A metaphorical insta-boner? There had been something tightening around my lungs when he smiled at me, that was for sure.

I was about to close the app when he accepted my request and replied with a pic of him in my shirt. He looked like he was in a bathroom. His face wasn't in the photo, not that I minded a great pic of his thick body in a too-small shirt. It was captioned *bro why is this so tight? If I sneeze it'll rip.* I laughed and snapped another photo, this time with his shirt pulled up, held in my teeth showing my torso. It's not like I had abs but I did have great tats, so it was a good photo. I said, *show off the goods, my guy.* Then I sent him a serious message in the chat.

How's your dad?

He replied. *Awake and angry. Still in with the doctors. They're tossing around the word stroke.*

Shit that's serious. Sorry Al.

We'll see, sorry I kind of ran out on you.
Naw, man. I get it, no big.
Thanks for asking.
Keep me posted.

I didn't expect a message back, and I didn't get one. Part of me felt like a goob for being excited that we were talking. And part of me felt like an ass for flirting with the guy while his dad was in the hospital. I put my phone down, lining it up perfectly over one of the skulls burned into the surface of the coffee table. The whole walnut coffee table had been inlaid with skulls, and they all stared at me. Everything was about alignment.

"Lou," Kyoko shouted, "I need help. I got green dye on my tits."

"How? You're wearing a shirt."

I went to the bathroom to try and help her.

I didn't hear from Al over the next few days. I thought about messaging him, but the only thing I could think to do was ask about his dad, and that felt weird. *Otherwise, what? Ask him out. Pfft. No. No.* This was probably a sign he didn't have room for me in his life. I honestly had written him off as best I could by Monday morning. My resolve to not think about him lasted until I reached one of the nurse's stations at the hospital in Valdosta.

"Hey there, handsome," Etta said. She came around the counter and hugged me.

"Hey, beautiful."

She smirked and strutted back to her chair. Then she gave me a look that said *spill it.*

"Why are you looking at me like that?" I asked, opting to play oblivious.

"A birdie told me you had a certain Asgardian in the campsite room." She fluttered her eyelashes and scrunched her lips into a kissy face.

"What's with the nicknames? Ky insists on calling him Khaki Daddy."

Etta sipped her iced coffee and sloshed it in affirmation. "I like that. But that doesn't confirm your involvement with him."

"Confirmed," I said, trying to catch her before she went too far, "but not much happened."

She pouted. "Aw, sorry. Disappointed?"

"Maybe," I said. She gave me side-eye, and I caved. "Yes, I did message him, and he responded…but he's busy."

She snapped her approval, then got down to the real business. "What're you doing here? Lunch with me?"

"No, the agency sent me. They have a client. I'm meeting with the coordinator, then the client at two."

She looked at the clock. "Don't bullshit me, Lou."

I really had come for lunch. She called over her shoulder that she was going to eat and grabbed her purse. The nice part of the smaller hospital in town was that it was slow enough for the staff to get away. Not that we went far. Etta and I grabbed some of the prepacked boxes from the cafeteria and had lunch outside. It was almost too cold, but Etta and I were both pretty warm-blooded. She was my workout buddy sometimes, a shorts-in-December type. Not that you'd know it through our scrubs.

"How's my baby?" she asked. She took off her cap, her short, purple waves bright against her black skin.

"I already said I'm good."

She glared at me.

"Lila's good. She's been with Ky's parents in Tallahassee for a few days. Ky flew out there this morning before she goes to Iowa, and I'm gonna drive down and meet the in-laws halfway to pick her up this weekend."

"Why Iowa?"

"Some farmers and developers have questions about the soil, so they called in the expert."

"She's so weird. Who studies dirt?" Etta groaned.

"It's not dirt, it's soil or planting medium, depending," said a soft voice suddenly at our table.

Etta and I practically cheered to see Rose Ness. She'd been my patient and was now about a year officially cancer free. I hugged her and stepped out of the way so she could hug Etta. She was easily a favorite amongst the nurses. Rose was Caucasian, blond, and wrapped in a huge, fleece-lined coat.

"You two are crazy, it's freezing out here," she said, joining us anyway.

"I like it," I said.

"I need it," Etta whined, shaking her salad. "The nurse's station is right under the heater, so it's ninety back there."

"What are you doing here?" I asked Rose.

"Volunteering on my old floor."

"I forgot you do that," I said. Sitting in a chemo chair would have been damned boring if it wasn't for volunteers. Rose usually sat with people she used to know from when she was regularly getting treatments.

"What's new?" she asked.

"Lou's seeing someone."

Rose raised her eyebrows. She was one of the few people who knew my marriage was open. I hadn't figured it out that long ago. And she had been one of the first I had bounced the idea off after Ky. Later, I had been surprised to find Etta, a nurse I had known for years, was in the community too.

"No," I said quickly. "Not dating. Made out with, that's all."

"Do I know them?"

"Ky calls him Khaki Daddy." Etta giggled.

"Oh my God, *stop.*"

"That has to be Al," Rose said.

"How?" I asked. Etta's giggling turned into full-on howling.

"No one else would fit that description and be worth making out with," Rose said with a shrug. "Tell me about it."

I looked at Etta and gestured with my fork. It was meant to say *if you're so eager to talk, you tell it.* And she repeated the events of the party without hesitation.

"Are you going to continue with him?" Rose asked when Etta had finished.

"I...I don't know."

"Why not?"

I looked at her, trying to find the words. "He's really busy. What if he doesn't have time for something like this? I wasn't lying when I said I was looking for someone to date. Maybe I should've talked to him at the party, but I was...distracted."

"How busy could he be? Really low stakes to false advertise at the party," Etta said.

"He has seven daughters," I said.

Etta stared.

"They're great kids," Rose said. "And the whole family pitches in to help each other, so there's no shortage of sitters for when one of them wants to date. Al's pretty good at figuring out how to make things work."

I shook my head. I didn't want to be strung along with promises of this happening, but then it never did. The more I thought of that particular outcome, the more awful I felt.

"You know," Etta said, "Bren says you left in a different shirt, so there must've been more than just making out."

"There wasn't," I said. I had seen Etta's wife, Brenda, when I was leaving.

Rose grinned. "I don't know, Lucas. Does everyone take off their shirt to make out?"

"I think it's a great thing he has seven kids," Etta continued.

I stared at her.

"He's got to be pretty good in bed if a woman like Dani would sleep with him that frequently."

"Geez. I'm done. I'm leaving," I said. Both women laughed so hard they had to hold on to each other just to keep from swaying out of their seats. Neither could say goodbye through their cackling.

❖

I dropped into the seat across from the coordinator. She was on the phone but welcomed me into her office anyway. I waited while she finished her call.

"Lucas," she said, setting down the receiver.

"Good morning, Mrs. Wright."

"How've you been? I'm sorry our caseload has been so slow. I mean, heaven bless us, it's a good thing when we don't have clients because it means people are keeping healthy, but Lord, it does make the time drag, doesn't it?"

"You're preaching to the choir," I answered, knowing her words were a show. In reality, she was the busiest one in the building and had learned to get small talk out of the way. She was a short, efficient woman with black hair and eyes like a bush baby, but in a pretty way.

"Well, I have an idea I want to propose to you," she said.

I shrugged and gestured for her to go on.

"The elementary school reached out to me. They're going to need a nurse next semester and want someone at least through the end of the year."

I blinked. I had been an institutional nurse for a year, and it was one of the hardest jobs of my life. I didn't know if I was ready to go back to that. Then again, Valdosta West Elementary wasn't the same as a youth correctional school. And it was steady work.

"What if a patient comes up?"

She shrugged. "What if one doesn't? Look, I'll set up the meeting and you can go talk to them. It won't hurt you to interview, right?"

I pointed at her in a *fair enough* gesture. She smiled, shaking her head, and stood to hand me the folder across her desk. I read the name.

"He was admitted a few days ago. It was decided to pursue treatment in-home. It's a short-term case but—"

"I know him." I held the folder up as if it were evidence against me. Then I realized I had interrupted. "Sorry, I just…didn't expect to know him."

The sticker on the edge of the folder read *Jefferson, Jeffery*. It was Al's father. To say I knew him was a stretch. I had only met Jeffery Jefferson once. We had crossed paths in a store while I was with Rose. But considering I had made out with his son only a few days ago, I figured knowing him was close enough.

"I'm friends with Alexander, his son."

"I figured. It was his sister, Betsy Casillas, who requested you."

"Requested," I repeated. *Well, that's a first.* I stared at the grains in her cherrywood desk. It probably would have been more unusual for me *not* to get Mr. Jefferson as a client given the size of Painted Waters and Valdosta. That knowledge didn't change the shock of it, though.

"Yup. Said she liked the way you worked with Mrs. Rose Ness and thought you'd be best suited to help them."

"Okay," I said because I had no reason not to. It wasn't like Al and I were dating.

❖

My heart raced as I went to meet the family. Al would be there. Of course, this wasn't about Al and the way he sort of hummed rather than moaned when you kissed him. I took a deep breath and dredged up my professional face. For a while I could get away with treating them like any other family, but then what? Would this change things between Al and me? Not that there was anything between Al and me. *Yet.* My brain inappropriately supplied a memory of a certain hardness pressing into my groin only a few nights ago, and I had to pause outside the semi-open door. I closed my eyes and counted to ten to try and clear my thoughts. There was a conversation I couldn't help overhearing going on in the room.

"You know him, Daddy. He's the same nurse Mrs. Rose had."

"That Black fellow?" a wheezy voice asked. I figured that was Mr. Jefferson.

"You couldn't find a girl?" another voice, deep like Al's but not quite his, added.

"There ain't nothin' wrong with a male nurse," the woman who spoke first said.

"'Cept they's all queers," the other voice said.

A third voice asked, "So what if he is?"

"Don't think there's room in our house for any more fa—"

"Watch your mouth, Gage. It's not *our* house, it's *my* house, and I'll tell you right now, Lucas is a friend, and he's who we picked for this job. You had your chance to have a say. So, keep your thoughts to yourself."

That was Al. And damn, that was hot. My hero, I thought, stunned.

"He's late," Mr. Jefferson grumbled.

I counted to five. I had been spoiled by Rose, but this wasn't my first rodeo. I had patients who were not thrilled to have a male nurse before. I had also had people be less than excited for a Black nurse. But homophobes too? Perfect trifecta.

"Hello." I knocked and stepped into the room. "Afternoon, I'm Lucas Laverty."

I made a show of looking first at the patient, then at the rest of the room. Jeffery Jefferson was a slight man, average height with a wiry frame. He looked like the type to be underestimated in a fight.

He was bookended by two immense men. One was Al in his work uniform. The words *Khaki Daddy* flashed through my mind. I tried not to smile at him. He smiled at me. My chest did that tightening thing again. The other guy was an older, slightly shorter reproduction of Al. He had a full beard and wore the bright colors of a man who works on or near the road. He was sunburned and greasy and had to be John Adams Jefferson, Al's older brother.

At the foot of the bed stood two gorgeous people. A woman stood near Mr. Jefferson's feet. She was the picture of professionalism in a bright blouse and pencil skirt. She was like a mix of Adele and Dolly Parton, with a curtain of blond hair flowing around her face. Betsy Ross Casillas. Next to her, backed against the wall, was a young guy who could have passed for Jeffery in build but was as beautiful as the woman. All his visible skin except his actual face was tattooed. He chewed on his lip ring as he looked me over. His hair, bone straight and white blond, was piled in a messy bun on the top of his head. I forgot for a second what I was doing there. *The whole Jefferson family is a pansexual wet dream.* Betsy broke the silence.

"Mr. Laverty," Betsy said and put out a hand, taking a few steps toward me.

"Lucas, please," I said, taking her hand.

"It's a pleasure to see you again. I'm Betsy Ross Casillas, of course. You can just call me Betsy. Mrs. Rose—well, I remember what you did for her, and when I called, she said you were just an angel. I thought, welp, we could use a little salvation, so thank you for takin' us on."

I think my heart melted. She was the definition of Southern charm. I had to remind myself to stop shaking her hand. "The pleasure's all mine. I'll do whatever I can to see to the comfort of the patient."

"I have a name," Mr. Jefferson snapped, crossing his spindly arms over his chest.

"Oh, Daddy," Betsy sighed, unfazed by his gruff tone. "I'm sorry. Mr. Laverty—Lucas, this is my father, Jeffery Jefferson."

"Good afternoon, sir," I said, offering my hand. He ignored it.

"Don't be such a stick in the mud. You better find your way to nice," Betsy said.

Jeffery stared and reluctantly shook my hand.

"I think you know Alexander," she said, putting a soft hand on my elbow and turning me toward her brother.

"Hey, Lou," Al said.

"Hey," I said. I shook his hand platonically. *Completely* platonically. No horny vibes. No homo. I might have cleared my throat.

"This here's my other brother, John Adams. Near to everyone calls him Gage," Betsy said.

"My *friends* call me Gage," John Adams said in a tone that clearly indicated I shouldn't. He didn't take my hand, and I withdrew it before Betsy could try and coax him into a handshake.

"Ignore him," she said to me in a small voice I'm sure he heard anyway. She turned me to the final person in the room. "This is my youngest brother, Thomas Jefferson—"

"Teach," he interrupted, stepping forward and shaking my hand.

"I'm glad to meet everyone. What say we get started?"

I gave my usual introduction, then I had John Adams and Teach leave the room. Betsy asked all the usual questions and Al nodded along. We discussed the layout of Al's house, where Mr. Jefferson was staying until they could get ahead of his condition. They explained some of the nuance in their schedule, and I went over the treatment plan I'd been given. Mr. Jefferson said nothing. He didn't even look up. He just lay there with his arms crossed and stared in the general direction of the window.

It wasn't the worst meeting. I was texting Kyoko about it as I crossed the parking lot to my truck when a voice called my name. I turned to find Al trotting toward me. The winter sky made it feel later than it was. His breath trailed him in the chilled air. Even though it was the coldest it had been for the season so far, neither of us had on coats. I remembered the heat that poured off his body when he was on top of me.

"Hey, Al," I said.

"I just wanted to…say thanks," he said, hopping to a stop in front of me. He pulled on the bill of his hat.

"It's no problem…it's my job."

"I know, but…I…Coach isn't the easiest person. I just wanted to say it now. No hard feelings if it comes down to you not wantin' this job anymore."

I was surprised. "Is he that bad?"

Al shrugged. "He has his hang-ups. Ask Orion about it."

Orion Starr was the partner of Franklin Ness, Rose's son. They had been in town last year, and I had met him a few times. I knew Orion had attended the school Coach Jefferson had taught at.

"I'll manage for now."

"I'm also sorry I haven't gotten back to you on the chat. It's been one."

"Understandable, I didn't expect anything."

"Naw? But maybe I did. Whatever plans you and I hadn't got around to makin' might have to go on hold till this is over, but I still want those plans."

I considered his words, and I thought about the reaction of the people in the room when John Adams suggested male nurses were all queer. "Out to your family?"

He laughed like it was the funniest thing in the world. He looked around and explained. "It's not that simple. It's more like don't ask, don't tell. Which I think is worse sometimes. I'm not hidin', so what they know they know—'cept the poly thing. They don't know about it mostly because it's been a while. I haven't dated anyone since we moved back. Well, I guess Teach knows."

"Oh yeah?" I asked, leaning against my truck, unsure of how to feel about the conversation. It was so easy and felt so natural to talk to him that I could almost ignore my disappointment. The cold metal of the vehicle felt grounding.

"Yeah. But for now, the real problem's that I need to figure out how to do this," he said, gesturing to the hospital. I got the impression he was gesturing to more.

"Can't sleep with the nurse," I said mostly to see if he would blush. He did. "That's not—"

"I'm just fucking with you. It's a good idea to keep it platonic. I can wait."

That came out of my mouth before I thought about it. Could I wait? I figured this couldn't be much more than dates and hanging out. I thought about the goofy way he'd collided with the fridge when I walked up on him. That caught more of my attention than anything anyone had done since I met Kyoko. Getting to know someone didn't have to happen on a schedule. I did a thumbs-up to back up my words.

"That'd be amazing. I…that's great news. My family's chaos. Between Coach and Gage—sorry for Gage bein' an asshole, by the way."

"I can handle it." I didn't want the conversation to end, so I said the first thing that came to mind. "Teach is fucking hot, bro."

Al cringed. "God, if I had a dollar for every time someone said that. He lives in Denver. That's how they look in Denver, I guess. He flew in for Dad."

"Betsy Ross is smoking too. A little her, little him, hoes in different area codes," I added, rubbing my hands together like a sleaze.

"God damn." Al laughed. "Don't call my sister a hoe. Also, she's married."

"Didn't stop me before." I winked.

"Good grief. Look, Betsy can hold her own, but that wouldn't stop Daniel, her husband, from taking you out if he needs to."

"Taking me *out* or taking *me* out."

Al gave me a clear look of annoyance, his willingness to put up with my banter breaking. I smirked, feeling victorious. His irritation almost felt like vindication for my disappointment. I quietly reminded myself that *not now* wasn't *not ever*.

I figured I'd let him off the hook. "Chill. I have my sights on one Jefferson. Betsy and Teach aren't it."

Al grinned. And we both realized in that moment we were almost standing toe to toe. It was too close to be platonic. Too close for a parking lot that could be seen from his father's room. Al took a step back, though I could tell he didn't want to.

"I'll see you next Wednesday?" I said.

"Yeah, but maybe I'll text you?"

Mixed signals much? I shrugged like it didn't matter. "Okay. Anyway, I have a new gym shirt to break in, so I better get going."

"Or you could just give it back," he said. It was obvious he didn't want it back from the way his eyes took in my face, then my neck, then my chest.

"I guess, but I already cut the sleeves off it." I could have got an Oscar for how well I played it off.

"I liked that shirt."

"It's been donated to a great cause. The gun show." I made a kissy face at him and got in my truck. I flexed, flashed him a peace sign, and drove away.

CHAPTER THREE

Alexander

I felt something connect with the side of my leg, and my eyes opened faster than my brain was able to see. The image of my daughter jumping on the bed, sucking two fingers, slowly clarified after a few seconds.

"Vicky, what are you doin'?"

"Hi, Daddy, I'm jumpin'," she said.

As more and more information began to accumulate, I understood the morning was already in a state of chaos. For one, the four-year-old shut in the room with me was wearing only a towel. Her wet, light brown hair bounced lazily as she hopped around my bed. Dani was gone and the clock said—

"It's six in the morning," I said, as if she would care.

"Morning."

"Why are you in a towel?"

"I took a shower."

"Why?"

She either said she threw up on her clothes or she threw up Cheerios. It was hard to tell with her fingers in her mouth. Either way, the "threw up" part was pretty clear. I took her out at the ankles, sending her sprawling and laughing on the bed. She righted herself, still sucking her fingers.

"Let me see your fingers," I said, holding up my hands. She giggled and showed me her widespread, tiny fingers. She must have had a nightmare. When she did, she sucked her fingers so hard she'd gag herself and barf.

"Let me see your bear claws," I sang, continuing the little dance that was more of a ritual now. She made little claws and growled at me.

"Let me see your wingers." I sat up to flap my wings.

"Let me see your kitty paws." We both pretended to lick our hands, then rub our hair.

"Hey, buttercup," I said, pulling her onto my lap.

"Hey, daddy-cup."

"Have a scary dream?" I asked. She nodded but didn't say more. I said, "Well, you're awake and I'm awake, so we don't have to be scared anymore, right?"

"Right."

"Let's go find some pants," I said, picking her up as I got out of bed.

I pulled on some sweats and went out of the room. Seven daughters was a lot. I knew that, Dani knew that. But our family never felt quite whole until Tessalee was born. My seven, Gage's five, and Betsy's three meant my father had fifteen granddaughters. And since he retired from teaching, he had been helping us with them. That was one reason I was able to go to the poly party in the first place. With Coach's help on top of the rotation me and my siblings had, Dani had time for her business and her other partners and I had time for my…whatever. But now with him sick? Lucas said he would wait, but could I? Seeing him in my house would be weirder than seeing him at the hospital. He made sense there as a nurse. But here in my house?

Vicky and I were met in the hall by two more partially dressed daughters. I scooped them into my arms and headed toward their rooms. All the girls slept in the bedrooms upstairs, the oldest getting her own room and the rest splitting the remaining three. We had one more room downstairs across from mine and Dani's. We had planned to rotate the girls through as they aged, but now it would hold my dad. *Well, sports fans, the game will never be the same.* A man doesn't get seven kids without thinking about sex, so I had made sure to soundproof both downstairs rooms this summer when I renovated. I didn't want a daughter to hear me and Dani be married any more than I wanted my dad to.

"Mama, where you at?" I called.

"Here," Dani said from one of the girls' rooms.

I carried them in and set them amongst their sisters. The five oldest milled about, dancing or walking or sitting, near Dani, who was on the floor trying to pull Tessalee into a pair of socks.

"Morning, Daddy," she said, grinning up at me.

"Morning, Daddy," the rest of the kids echoed.

"We have school today," my seven-year-old, Ysabel, reminded me.

"True. What stage are we in?" I asked Dani.

"The food for anyone who is dressed stage."

I nodded at Dani and shouted to the girls. "I'm so hungry I could eat a…?" Then I pointed at Vicky.

"A cow," she said. So, I mooed at her and chased her to the door.

Then I repeated the chase as a pig, a dragon, a horse, and a turkey until the middle five girls waited for me at the top of the stairs. My oldest, Zara, sat on one of the beds, picking at the hem of her pants. She was nine going on ninety.

"Zar, I think I need help making breakfast. Wanna crack a few eggs?" I asked as I scooped the three-year-old, Ursa, into my arms.

"I guess," she said with all the enthusiasm of an embalming. If I had to guess, she was going to switch to an all-black wardrobe soon.

"I'll be down soon. What time do you need to pick up Coach?" Dani asked as she finally got Tessie into her outfit for the day.

"Eight, then Lou'll be here by nine. That gives us just enough time to stop by the pharmacy."

She made a few clicking sounds with her tongue. "*Lou.*"

"Naw, it's not like that. I told him whatever's between us was on hold till Coach is settled."

She covered Tessie's ears. "I bet he's got something you can hold."

"Yeah, a polite and platonic conversation about medicine." I had meant it as a warning for her to stop teasing, but it came out too prudish for either of us to take seriously.

"I love you."

"Love you."

I carried Ursa downstairs tote bag–style by her overalls.

Zara and I made breakfast while Dani put the finishing touches on the girls' outfits as well as her own, and she even brought me a shirt and real pants. At seven fifteen, Teach wandered out of the guest room. Really it was a mother-in-law suite the landlord let me build over the garage. Having Orion Starr as a landlord had its perks. He didn't care what I did to the house so long as it was an improvement.

"Morning, Teachy," the girls screamed at my brother.

"Hello, kiddos," he said. He was surprisingly cheerful, which made me suspicious.

"Did you sleep?" I asked him.

"Do you want some eggs, Teach?" Zara asked.

"Two pre-birds, make 'em run," he said, patting Zara on the head. He didn't answer my question. Instead, he went to find a seat at the table, which meant putting one of the toddlers on his lap. At least he was wearing the uniform.

"I'm going to make you scrambled eggs," Zara decided for him.

"Teach, you look like you didn't sleep at all," Dani said.

He grinned at her. "I didn't, but staying up all night's easier."

"You look like you haven't slept in a while." Dani inspected him as if he were one of the kids. He kind of was. He was younger than me by six years. Dani, Betsy, even Rose mothered him. He gave her a small smile, which got her to leave him alone.

"Do you have any questions?" I asked him, helping Zara pour the eggs into the pan.

"I remember, not like it's hard," Teach said, helping Vicky with her toast. "Besides, Paul'll be there."

"That's not what I asked."

He rolled his eyes.

"I just mean—"

"Al," he said with a glare.

His look clearly read *Is this about me or you?* Maybe he was right. He might have agreed to help run my late grandfather's appraisal business, but I had only needed coverage so I could help Coach. I couldn't picture the future. Lucas would meet us and show me and Coach how to set up his equipment. The rest of this week and next would have Lucas showing Dani, Betsy, and her husband how to help Coach with his breathing machine, and what to look for in case of seizures.

"Daddy, you're burning the toast," Zara said, pointing to the slice of bread I had pushed down in the toaster for a third time.

"Right, here I think that's the last of it. Take these to Teach and go eat your breakfast," I said, handing her the remainder of the good toast.

"We got this," Dani reassured me, coming to pat my arm. "Coach'll come around too."

I sighed and tried to focus on not burning the rest of the eggs.

❖

Dad was sitting in a chair across from the bed, winter coat and hat on, waiting for me. He hated hospitals. As soon as I stepped in the door, he stood and started toward me. *Good morning, friends and family, another day at the ballpark. You're in for one hell of a game tonight. Our MVP takes on the Ill-men, a team from just north of—*

"Mornin', Coach," I said.

"Morning. You bring the truck?"

By the truck, he meant *his* truck, which really meant he wanted to drive. That wasn't going to happen, but I didn't want to tell him outright. "Naw, I brought the SUV."

He grumbled. The ride to the pharmacy was silent, and he didn't get out of the SUV to help me pick up the equipment. It was a long list: a breathing machine, inhaler, medication, tubes, cords, and wires. I tried not to think about it all. I just carried it to the SUV and started the thirty-minute drive home.

"This nurse," Coach said suddenly.

"What about him?" I hoped I sounded neutral. I couldn't forget Gage's comments about Lucas. I knew he was a risk, but he had made a good impression with Betsy. Anything Betsy wanted, Coach usually abided. That didn't mean I wasn't worried. Gage was one thing, but Coach's track record was far from politically correct.

"He a friend of yours?"

"I said as much."

"He do right by Mrs. Rose?"

I had the sudden and bananas idea that my father was nervous. I looked at him, but his face was stoic and unreadable. He had always been a hardass, but since his wife left when I was eighteen, he had grown steadily quiet. Unless he was with the girls, he was almost silent. That made this sudden bout of questions both surprising and suspicious.

"Yeah, Coach. She loved him. She sends her best, by the way. And so does Frank." I hadn't planned on hesitating before I added Orion, but I did. "Orion too."

He harrumphed.

I sighed. "Orion really did, Coach. You might not like each other, but he doesn't want you to die."

To my surprise, he laughed, even though it was quiet and mostly to himself. Maybe the loss of oxygen during his seizure damaged his brain. When was the last time he laughed? He had been living with Gage for the last two years. I couldn't really blame Gage for Coach's condition, but I didn't think he'd laughed since moving in there.

"Coach?"

"Son?"

"Uh…never mind." I backed out of asking the few half-formed questions that floated around in my brain. Mostly because I didn't know what to ask.

"Orion and Frank still together?" he asked.

I again looked at him. "Yeah."

He nodded. I remembered talking to him about Orion years ago. Fin was the first gay guy I had ever known. At the time, I didn't know what he meant by telling me he was gay until he met Orion, and I watched them fall for each other. I remember Coach quietly talking with my mother about how Fin shouldn't hang around Orion. My parents treated Fin like one of my brothers until Orion showed up. After it became indisputable that Fin was gay, my mother tried to get me to stop talking to him. I blinked a few times and tried to remove her from my thoughts. If she didn't want to be in my life, she didn't get to live rent-free in my brain.

"Where're they living?"

"Who?"

"Franklin and Orion."

"Why do you care?"

"It's just a question. I'm making conversation," he grumbled. He sometimes had a Christopher Walken way of speaking, his words staccato in a disjointed pattern. Most people didn't hear the New York in his voice. His father moved him here when he was a small kid, so most of the time, the Southern stuck, but every now and again there was New York in there.

"They live in Rhode Island."

"Near where?"

"I don't know—Massachusetts."

"What city?"

"What're you gonna do, send 'em a Christmas card?" I said, sounding more like an annoyed teenager. He snorted again, louder. I blinked at him. He put up his hands in a way that suggested we could talk about something else.

"About Lou," I said.

"What about him?"

"He's a friend."

"So you've said."

"He's also a professional. You listen to Marty, our mechanic. Treat Lou the same."

"You forget who has more grass under their porch, boy," he said, his tone even.

I didn't answer. He left it alone, and the rest of the drive was quiet. When we got to the house, Lucas's truck was already in the drive. He was standing outside it talking to Teach. They both looked over.

"Mornin'!" I called out the window as I pulled the SUV in.

"Morning, Al," Lucas said.

"Hey, Coach," Teach said.

"Good morning, Mr. Jefferson," Lucas added.

"Most call me Coach," Coach muttered as he bypassed both of them and went into the house.

"You could help," I shouted after Coach.

"Can't lift. Doctor's orders," he said.

I groaned. "That's what I'm gonna say next time I have to lift your ass off the floor."

Teach snickered.

"Why're you here?" I said to him, looking at my watch. "You're late."

"Good thing the boss is off today. I forgot the key," he admitted, holding up the keys by the bass fish keychain.

"I'm glad I left our grandad's legacy in such capable hands."

"You don't even know the half of it," Teach said, winking at Lucas. He pulled a sixteen-ounce energy drink from the back pocket of his jeans. Using the office key, he stabbed the can, pulled the tab, and shotgunned it. He burped, handed the can to me, finger-gunned Lucas, and skateboarded away.

"That is a cryptid," Lucas said, amused, after Teach had gone.

"God, do you even remember being twenty-five?" I asked.

"Sure. I'm twenty-seven."

I stared.

Coach shouted out to us. "Y'all holding the grass down? Expect to sprout roots?"

I sighed and Lucas laughed. I grabbed a handful of the stuff from the pharmacy and he grabbed the rest. Then my phone rang.

"Shit," I said. I pulled it from my pocket as best I could, balancing the bags. Lucas started for the door.

"Hello, you got Al."

"Al, it's Paul."

Paul had started with my grandfather forty-ish years ago. He owned some of the company, though I owned the majority. He was rugged and somewhat intimidating, like a cowboy from an old cigarette ad. I liked him because he never minded that I was bisexual even though my family ignored it.

"The company truck won't start," he said.

I nearly dropped the super-expensive, super-important breathing machine on my way up the porch. "Well, use the van, the keys are in the desk. If it doesn't turn over, take the day off, I guess. Shit, Paul, I have to go, just have it towed," I said as the bags of supplies slipped. I tried to adjust but was making it worse. I didn't have enough hands to hang up, so I just let the phone fall on the pile of things in my arms. Paul would disconnect on his end.

"I can take something else," Lucas offered, coming back to the porch.

"Just get the door," I said, trying to sound polite.

He held it open. "Let's put these things in the room Coach will be staying in and have a chat about how the day will go."

He was talking to me, but he spoke louder than necessary to make sure my dad heard from where he sat on the couch. He was still in his coat and hat. I showed Lucas where the room was, and we set the equipment down.

"My goal for some of this is to assess Coach's willingness to participate. Like we talked about in the hospital, things are different at home." Lucas had almost whispered it, sounding conspiratorial. "But if he puts in the work, the changes won't limit him."

"Right," I said.

He had beautiful eyes. *Lord, the Gunner did not account for a demigod like Lucas Laverty playin'—* I shook my head to get both the sports announcer and my libido to chill. I couldn't argue with either, though. He was fucking handsome. While I was trying to focus on the tasks and not Lucas, he crossed his arms and looked around the guest room.

"How long do you plan on him staying?" he asked.

"I don't know. I guess I didn't plan on him leavin'."

"That's fair. Some people get a cart to put some of this equipment on. It makes it easy for him to use anywhere he needs it."

"Okay, we can do that."

Lucas just nodded and moved out of the room. I followed. He went to the door and picked up his bag before we went into the living room.

"All right, Mr. Jefferson, I'm going to start with vitals," Lucas said. He put his bag down beside the couch.

"Vitals," Coach repeated.

"Yeah, but you're going to have to take off your coat."

My phone rang. "Coach, do what he says. It's the girls' school, I'll be right back."

I stepped out of the room.

"Hello, Al speakin'."

"Hello, we're calling because Ysabel doesn't seem to have her backpack with her. She says her glasses are in it."

"Good grief." I looked around the kitchen, and there it was. "Yeah, it's here, but I can't get to the school right now."

"She won't stop crying about them and insists you have the day off."

"It's not like that, I…" I pinched my nose. "Tell her I'll find a way."

"Okay, sir."

The elementary school was fairly understaffed, so one crying child could seem like a lot. I stared out the kitchen window trying to figure out who could take the backpack. It didn't make sense for Dani to come all the way back from Valdosta. Glasses weren't the end-all be-all, but Ysabel was a perfectionist and without her glasses, she was—

"Al."

I jumped and turned to Lucas. "Yeah."

"If you're ready, we can move on to the equipment."

"Yeah, I just have to call Teach really quick. Five minutes, please."

Lucas nodded and started pulling papers out of a file and setting them on the kitchen table. I dialed the office.

"Jefferson Land Appraisal: The beauty of your land and a list of the Indigenous you stole it from, this is Thomas speaking."

"Jesus Christ."

"No. Thomas."

"I hate you. Is Paul there yet?"

"No."

"Call him. Have him come pick up and deliver Ysa's glasses to her."

"Righto, boss."

"I know better, but you aren't answerin' the phone like that for real, right?"

"Naw. Last call I said, 'the slaves your forefathers owned.'"

"You're fired."

"Get off my ass."

The line went dead.

"Sorry, I'm ready," I said. I turned to Lucas and Coach, who looked at each other in a way that was weirdly annoying. It's like they knew something I didn't. "Let's start."

Lucas explained the pages he had laid out on the table, putting them in a binder for easy access. He systematically explained the medications, the inhaler, and the breathing machine. And Coach listened without a word.

I listened too, enjoying the bright tenor of Lucas's voice and the way his muscles, muscles I had seen and touched, moved beneath the long-sleeved shirt he had on under his scrubs. He looked more toned down today. No visible tattoos, skin-colored plugs in his ears, no polish on his nails. He'd been much less reserved with Rose, so I knew it was for Coach's benefit, but I didn't like thinking he was being forced to hide or something.

"Al."

I tuned into my name. I blinked. "What?"

"You ready to move on?" Lucas asked. Maybe his voice was a little annoyed. *Oh no, sports fans, is the Gunner getting a penalty?*

"Yup, I'm with ya," I half lied.

We filed into Coach's room. Lucas walked us through putting the machine together. He had just started explaining how to clean it when, of course, my phone rang. I tried to ignore it, understanding it was getting me into hot water with the hot nurse. I didn't even look at it. But the look Lucas gave me, while not judgmental, was knowing. He continued explaining through the call.

"Okay, well, that's it. What do you say we take it for a spin," Lucas said to Coach about twenty minutes later. Coach looked at him and crossed his arms. He looked like he would rather be punched in the nuts than test out the breathing machine.

Lucas put his hands up in a show of good-natured peace. "Not for long, promise. I want to coach you through getting set up for sleep. If you arrange your pillows a specific way, you won't have to worry about the cords. Ten minutes, then I'll show you the exercises."

"I don't need exercises," Coach offered. "Aside from this lung business, I'm in the best shape of my life."

"Coach," I said, ready to intervene.

"Yeah, same, but that doesn't mean I won't go to the gym later and make sure I *stay* in my best shape," Lucas said. To make his point, he crossed his arms over his chest. There was no missing the muscles when he flexed like that. Coach let out a slightly wheezy breath that was probably more sigh than anything else. My phone rang again.

"Shit, I'm sorry."

"Just answer it, son. We're going to test out this contraption," Coach said.

I left the room, grateful and embarrassed. "You got Al."

"Hi, hon."

I had intended to only walk a short way down the hall, but that stopped me in my tracks. I felt suddenly like I couldn't breathe. I was half tempted to knock Coach out of the way and take a few swigs on his breathing machine. "M...Mom?"

"Hi, hon," she repeated.

I threw my hat to the floor and kicked it down the hall, then followed it. Mouthing the words "fuck my life" didn't provide the same relief as saying them out loud. I wish I had the ability to hang up. *Our MVP is in a real pickle now.*

"What do you want, Wynona?" I said, schooling my voice to neutral.

"Well, I got a call yesterday from Jenny. You remember Jenny? She says she saw that father of yours in the hospital. I wanted to call and check on him."

The sarcastic huff was out of my mouth before I could stop it.

"Come now. I'm worried about him."

"Why didn't you call *him*?" I asked. I barely held my phone to my ear, as if her voice produced a toxic acid that could seep through the phone and burn me. I went to the back porch where I could breathe the winter air.

"I tried. He didn't answer," she continued.

"Guess he doesn't want you to know."

"Gage says he's staying with you now."

Her voice was too methodical. It was pissing me off. She had a world of ulterior motive in her voice, but I couldn't even begin to guess what she wanted.

"He is," I said.

There was a long pause as if she were waiting for me to offer more. There wasn't more. She left him, but that hadn't meant she would leave him alone.

"What's he diagnosed with?"

"A sickness."

"Yes, I gather that much. You know, I'm still married to him. I could demand answers if I was so inclined."

Was that it? Was there something she could use in this for the divorce they still hadn't settled? I took a guess. "Maybe, but if you're worried about him dying before you can divorce him, it wouldn't matter. His will doesn't include you."

I could hear her acrylic nails on some solid surface. She usually tapped her nails when she was irritated. And she would run her tongue over her teeth as if she was trying to get lipstick off them. She hated talking about the divorce Coach wouldn't grant her more than I hated talking to her.

"Look, Wy, if that's all, I'm gonna go."

"Well, son, it was good talkin' with you—"

I didn't need to hear any more. I hung up. I sat down with a huff. I hated when she called.

"Hey," Lucas said. I heard his footsteps across the porch but hadn't registered them. He sat next to me.

"Hey."

"You okay?"

"Yeah. Why?"

"Your face."

I rolled my eyes. "Most people like it."

He smiled at me apologetically. "I do too. I just mean you look troubled."

"It's fine."

"Okay. Look, can I ask you something?"

"Sure." I preened a little at his *I do too* about liking my face.

"Asking as your father's nurse?" he added, like he'd heard my internal excitement. I appreciated the clarification. It made it easier somehow to separate the man I had hired to look after my dad from the man I'd held and wanted to hold again.

"Yeah, by all means," I said, hoping he couldn't track my thoughts.

"You and your family have agreed to take care of your dad."

"Right…"

"Do you think you're up for this?"

"What? Of course, how hard could it be? It's not like there's a commute." I tried to deflect with a joke.

He shook his head. "That's not what I meant. Today you were

supposed to learn, right? But you've spent most of the time answering the phone."

"Oh."

"I've had families overestimate themselves before, but my job is to think about one person's well-being. You have a business and a family. Can you make room for this?"

"Does he have to be watched that intensely?"

"No. He may not even need it someday, but it takes time. You have to be in a place where you can react to any needs that arise."

"Right, this is just a settling in," I said. "It'll be different once we all get used to it. It's a lot of moving parts still."

"Why not Teach? You and Dani and Betsy all own businesses. It doesn't seem like Teach has much going on."

I tried to smile. "Teach and Coach are still working on a civil relationship. 'Sides, Teach lives in Denver."

"Oh," he said. His tone gave away his curiosity, but he didn't ask for details. "Right, okay. We'll see how it goes, but I won't hesitate to tell you when it's not going well."

"That's what I pay you for."

He grinned. "All right, now, *as your friend*, how are you doing?"

"You already asked that."

"Not going to tell me, then?"

I looked at the field behind the house. The air was cold, and the green was gone from the grass. It wasn't hard in that moment to separate the friend from the nurse. It seemed so easy for Lucas to make the switch. It was as if his voice changed to accommodate the role he was taking on.

"It occurred to me a long time ago that he was human and not some *deity* I had to contend with. But this is the first time I realized he was mortal. There might really be a time without him."

"That's scary."

"Yeah, especially when I spent years wishing he'd get out of my life. But it's refreshing too, you know, to know maybe my father and I are finally equals. What do you think about your father? How old's he?"

"Oh, um…I don't think about him. I don't know him."

"Oh?"

He grinned at me. "I have two moms."

I think my brain shorted out.

CHAPTER FOUR

Lucas

I wasn't surprised by Al's reaction. It was part of the fun of announcing I had two moms. "Yeah, my birth mom is Jojo, and my other mom is Silvy. They had a friend donate sperm. Well, donate is kind of a loose term. He hung around until I was seven. He's moved on with his life, though, and I haven't heard from him since."

"That's...wow, I...um..."

Al's inability to speak was endearing. "I know, it's a lot."

"I've never met anyone with same-gendered parents."

"I haven't either. So..."

Al looked at me. I didn't know what to say, so I didn't say anything.

"Where's Coach?" Al asked after a second.

"Napping."

"Really? How'd you manage that?"

I brushed my shoulder off. "I have my ways."

He squinted at me. "You drug him?"

"No. I just had him try the breathing machine. Some patients get out of the hospital and have a hard time resting at home. I usually put them in bed under the guise of teaching them how to sleep better, then I just talk to them about boring things until they fall asleep. The oxygen helps a lot."

"How long you goin' to let him sleep for?"

"However long he wants."

"What're you gonna do in the meantime?"

"I'm going to work on my reports." I stood to leave, but he caught my hand. It was hard to ignore the flash of warmth the contact created.

"Um, thanks for this."

"You're welcome." I didn't pull my arm away.

"And I was thinkin', would you want to go to dinner with me two weeks from now?"

I gave it a thought. Well, more than one. Here was a man with a thousand things on his plate asking if I wanted to be another. Of course I did. But I also wanted someone to spend time with. Would it be that different in two weeks? There was only one way to find out. "Okay, name the day."

He looked hopeful. He said he would coordinate with Dani and let me know. I left him on the porch presumably to think or make more phone calls. When he finally came back in, he read through the instruction packets I'd brought. Then he asked me to walk him through the list of pills again. He seemed more focused. The phone calls didn't stop, but he was less aware of them, his phone on silent. A guy did come by for something, but that was really the only interruption. Mr. Jefferson ended up sleeping for three hours.

The weirdest part of the day was simply sharing space with Al and his dad. Or maybe it was just being around a dad generally. My moms didn't have their dads; all my grandfathers died when I was a baby. Grandmothers, moms, wife, daughter. I had somehow become the only person in my life who identified as a dude. That realization came to me halfway through the exercises I was trying to teach Al and his father.

Coach was sitting on the couch, stretching in a seated position. Al was lying on the floor. I had just instructed Coach to lean forward and work on reaching for his feet. I was supposed to be counting, but I was too distracted by the concept of fathers. Ten seconds after the thirty-second deadline, I came to. I was about to apologize when I noticed a subtle sound.

I looked at Coach, who was looking at me. He gave me a mischievous expression, a smirk disguised as indifference. With his head, he directed my gaze to the floor. Al was supposed to be practicing the exercises. Instead, he was sleeping. The sound was him snoring.

Carefully, Coach stood and walked around the oak coffee table. He had one of the pillows from the couch in his hands. I watched him. He held the pillow above his head as he stood over Al's face. He didn't throw it down so much as let it go. As soon as it was out of his hands he shuffled back to the couch. It hit Al, who leapt up with a gasp.

"Wh–what's up? Was I asleep?" Al asked groggily.

I nodded. He looked at the pillow, then at me. I jerked my head toward his dad. And that sneaky bastard had the audacity to look disapprovingly at me, like I had been the one to drop the pillow. Al looked between us like he didn't know who to trust, but he smiled anyway. Al apologized and went back to lying on the floor, this time with the pillow under his head. Coach went back to trying to touch his toes, that smirk still on his face. I wasn't totally sure what I had just witnessed or why it made me feel something.

❖

I was still thinking about fathers when I got home. I changed clothes, went to the gym, then went to pick up Lila. I spent a lot of time as a kid not thinking about fathers, even though I knew most people had one. My brain replayed the scene between Al and Coach over and over. I blinked when I heard Lila shouting across the parking lot of her day care.

"Hi, Lou," she said, sounding more and more like Jojo every day. I waved at her teacher. He waved back.

"Hi, Lila. What's in your hands?" I asked. Last time it had been bird feathers. She unclasped her tiny fists and showed me two painted rocks. They looked like ordinary stones a toddler had painted green with brown spots.

"What're these?" She wouldn't let me take them as I carried her back to the truck.

"Eggs. I'm going to hatch one chicken dragon and one duck dragon."

"Okay, well, put your eggs in your pocket and put your seat belt on."

She did as she was told and snapped herself into her car seat.

"We have to go see Gran and Gam," I said as I checked her belts.

She screamed with excitement. As I drove, she talked about school. She was a very social kid. Ky and I were generally introverts, but Lila was born talking. Even as a baby, she babbled constantly. I wondered if you could really be a good dad without having a dad. I had to assume yes, historically and statistically. But my brain wouldn't stop repeating the question.

My moms lived in a tidy Craftsman with a sprawling garden wrapping around the house. And it was a *garden*. Jojo made a point of planting only edible things in the yard, so it was teeming with leaves, fruits, stalks, roots, and anything you could need as a vegetarian—not that they were vegetarians. Also, it was winter. Right then it looked like an evil witch's cottage. I let Lila out of the truck, and she went screaming into the house brandishing her two eggs.

"My baby girl," I heard Jojo call.

"Psst," someone hissed from the side of the house. I stepped back and saw Silvy waving me over to the garage.

"What's up, Mom?" I said, kissing her cheek.

She smiled. She looked like she could be a dwarf in a fantasy movie or blacksmith in a medieval drama. In reality, she was a carpenter. I towered over her by nearly a foot and a half, but I was pretty sure she could kick my ass. I followed her through the garage out to her backyard workshop.

As soon as we got into the shop, she turned her ball cap around, flashing her brown hair, cut into a mullet, of all things. She also adjusted her glasses against her nose. They were just safety glasses, but she wore them all the time as if she needed them to see. She picked up a pencil and a square and looked at me down the length of the hickory table she was working on.

"What's up?" I asked again, looking at the assorted half-finished furniture around the shop.

"I thought you might want a practice run before Jojo gets hold of ya."

I sighed. "It wasn't all that exciting."

Silvy Laverty knew me better than that. She just stared.

"I met a guy, but now I work for him," I said. "So…"

"Naw, see, that's why you need the practice. Sounds exciting enough, ain't mine or your mom's fault you tell it bad. Start again."

"Let's just go inside, and I can tell you and Jojo together," I said.

She laughed. "I'm not going in there. She has the blender out."

I gulped and felt my stomach turn. Juicing and smoothies and whatever were not the problem. Jojo's ability to make them was a whole different story. She'd tried to make me a leaf, seed, and stem juice once from random garden items. It was like drinking wet hair and sand.

"Yikes. Fine."

I told Silvy everything that had happened between me and Al and about working with Coach.

"But you have a date already, so why the long face?"

"I don't have a long face."

"You don't have a short one."

"Well, it's not even like he set a time."

He had said at the hospital that *we*, this unsolid idea of us, would have to wait until things had settled with his father. Then just today, he said two weeks. I get that that was the wait, but would things really be settled?

"Why didn't *you* set one?"

"I don't know."

"Playing hard to get?"

"Not intentionally."

"Waiting for something else?"

"No, at least I don't think so."

"Scared?"

I didn't answer, which made Silvy laugh. I watched for a while as she worked on the table. Mom and Ma weren't really the settling type and had moved every few years when I was a kid, but they fell in love with Painted Waters when they came to help Ky through her pregnancy. When Silvy got a few commissions from a local house flipper, they committed to staying.

"*Dad! Gam!*" Lila shouted, breaking our concentration. We looked out into the yard. She was crossing the grass with an old Easter basket in her arms, and her rocks nested safely inside.

"Gran wants you to come inside," Lila told me in a tone that was all business. When she made it around the table to Silvy, her tone shifted. "Gam! Look at my eggs."

"Very nice, did you lay them?" Silvy asked.

Lila giggled. "No!"

I smiled at Silvy. She picked up Lila, and the three of us headed back into the house. Jojo was sorting through things in her pantry. I tiptoed up behind her, grabbed her sides, and roared. She screamed and slapped my arm when she realized it was me.

"Don't do that," she said. "I'll pee."

"What're you looking for?" Silvy asked her.

"Chia seeds," Jojo answered, shaking a Mason jar. Silvy gave me a knowing look. Jojo laughed, kissing the top of her head. "Don't worry, sourpuss, they aren't for you."

Jojo was nearly as tall as me. She had brown hair and long limbs. She reminded me of slightly out-of-proportion cartoon moms. I remembered a photo of them in college, one of three that had my father in it. Jojo and Silvy had been so close with him.

"What do you say, son? How about a health drink?" Jojo asked.

"I had a shake at the gym, so I'm good," I said. It was a safe little lie.

She frowned, then shook it off. "My rhubarb is going to be so nice in the summer. It helped that I looked up the recipe for that natural pesticide. Not that I want to get rid of all the bugs, but sometimes you need bugs and sometimes you need nice rhubarb."

With that, she hit start on the blender, adding chia seeds as the assorted frozen veggies and fruits minced, then liquified.

"So, how was your party?" she asked when the blender stopped.

"It was fine. I met someone. Ma, what was DeAndrew like? I mean, I can't really remember him."

Both Silvy and Jojo paused mid task. Silvy was pouring a beer, and it spilled over the glass. Jojo was trying to get the contents of the blender out with a spoon. They looked like I paused the TV in the middle of a lesbian sitcom.

"That's not what we rehearsed," Silvy said finally, licking the beer she'd spilled on her hand.

"You met someone? DeAndrew? What makes you ask about him?" Jojo asked at the same time. After a moment of silence, she added, "You haven't asked about him in years."

I shrugged and picked at the remains of the smoothie veggies littering the counter in order to occupy my hands. "I have a new client, the dad of the guy I met at the party. I was just thinking about dads."

They both blinked at me again.

"Here," Silvy said, sliding me the beer. "Why don't you start that story over?"

I sipped. Then I explained. I obviously kept it within HIPAA protocol, and I didn't go into much detail about the events of the party. I did try to explain my thoughts as clearly as I could.

"My," Jojo sighed when I was finished.

"I think you should call him—Al, not your dad," Silvy said, slightly missing the point.

Jojo took over. "Well, you know most of the basics. DeAndrew was the graduate assistant for my accounting class. He was this fantastic guy, active in the community at school, Student Pride Center and all. That was how I met him. He was at the wedding. Then right before we graduated, I asked him if he would donate to us. He said sure—"

"He said *sure*?"

Jojo nodded.

"*Sure*. That's it? Just sure?"

I don't know why I was getting angry. I literally hadn't given DeAndrew Nation a single thought in over a decade. It seemed like he hadn't given me one either.

"Well, there was more than that," Jojo said gently. "He was around for a few years. Then he needed to come home. Help his family. You know all of that."

"We've sent him a few photos over the years," Silvy said.

That didn't make me feel better. *His family.* Like I wasn't someone in his family. I had never asked if he had even wanted to be my father. Maybe I figured if he hadn't wanted to, he shouldn't have been around till I was seven. I remembered a birthday or two and some bitter feelings. I couldn't even really fill in the face in the photo I remembered, just Jojo and Silvy, then a dark patch where DeAndrew Nation stood—no pun intended. He was a tall Black man and had chosen two white lesbians to be his friends and the mothers of his child.

Silvy looked at me critically. "You know, I'm surprised you haven't asked about him more since moving here."

"I mean we only talk every day, Ma, when would I have asked?" I told her sarcastically. Mostly, I didn't have a reason to ask about him until now. She squinted at me like I was speaking nonsense.

Jojo came around the counter and put an arm on my shoulder. "Listen, I know it's not easy to accept, but we've never stopped him from seeing you. We've invited him to all the important things. His involvement or non-involvement was his choice. It has nothing to do with us and especially nothing to do with you."

I stared at them and they stared back. I could see only the same love and honesty they had always given me. I tried to take them at their word.

❖

"Hey, bae," Ky said, greeting me and Lila at the door.

"Hey," I said, and handed her Lila's eggs. She'd carried them around Ma's house for three hours. Now it was my turn to cart them around. She had moved on enough to hand me the basket but not enough to let them get lost.

"A basket of rocks, how thoughtful," she said.

"They're eggs, Mommy."

"Oh, got it."

"How was writing?" I asked. Lila went to day care Monday through Thursday so Ky could use the house to work on her research. She also rented a desk in a community office space when she needed it or wanted a change of scene. Her officemates were a local hemp dealer and a middle-aged housewife who did tarot readings over the phone. She was home with Lila Friday through Sunday unless she was traveling.

"It was fine. I got in a rabbit hole because of a discussion about biosolid runoff, but other than that, I made progress. Why do you look like someone shit in your pocket?"

"It's called *biosolids*," I corrected, trying to distract her.

She laughed. "Okay, so was it the *client*? Word around the office is that Mr. Jefferson is low-key the worst."

I gave her my HIPAA look, and she rolled her eyes.

"Peter says he went to school with Al," she continued. I'd met Peter, and it was hard to place the Willie Nelson knockoff in the same location as the business casual Al. "He also said Coach Jefferson is a bigot."

Despite all that was said in the hospital, Coach himself never said anything. I stared, unresponsive.

"All right, if not him, then what?" she pressed.

Lila was talking around us. We were so used to her noise, we'd learned how to continue the important parts of a discussion over her. She never seemed to notice. I pretended to let her chatter distract me. I wasn't in the mood to have another conversation about my dad. I corrected Lila on the right way to say ostrich and looked at Ky.

Finally, I said, "Al asked me to dinner when I'm not working for him anymore."

She followed me into the living room. "I'd say that's great, but you don't sound that excited."

"Is it weird for you to talk about this?"

"Lou, you can talk to me about anything. I promise I don't feel like I'm not getting my due focus from you." She held up three fingers. "Scout's honor."

I fell onto the couch face-down in the cushions. "Would he even have time?"

"He seems irresponsible for a guy who wears polos," she said.

"He's probably too responsible, but it's all for other people. I can't really tell what he does for himself."

"That's a read," she said. I pulled her down as I rolled over so she was lying with me. "Wait, no, I have to make dinner."

"I got something else you can make," I teased.

"Crafts?" Lila butted in.

We laughed. I tried to hold on, but Ky escaped by pulling my arm hair.

❖

When I walked into the house, I realized this session with the Jefferson family would be showing Dani everything I'd shown Al the day before. I'd never hung out with a boyfriend's wife before. *Not that we we're hanging out. Not that Al's a boyfriend.* I took a deep breath and tried to focus.

"Hi, Lucas. Looking good. What gym do you go to? The one here or in Valdosta?" Dani's ponytail flapped behind her as she trotted away from the door. Every worry I had dissipated. She was wearing leggings and a loose-fitting tank over a sports bra. I forgot she was a personal trainer. It was easy to overlook when she was flirting with dudes at a party.

"Um, that wasn't the first question I was expecting."

"Figures, but I've been dying to ask, and since you were *occupied* the last time I saw you, I didn't want to miss my chance." She winked.

I laughed out of embarrassment. "I go to the gym here."

She made a face. "Why? If you went to Beast, you could hang out with me."

"First of all, here's closer to where I have to pick up my kid. Second, we aren't here so you can recruit me."

She pouted, then grinned. "I guess you-know-who has a type."

"What? Gym junkie?"

"I was going to say *physically acclaimed professional*," she answered playfully.

Our laughing was cut short by a loud bang. Teach came running down the stairs from the apartment over the garage, sliding the pocket door open with so much force, it rattled. He was half dressed, with one arm in his jacket and his polo draped around his neck. His white hair was like a crazy curtain around his face.

"Shit, did he leave?" he asked Dani.

"Yeah, kiddo. It's, like, almost ten."

I looked at my watch. It was five after nine. Teach groaned and ran into the kitchen, coming back with an energy drink in his fist and a muffin in his mouth.

"Slow down. You'll choke on that. Al's gonna be angrier if you're dead than late," Dani warned him.

"Good thing I'm his favorite," Teach said, winking. He gave me a once-over and a sly grin, then bolted out the door.

"Did he just…?" I asked, pointing after him.

"He did." She shook her head like it was something that happened all the time.

"Huh," I said, surprised by the drive-by flirt.

"Good morning."

We both turned to see Coach come out of his room. He was dressed much the same as yesterday: jeans, thick flannel, hat. The way Dani and I were dressed, you'd forget it was November.

"Good morning, sir, ready to get at it?"

He grumbled and marched past us into the living room.

"I'm going to take some vitals. Start with this," I said, pointing Dani to the kitchen table, where the medication instructions were located. As I set up around him, Mr. Jefferson eyed me.

"You're what—twenty-two? Twenty-three?"

"Twenty-seven."

He nodded as if he had guessed right and wasn't surprised.

"Roll up your sleeve, please."

"You got all your degrees?" His eyes were on his sleeves not on me.

I tried to answer and work at the same time. "All that matter for an RN."

"Why don't you work in the hospital?"

"I do sometimes."

"But?"

I took a slow, patient breath and sat back on my heels, letting the air out of the blood pressure cuff. I was going to have to retake the measurement. "I had my fill of institutions my first year out of school. I worked at a juvenile correction facility north of here. It was a lot. I guess I'd rather help people live their best lives than patch up kids after they decide to beat the shit out of each other—sorry for cussing. Hospitals here are ER heavy, and I didn't want that."

He again nodded. He let me finish most of my checks in silence. But when I started to listen to his breathing, he asked, "And this is good work for people like you?"

My grip on my stethoscope faltered for a minute, and I had to sit back. *People like you* could mean a million things, and after what Ky had reported I felt a slight panic.

"Coach," Dani warned from the kitchen.

"What? I was just wondering if Black people"—he eyed me and corrected himself—"colored people get treated all right. I know that weren't always the case. I was just making conversation."

In his tone and in his expression, I recognized someone who was asking to understand but didn't have the language to do it without offending.

"School was fine. I went to an HBCU. I had a harder time in high school than college. And yes, people of color are treated better in ways. And in others, we're treated as you would expect."

"You aren't full, right?"

"Coach, this ain't a church social. Mind your business," Dani said, poking her head out of the kitchen.

"It's fine," I said. I decided to answer his questions. I felt like I was learning something about him. I also gave up on trying to listen to his lungs. "No, my mother's white."

"She live here?"

"She does." And in a fit of insanity, I added, "She moved here with her wife around the time my daughter was born."

I could hear Dani choke on her drink. Mr. Jefferson only raised his eyebrows and nodded, as if finding out his personal nurse was raised by lesbians was no big deal.

CHAPTER FIVE

Alexander

I came home to the sound of arguing. My living room was just a short hallway down from the front door, so I could see Coach sitting in his armchair as soon as I walked in. He was watching the arguers with an amused smile. As I came into the house, I could make out Lucas and Dani wrapped up in a semi-heated conversation about stretching.

"Hey ya, Coach," I said kneeling by his chair.

"Son."

"What's with them?"

"One says do it that way, the other says this way."

"Don't they know you're literally a coach?"

"So far...no one's asked me."

"And you didn't think to stop 'em."

He scratched his chin with his palm. "If they keep it up, no matter which way's the right way, I don't have to do it."

I think I fell in love with everyone a little more in that moment. Everyone being so themselves around each other was surprising but welcome. I pulled a pile of scratch tickets out of my back pocket and handed them to him. It was part of the Thursday ritual, only he didn't know it was a Thursday thing. I stopped weekly on the way to pick up the girls to get Dani flowers and buy scratchers for Coach. I would give them to him whenever I saw him next, so to him it was probably random. Now I guess he'd get them day of.

The other two didn't even seem to notice me come in. They were almost exact opposites physically: tall and short, white and Black, so on and so on. But listening to them argue was jarringly similar.

"Well, shit," I said loudly, disrupting them both. They turned to me. I got to my feet.

"What's the matter?" Dani asked.

"I don't know. Doesn't seem safe having two meatheads in the house. Pretty soon you both are goin' to have all of us running laps."

They rolled their eyes.

"Where are my kids?" Dani said, walking toward me. She turned back to Lucas. "This conversation isn't over."

He nodded.

"Teach offered to drive the bus," I said. The bus was the church van we bought as a family to shuttle the kids to and from school and day care. Some days I drove it, some days Daniel did. It almost wasn't enough, but with the right placement of children and car seats, we could get two adults and all fifteen girls in it.

"Aw, Teach." She took her flowers and kissed me.

I watched her go into the kitchen, and then I waved at Lucas. "Hey, Lou. How was the day?"

"It was good. He—"

"*He's* going on a walk," Coach said, rising.

"Wait, what?" I looked at Lucas. "Is he allowed to do that?"

"Yes. As long as he has the inhaler with him."

My dad pulled it out of his front shirt pocket and waved it as he got to the door.

"He should have someone with him," Dani said.

I looked at Lucas, who looked like he was on the verge of leaving, his bag over one shoulder. I didn't want him to leave.

"I'll go, just make sure the girls start their homework," she said. Dad, who spent every moment out of bed fully dressed, shoes and all, was out the door with little delay. Dani had to rush into shoes and a coat. Not that he could outpace her.

"She's almost too honest," Lucas said. "She said my form was off."

I winked. "I think it's pretty good."

He opened his mouth, surprised.

"Um, you want to talk a minute?" I asked, feeling my blood start to race.

He looked at his watch, then at the floor. It only took him a second to make whatever calculation he needed to before he nodded. I looked around the room and felt too exposed. We were watching Betsy's and Gage's kids for the evening, so we'd have a typhoon of girls in a matter of minutes. Not to mention Coach would be back.

"Come with me," I said.

He put his bag down and followed me down the hall into the stairwell connecting the house to the mother-in-law suite. The hallway and stairs were new, since the house hadn't been connected to the garage before I renovated. It was a wide staircase, and the light from the many windows above gave it a cool, gray coziness.

"Hi," I said turning to him on the stairs. He slid the pocket door closed behind him.

"Hey."

The stairs were a normal width for a house but seemed small with the both of us there, so I sat a few steps up, eye level but not crowding him. "So, I was thinkin' dinner next Saturday?"

I watched him think, but it didn't look like deciding whether to say yes or not, which was reassuring. He looked more like he was looking at a calendar in his head. His last day working for us would be the Friday before the date. So that meant there'd be time to give this a chance.

"I can swing that. What time?"

"What time works for you?"

"Seven?"

"Seven."

"Where?"

"Wherever works for you."

He cocked an eyebrow at me.

"Well, what're you into? I don't even know. Are you a wings and beer type? Or, I don't know…Italian?"

He smiled and said, "I'm into…"

Then he leaned forward just enough to press his lips against mine.

"You've got to be the most impressive flirt I've ever met," I said when he stepped away.

"Beer and wings," he said.

I nodded. "Great, love it, good, cool, so should I pick you up?"

He crossed his arms. His smile was enough to show that he was happy with the plans, although something behind his eyes looked like worry.

"I'm goin' take that as a yes. Is…is it actually a *yes* or is it a *yes but*," I asked, standing, coming too close all at once.

"You're sure it's not too soon? You're the one who said life was a lot right now."

"Right, yeah, but this is goin' better than I thought."

"It's been two days."

"Knowing my dad, it would've gone bad day one if it was gonna go bad. Maybe I overestimated how overwhelmed I'd be."

He squinted at me, but I could tell he was relenting and not challenging. *This is it, guys, gals, and nonbinary pals, our MVP makes the play of a lifetime.* Feeling hopeful for the first time in almost a week, I stepped closer. He let me, his eyes on my mouth the whole time. I kissed him, our mouths the only parts of our bodies touching. This kiss was somehow different. At the poly party and even the peck before this kiss, there had been warmth. That was just lust, though. Right then, in the stairwell, I felt a flutter in my stomach, like butterflies made of light. Then I heard a cough. I hadn't heard the door open. We jumped apart and stared at Teach. He grinned and squeezed past us.

"Damn, disappointing," he said to Lucas in a way that made it clear seeing us together was somehow a loss for him. He walked a ways up the stairs, then turned and looked over his shoulder. "Then again, you must be poly too, so a guy can hope."

"Fat chance," I said, looking to Lucas to back me up. Annoyingly, he was looking after Teach.

"Oh, what? Come on," I groaned. Teach laughed and disappeared into the suite.

"That's," Lucas whispered, "the best flirt *I've* ever met."

I tried not to laugh. "Go home."

He was chuckling as he led the way back to his bag. He had to fight three toddlers for it and then had to wade through a tide of blondes and brunettes. He didn't seem to mind it all. And just before the door closed behind him, he winked at me.

Two weeks passed fast. It was so fast for me that it wasn't until after ten a.m. on Thursday that I realized the next day would be Lucas's last. It was nice seeing him every day—well, nearly. I had started putzing around the house a little longer in the mornings just to see him. He was at the house today with Daniel. I was actually jealous.

I looked at the calendar on my phone. Today was full of notes for the girls, the biggest one being that they were going to be over at Betsy's to help make cookies and brownies for a school fundraiser. That meant Dani and I would have the house to ourselves since Coach would probably go with them. I had to stop by the store for Coach's prescription refills, and Dani was launching the rock wall at the gym and would have a busy weekend. And about ten thousand other things were on the list. At the start of the day tomorrow, though, was a small reminder for Lucas's last day.

Coach was getting better, and even Lucas agreed we didn't need him anymore. *I* wanted him, though. Lord, did I want him. I looked around my office, suspicious that someone could hear my thoughts. I was alone. And for the first time in a while the phone hadn't rang once, my personal one or otherwise. *To recap for those of you just tuning in, our MVP has the opportunity of the century. Now, Lucas "the Tank"—*

"The Tank? He gets the Tank and I get the Gunner?"

—is one of the finest we've seen in the arena since Danielle "the Crusher" Cullen. I snorted a laugh at my thoughts. *We have no doubt these two will be a perfect pairing for the upcoming game. Now, what do folks at home have in common with our friends here in the arena? We're all wondering where the matchup is gonna take place.*

Crap. Sports announcer voice was right. Where was I going to take him for dinner? Wings and beer was easy enough, but I didn't really want anything here in Painted Waters. The restaurants were good and all, but in the same small-town way. Atlanta, though, was too far. Right?

I opened a browser on the computer and typed in *wings*. My phone buzzed as I was searching. Dani's text asked *What tool does this take*, then a picture followed. Giggling to myself, I unlocked the phone and texted *my dick*. Then I went back to looking at restaurants. A second later, my phone buzzed again. It was from Lucas. There was a blushing emoji, and it said *most people say good morning first.*

I felt a piece of me die with embarrassment. Hurriedly, I opened the message. Somehow my phone had opened to my chat with him rather than Dani. I groaned and slowly typed, *my bad. I was trying to text Dani.*

Dang she gets all the good texts.

Well there's plenty to go around.

I went back to the restaurants. There was a decent-looking one about thirty minutes from my house. Maybe there. I sent Lucas a message. *How about Wing Central?* It took a little longer than I anticipated for him to respond. Maybe he was looking it up. Enough time passed that the phone had put itself to sleep. I thumbed it open when he finally replied.

What do wings have to do with the tool? I read. It took a second to register what was going on. I had texted the wrong person twice in twenty minutes. I face-palmed. "Lord baby Jesus, give me strength."

I looked at the photo Dani sent and told her I had no fucking clue and I did most things with an adjustable wrench. Her response was: *maybe it's a bolt thing…needs a bolt thing? I want wings now. Let's go out to eat since the girls won't be home. We can Venmo Bets to get them pizza or something.* I agreed, then copied the photo and sent it and the name of the restaurant to Lucas.

Building something? he asked. *Restaurant sounds good.*

I cheered for myself then explained that Dani was trying to set up a rock wall. The gym had a professional team come and build it. Test climbers came on Wednesday and made some suggestions Dani and her team were trying to implement. It didn't seem to be going well.

Tell her to get a hammer. J/k, it's a bolt-thing but that's the nut part.

I smiled and sat back in my chair. *Lou says it's a nut*, was all I texted Dani. Then I got a notification that she added me to a group chat with Lucas. I spent the rest of the morning watching them banter in text messages.

❖

Dani and I decided to eat in Painted Waters for dinner. She found a pop-up restaurant in an empty building near town hall. I didn't care—it sounded like food I didn't have to cook, which was good enough to me. The city was crowded for once.

"Shit, I forgot they were opening the Winter Park today," Dani said, gesturing to the square in town. It would eventually have an ice-skating rink, but for now it was hosting a dozen or so ice sculptures. "Should we go to a different place?"

"We should at least see what the wait is."

The restaurant was crowded. I opened the door for Dani, and we stepped into a makeshift lobby. It didn't look like much. The pop-up organizers hadn't changed the building from the empty restaurant husk that had been there. It was a big room with rows of tables. On the walls were paintings from local artists, but that was about all. I tried stepping around the crowd of waiting patrons to find the host.

"I'm sorry, I don't work here."

I caught the voice before I saw the man. I turned to see Lucas waiting off to the side.

THE SPEED OF SLOW CHANGES

"You don't work here?" an older man asked.

"No, sir."

"I just want to know the wait," the man grumbled.

Lucas shrugged. "They told me thirty-five minutes, but that was twenty minutes ago. I bet it's changed."

I decided to interrupt the awkward encounter the best way I knew how.

"Look," I said, nudging Dani.

"Lou," she shouted, trotting over. She all but shoved the older man aside as Lucas smiled and hugged her. The old man scooted away.

"What're you up to?" she asked him, making room so I could shake his hand.

"Ky heard from one of her officemates that this place was pretty good."

"Where is she?" Dani asked, looking around.

"Bathroom. What're you two up to?"

"Same idea, but hell if I know when we'll get a table," I said.

"Lila with you?" Dani asked.

Lucas shook his head. "She's with my parents. I don't know why they even bother bringing her back to us."

Then I saw Ky wading through the tables. I waved at her. She grinned and waved back. She stepped up to Lucas. They were a good-looking pair and complemented each other nicely. Ky looked like every volleyball player I had known in college save for the green hair, tattoos, and gauged ears. They both had on band T-shirts and were the fucking coolest. With Dani in her tight jeans and her flowy red top, I was looking like a fine dork in my work clothes. At least they didn't have the logo on them. Then Lucas grinned at me, his brown eyes shining with genuine affection. What I was wearing didn't really matter anyway.

"Hey, Jeffersons," Ky said.

"Hey, you've met Kelley, right?" I asked, shaking Kyoko's hand.

"Once or twice," Ky answered.

"Dani, please. We are friends now." Dani dug her elbow into my rib for introducing her as Kelley.

"I—"

"Laverty?" the waitress asked as she approached.

"Yup," Lucas said.

She looked us over. "You're a table of four? I have you down for two."

Dani and I were about to protest, but Kyoko beat us to a response. "Yes, four. Is that okay?"

"Sure, I just…I'll have to grab two more menus."

"Is that okay?" Ky said as the waitress got more menus. "Come on, we can share a table."

"How'd you know they could fit us?" Dani whispered.

"All the tables seat four or six. I noticed when I went to the bathroom."

Dani grinned at me, Ky took Lucas's hand, and we were all seated at the table. The menu was a limited selection of barbecue, but it seemed like a fairly fancy take on barbecue, the pulled pork coming with whatever kale salad was. They did bring cornbread rolls to the table, so the menu could have been a selection of fancy ice water, and I would have been excited. I shoved a roll into my mouth without much formality.

"Gonna fill up on bread?" Dani asked me.

"Maybe."

"Did you get the wall finished?" Lucas asked Dani.

She groaned and regaled the table with the shenanigans of trying to finish the rock wall. My hand fell over hers and she held it, barely pausing in her story. After a moment, someone's foot slid against my boot. I looked at Lucas. He met my gaze but didn't hold it. Instead, he grinned slyly and looked back at Dani. I slid my foot more completely against his. It had been the simplest thing in the world. All I understood about my feelings for Lucas was the potential. With both of them in contact with my body, I lost the thread of the story fairly quickly.

Dani and Ky ended up mostly talking to each other while Lucas and I fought over the honey butter and rolls. Lucas tried a little harder than I did to stay in the conversation, but eventually they kicked him out too. They were talking about Ky's research. Ky was a soil scientist and was studying something or other. I would have to ask later, but it was hard to draw my attention away from Lucas. Eventually we ran out of bread and ordered dinner. Ky and Dani left us out even more after the food came. I inspected my brisket. It all looked good even though I wasn't sure what made a potato purple. And who put white gravy on mashed potatoes?

"You gonna eat it or appraise it?" Lucas asked.

I looked up to retort, but he started to pull the meat off the bone of his ribs with his fork. "What're you doin' there?"

"Eating," he said, gesturing with both bone and fork.

"You aren't gonna pick it up and bite it like normal?"

He accused me with the bone. "That's racist."

I blinked. "Oh shit, is it?"

He grinned and put a hunk of meat in his mouth. "Naw. I just don't like sauce on my face."

I squinted. "Not on the face, huh? That apply to all sauce?"

He choked slightly. Then he laughed and gestured to Ky, who was paying him zero attention. "Hey, can't you see I'm on a date here? Keep it clean, pal."

Dani and Kyoko had moved on to talk about a romance book series they both liked. I'd read it too, but it was too creepy for me, vampires and sun-elves or something.

I put my hands up. "Fine, fine, do you."

He bowed with mock gratefulness. I dug into my own meal. The meat was great. The potatoes also. I hadn't expected the corn on the cob, so that was a nice surprise. I picked up my knife and started trimming off kernels. When the cob was naked, I scooped the kernels with my fork. With the fork halfway to my mouth, I looked up. Lucas watched me, somehow both annoyed and amused.

"What?"

"You know what," he said, sounding stern. "Get up."

"What?"

He tossed his napkin on the table. "I said get up, we're going outside."

I stared, confused. His seriousness broke. "You get on my ass about *my* ribs, then proceed to defile corn on the fucking cob. It's on a cob for a reason."

"I don't like kernels in my teeth."

"You pick it up...no, you know what, it would be easier to fight you. Get your John Cena–lookin' ass up."

By this time, I was practically on the floor laughing. Some of the kernels still in my mouth slipped into my lungs, and I started to choke. I wouldn't die, but I gestured for Lucas to help me anyway.

"No way, that corn deserves a chance to get revenge after what you did. CPR is what you get later after the corn finishes the job. The Heimlich isn't for corn-defilers."

Eventually he laughed too and handed me some water. We probably overstayed our welcome at the little restaurant, but we tipped well. We went out to the sidewalk. It was a fairly cold night, our breath lingering in the air. I stood by talking with Lucas and Ky while Dani went to the restroom.

"Hey, Al, can I drop you off at the house?" she said, coming out of the restaurant, looking at her phone.

"Yeah, but where're you goin'?"

"They're having problems at the gym. Something about belay ropes. Two trainers are stuck in the air."

I tried not to laugh.

"I can take him," Lucas offered out of nowhere, the rest of us turning to stare at him. He rubbed the back of his neck, shyly. "Dani would have to backtrack. My truck is right here."

He pointed to the apartment above an office, literally right next to the restaurant.

"That works for me," Dani said, looking at me.

I nodded. I was so enamored by his small, bashful gesture that it almost made me happy she ditched me.

"I need to stop by the office to get my laptop charger, so have fun," Ky said, kissing Lucas on the cheek. She waved at the rest of us and was on her way up the stairs. Lucas followed her into the stairwell, propping the door to the street open with his foot. A half minute later, his wife dropped his keys down to him.

"Thank you," Dani said to Lucas. She hugged him then kissed me, taking my keys, and trotted across the street to where the truck was parked.

I didn't say anything to Lucas. I couldn't really find the words. It was the second simplest thing that had happened that night, and it gave me an overwhelming sensation of joy. I just followed him to his truck. The drive was short—our houses were only ten minutes apart—but we spent most of the time in a nice sort of silence.

I was almost disappointed to arrive in my own yard. The house was dark. Bets would bring the kids and Coach home at nine, and it was only seven thirty. Teach might have been home. The light was on, but that didn't mean much. I looked at Lucas, who put the truck in park but didn't turn off the engine. I guess even our dates wouldn't go a usual way. It wasn't like I could invite him in. I could, sure, but not for...

It was time for a subject change. "Thank you. I hope this didn't ruin your date night with Ky."

"Naw, it was more of a necessity than a date since neither of us wanted to cook. Besides, I had fun. I've never done that before."

"What? A double date?"

He shrugged and for the first time looked confused, but in a charmed way.

"I mean, that was a bit more in a way, wasn't it? With you and Ky."

Dani and I had different approaches to our partnerships. When she dated someone, they tended to stick around even if she stopped dating them. So ultimately, she had a lot of friends who were former lovers or metas. She'd even dated one of the guys who co-owned her gym. That's how she was able to buy in. They broke it off, feeling more like friends. He was a great guy. We sat for his dog last summer when he went out of town. Brandon was a friend. I guess I could see Ky becoming a friend. But was that what Lucas wanted? I didn't figure out how to ask before he moved on.

"It was fun, though I can't stand the way you eat corn on the cob. Big red flag."

I smiled. "I'm glad it was fun. I'll see you tomorrow. Now that I know you're a good time."

"Oh, *now* you know? Half-naked at the party wasn't enough of a sign?"

If I thought too much about the party, a hard-on was a guarantee, so instead I reached for my keys— "Oh, shit."

"What?"

"Dani took the house keys. I guess I'll see if Teach is inside."

"We can try to pry open a window," Lucas offered, surveying my house.

I pulled out my phone and called Teach.

"You have three seconds," Teach said after only one ring. "Three."

"What're you doing that you answer the phone like that—"

"Two."

"I'm locked out. Come let me in."

"Sorry, bro, I'm not home. Use the garage key."

Then he hung up.

"Oh, right. There's a spare somewhere in the garage," I said to Lucas.

"The garage isn't locked?"

"Naw, there's nothin' in it. I had it cleared out to make a workshop to build the mother-in-law-suite, and the girls like to play in it, so we keep it pretty clear."

"Got it."

"Thanks for hanging around until I got it figured out."

He grinned. "I kind of wanted to see if we could get you through a window."

I couldn't decide what to say, so I just waved and got out of the truck. Every molecule of me screamed to go back and kiss him, hug him, something. I went around the side of the garage and entered, losing the high white glare of the headlights.

The blackness of the garage was absolute. I sighed, trying to remember what it looked like so I could navigate the darkness to the switch by the door that led to the house. I took a step. Then another. About a third of the way through, I realized I could have made the shorter, safer trip to the garage doors, opened them, and had Lucas use the headlights of his truck to help me see. I stilled. I didn't hear the truck anymore. I guess he'd left.

"Al," Lucas said from behind me.

I turned, surprised, and stepped on the most dangerous thing a thirty-one-year-old man could step on. I couldn't say what it was specifically, but it had wheels. I landed hard on the cement floor.

"Fuck me." I groaned and flopped onto my back to take the weight off the wrist I'd caught myself on. My right hip and my left wrist ached in unison.

"Shit, Al, are you okay?"

A small, warm yellow light blinked to life. I put a hand up to try and block out the sudden brightness. A big, light brown hand closed around mine and hauled me to my feet.

"Why are you always hurting yourself?" Lucas asked.

"I would've said somethin' about fallin' for me," I told him.

He grunted. The flashlight attached to his keys was pointed down now, illuminating our boots. But the back flow of light was enough to allow me to see him. He was fucking handsome, skin glowing like precious metal.

"What're you doing in here? I thought you left," I said, my voice betraying some of my awe.

He grinned. "Your wallet was on the seat. Thanks for the cash."

"You wish. I haven't had cash since I had children."

"Are you okay?" he asked in his nurse's voice.

"Yeah, I'll probably bruise is all."

"Why didn't you use the flashlight on your phone?"

I could have cried with embarrassment. "Cuz my brain is mostly for show."

I don't know if he'd started it or if I had, but I noticed we were practically whispering. It forced us closer to each other. By the end of my sentence, we were standing almost chest to chest. The only thing separating us was his hand still holding mine. His body was a warm beacon in the cold, and I wanted to wrap myself around it. I watched his eyes dart between my eyes and my mouth. I wanted so badly to feel his lips again.

"Al," Lucas said, his voice air soft and almost worried.

"I'm really fine," I said, misunderstanding.

"I...yeah...Um, tomorrow's my last day."

"I know."

"I don't usually make this offer to clients but—"

"Yes," I said. My pulse went from zero to sixty in half a beat. *Breaking news, folks, will we get to see some of our newest duo, Jefferson and Laverty, before their scheduled match?*

"You don't know what I'm going to say," he said.

That didn't stop him from leaning in. I became aware of the faintest fragrance of cedar and leather. It was like breathing air from somewhere I had never been, like the smell before a thunderstorm. I took a deep breath of it. Lucas smelled so enticing.

"I can't think of anythin' I'd say no to." And that was a slutty fact.

Lucas gave me a half grin, as if he would argue. I almost couldn't breathe. It was like the blood in my body was moving too fast for my cells to get any oxygen. I was light-headed and rooted in place, all because of his smile.

He let out a breath like he had convinced himself of something and let go of my hand. His drifted around my waist. That small opening was everything, and I stepped into it like walking into a warm house on a winter night. His mouth met mine, lips already parting.

He let me in his space, let me in his mouth, my body flush with his. It took less than two steps before he was against the doors to the garage. They were thick, barn-style doors, strong enough to take the force of our bodies without give or noise. Not that anyone was home to hear.

He practically melted into the kiss, breathy moans escaping him as he pulled me hard against him. He was sinking against the doors in a pliant, eager way, and I felt like I was looming over him. I liked the feeling of kissing down into his mouth and the long feel of his jawline as he kissed back. I shifted to hold him in place, my leg coming in between his. He hummed against my lips. This new position slotted our bodies against each other in a familiar way. *It's a classic move but we love to see it, the old thigh straddle. Been doing it since he was twelve—*

Lucas groaned almost inaudibly, grinding into the contact. I followed that groan with a thrust. His answering thrusts were almost overwhelming. The more I explored his mouth and pressed him into the doors, the more he rutted against me. That was making this go way faster than I thought possible. I was hard and ready to come in a few thrusts of his cock on my thigh. I needed to back out of the contact, pull back to regain some control over my orgasm. I was ninety percent sure he was going to ask to kiss me when he started talking about tomorrow being his last day, but that didn't give me consent to dry-hump him.

His hands on my hips, though, were tight, and he wouldn't let me back up much. I opened my eyes and tangled my hands in the perfect brown curls at the base of his neck, his hair long enough to wrap around my fingers. I grinned at him. "Holy fuck, you're beautiful."

He groaned. "I know. Now, shut up and kiss me. Please don't stop."

I did kiss him, softly, slowing myself down because I didn't want to rush through. He didn't force anything faster, either. The slower I went, the more he seemed to melt. He shifted, his thick thigh rubbing the full length of my hard cock. "Lucas. God. Fuck."

"It's like being seventeen again, right?" Lucas breathed, his lips coming to my neck.

It was my turn to melt. When I was a teenager, no matter who my partner was, this grinding against each other, the sex without sex, always seemed like such an advanced step. Any partner I'd had since sophomore year of college usually went from kissing to naked, skipping right over plain old rubbing together as a possible means of getting off. But it was fun. Why do people quit doing this?

"Do you want me to stop?" he asked, probably interpreting my thinking as hesitation.

"No. Fuck no."

I tipped his face back up to me and continued enjoying his mouth. He palmed my chest and rubbed my sides, tracing back to the top of my jeans. Fuck, I wanted to let him shove me against the door, I wanted to feel him inside me. Since that wasn't on the table, I rocked into his body, hips grinding on hips. The sensations on my dick were overwhelming, the fabric of my briefs, the seam of his fly, the heat of my own body.

He responded by pulling my hips back, dragging me against him, and rocking into it. Everything faded, and the only things I could process were his dick, his thighs, and his mouth. I gave over to the rhythm he was setting. Light burst behind my eyes with every push.

"Uh—fuck, so good," I heard myself babble in between kisses and breathing. Even my own voice was receding in my mounting orgasm. I was so worked up, I had the sporadic but recurring urge to climb him or to sink to the floor in some sort of fuckable puddle. I had to focus on not coming if I wanted to last. I didn't want to be the first to come.

Just when I thought I was going to lose it, Lucas's head fell away from my mouth, and his thrusting quickened to almost double. My eyes shot open to find his shut tight, mouth soundlessly open. A warmth, like the echo of his orgasm, rocketed through my body. In my pleasure of watching him come, I lost track of one of his hands. I became very aware, however, when he palmed my cock.

"Fuck, fuck, fuck."

My reaction was to jump back, surprised. But he caught me around the waist. And again, everything was gone, and I only understood the points where our bodies connected. His palm stroked, working my cock, dragging all of my pleasure south. But it almost wasn't enough. He seemed so much further away. His thrusting against me had made it perfect, and now, while it was still great, I felt a small worry creep in.

I opened my mouth to say something, ask for more or maybe less, or maybe I didn't get to ask for anything. His mouth was back on mine and his tongue entered like he lived there. And that was it.

I was lucky to both have my mouth busy and have no one home because I probably would have screamed through that orgasm. Instead, I chased it into Lucas's mouth. After the crest, I rubbed against Lucas a few more times, aftershock sparks rocketing round my guts. Lucas and I looked at each other. It was funny, I felt like I had been able to see so much when hard and needy, but by the time we had come, he was barely a shadow against the barn doors.

"I think the flashlight died," Lucas said.

"Oh, that makes sense. I thought maybe I was going blind."

"That good, huh?"

The flashlight was dead, so we both dug out our phones and turned on the flashlights. He helped me find the spare key, and I watched him leave the drive before going into the house. I knew I was in deep for this guy, and not just because of garage humping. I thought about dinner and how much we laughed but also how capable he was and how his focus and seriousness could shift in an instant. I had to hope he felt the same.

CHAPTER SIX

Lucas

"I feel stressed," I said to Ky. "Maybe I should text him."

"So, text him." She was focused on the laptop in front of her. Her deadline was Monday. She'd reminded me hours ago she'd be busy. But I needed help.

"Wouldn't that seem...I don't know...*needy*?"

"So don't. Or call him."

"What if the plans changed?"

"Lou, I really wish I had the bandwidth to go back and forth on this particular paradox, but I don't. My definitive answer is text him." She looked at me, irritated, then looked back at her computer.

I pulled out my phone. I opted for a Snap since he seemed to be on that app the most. *Still on for tonight?* I sent a pic of half my face. There was still two hours before our date. He just hadn't said anything about it on Friday, which was my last day of work, or all day today.

Shit I'm sorry.

I waited, not sure what he meant. The sinking feeling was instant. Over the last two weeks, I'd learned Al usually texted in long paragraphs and not sentence by sentence like I did. So, the short reply was stressful.

I've been dealing with the girls. Four of mine have fevers.

I took a breath and let go of my disappointment. He couldn't help that. I called him before I lost the nerve.

"Hey," he said.

"Hi."

"I'm really sorry, but raincheck? I've got to figure out what to do with the kids."

"Is your dad there? Cuz he probably shouldn't be."

"Naw, Gage dropped him off at Betsy's when he brought his girls over this afternoon. It's a mix here. The non-feverish are with Bets. Dani has the big launch at the gym and I just…the fevers won't break and a few of 'em have barfed. We've been at this since eight a.m."

"Tell me more."

He explained all the symptoms, and I gave him as much advice over the phone as I could, pacing a small circle around my living room. When I hung up, Ky was staring at me.

"What?" I asked.

"What do you mean *what*? Go over there and help that man."

"What?"

"Stop that. You heard me."

"You only want me to leave because I'm annoying you."

"Yes," she said without hesitation. "Plus, he's losing it."

"He didn't invite me."

"Go anyway."

"Ky, I'm not gonna just barge into that guy's life." I sat on the couch and tried not to look at my phone, as if I could see Al through it.

Ky made an interested sound. "Why not?"

"That's not how I do things. Like you and I have this here, and he probably won't have any reason to come and, I don't know, read a book to Lila or something. He's got his own box."

"You and your boxes. You remember how worked up you got at the idea of our laundry mixing before we were married?"

I snorted.

She cackled, then mocked me. "I didn't think boyfriends and girlfriends mixed laundry."

"Okay, okay. I know how I am. I just…" I did not know how to finish that sentence.

"Lou. I love you. I think it'll be safe to go over there. I think he'll like it."

"Yeah?"

"I'm a literal doctor. You're a nurse. Who're you going to trust?"

"You have a PhD, not an MD," I sighed. I considered her suggestion. I was already dressed, and since he had been my plan anyway, it wasn't like I had anything else to do. I could go get Lila, but my moms were possessive. Then I thought about the gym, but I remembered I already went. "Maybe I'll stay here and job-hunt. I don't know when the hospital will have something."

Ky stood and went to her backpack hanging by the door. She

rummaged inside until she found her wallet. She crossed to me with a twenty in her hand. "I love you. And I want this grant. It is literally worth my next three years' salary. So, you can either take this as a nice hint to leave—go anywhere, go to a movie, go to Al, go walk around the Walmart with the rest of the townies—or you can take it as a bribe to shut up."

"Any chance I can get five more?"

She glared.

"Well, if I go to the movies, I'll need a snack."

"Sure, here," she said, digging back through her wallet. This time she came up with a middle finger. I sighed and stood. She let me kiss her before she went back to the table and turned up the music coming through her computer. I grabbed my keys.

I went to the store and gathered some things I knew would help, then I headed for the big farmhouse Al and his family lived in. The thick, gray twilight was just starting, but the light glowing from the windows made the house look welcoming. I considered backing out.

I was too late. Al stepped out on the porch and stood in a beautiful yellow rectangle of light, watching me get out of the truck. I couldn't see his face right away because of the shadow of his hat. He wasn't in work clothes but had on a black shirt with a pair of black jeans. As I approached, I could feel his smile.

"What're you doin' here?" he yelled.

"I thought I'd help, and since my date canceled, I didn't have any other plans."

"They probably sucked anyway."

"I hope so," I said, winking. He actually blushed.

I met him on the porch, surprised when he hugged me. It was platonic feeling. Not like the other night with his arms around me. I swallowed and refocused. He sort of pushed me away, his hands burning on my shoulders as he held me at arm's length.

"No, seriously," he said.

"I'm a health care provider. Not that I'm practicing medicine or anything, but I'm also a certified first responder, so it's my duty." I put the bags from the store in his arms and patted his shoulder.

"Well, thanks. Gage's Megan and Bets's Margret are both in my Zara's grade. All the other girls are in different classes. Then of course

Zara's sisters probably got it from her. I tried callin' some of the other parents to see if their kids aren't feelin' well. I was thinkin' it was food poisoning from the cafeteria. You know you're supposed to…"

He talked all the way into the kitchen. Generally, you couldn't take a step in his house without running into one of his daughters or nieces. But tonight, not a single child was in sight.

"Where are the kids?"

"In Al and Dani's room," Teach said. He closed the fridge and looked at me. If it were possible for him to look paler, well, there he was.

"Dude," I said. "Give me those bags, Al." I put them on the counter and pulled a thermometer out of one, cracking open the plastic.

"We have one of those," Al said almost defensively. He grabbed one off the counter. It was nicer than the one I had bought.

"Good, we can tag-team," I said, popping in batteries. "Starting with Teach."

I gestured for him. The closer he got, the smaller he seemed to look. And the more he looked like Coach. He opened his mouth without a word.

"Naw, not that kind."

He closed his mouth and closed his eyes, looking like he might fall over.

I swiped the device across his forehead. "One-oh-one on the dot."

"What do I win?"

"A Popsicle," I said. I handed him one of the slightly melted freezer pops out of the second bag.

"What?"

"Two birds," I said. "It's cold, so it'll help with the fever, and it's Pedialyte, so it'll rehydrate you."

"I didn't know they made those," Al said. "These would've been a godsend over the years."

"Well, now you know," I said, grinning at him. He was too close and his eyes too intense for a moment, but his phone rang.

"Hello," he said quickly. "You got Al."

"He answers every call," Teach said, chewing the plastic on the freezer pop.

"Bro, use your evolution," I said, snatching it away. I grabbed the scissors out of the knife block on the counter. "Use a fucking tool."

I opened it and handed it back. He just grinned, looking younger than he was.

"That was the principal. She says several kids have fevers, but they don't think it's linked to the food," Al said.

"I agree. Why would this guy have a fever if it were foodborne?" I pointed at Teach.

"Oh! Right. Also, two other kids went to the doctor but are waitin' on results. Do I need to take them to the doctor?"

Al looked desperate. I couldn't imagine this was the first time a guy with seven kids had had more than one kid sick at once, but any sick kid was a sick kid. I thought about dads and their kids in a broad clinical way for a moment, seeing the faces of dads who had to come to the hospital for one reason or another. I thought about Lila. Dads and kids, my brain uselessly repeated.

"Well, you can take them whenever you want for whatever reason, but I'm sure you called their pediatrician."

He nodded. "She said their fevers are mild, and even though each of 'em barfed, it was only once so far, so she said monitor them. And if they get worse, bring 'em in."

"Welp, kids get sick and barf all the time. So let's do what she said, let's monitor." I slung my thermometer around like a Western gunslinger. He smiled. I gestured for Al to lead the way. He grabbed his thermometer and the bag of Pedialyte pops. I took the scissors from Teach, who was working on a third freezer pop.

"Did you barf?" I asked him.

He shook his head.

"Good...don't."

He saluted me, then went back to leaning into the fridge.

"Hi, Daddy," one of the girls said when Al entered the room. Children were draped everywhere. Several were sprawled on the bed and two were lying across armchairs in the corner. One was on the floor. All of them stared right at me.

"Nurse Lucas. Are we sick like Grandpa?" Winifred asked.

"You're sick, but not like Grandpa," Al answered.

"You take Meg, Mag, and Winifred. I'll take X, Y, and Z," I said, referring to Zara, Ysabel, and Xander. Al nodded.

"What's that?" Zara asked, looking at the thermometer.

I explained. Then she wanted to help, so I showed her how to take her sisters' temperatures. They were all between 99 and 101. I asked them to open their mouths, and I looked inside with a flashlight I kept for kids that had googly eyes on it. Al watched me, cutting the tops off freezer pops. His expression was a mix of awe and urgency.

I hesitated, then I checked Meg and Mag along with the others. Meg, John Adams's nine-year-old, didn't seem to share her father's revulsion toward me, which was good because she looked a bit worse than the rest. Her fever was 101.5.

"Anything hurt?" I asked Meg. She shook her head, twin braids flopping around her face. The kids were easy enough to tell apart. Betsy's kids all had curly hair. Al's had bone-straight hair that ranged from white blond to brown. All of Gage's had black hair.

"Can you swallow okay?"

She nodded.

"What did you eat today?" I asked.

"My breakfast my dad made."

"And your sisters?" I continued, while I opened a freezer pop for her.

"They all got the same breakfast as me. Dad always makes us food when he's home. Then Uncle Al gave us soup."

Dad. Again, the word bounded around in my brain untethered. I knew the rough, homophobic, racist John Adams was a father of five, but the image of him putting together breakfast for his kids didn't really compute.

When we had entered, the room had been almost silent except for the TV. Now it was noisy with the sounds of kids talking about their temperatures and eating freezer pops. The younger two were now under the care of their older sisters and cousins who wanted to play nurse. Winifred let Zara repeatedly take her temp. Zara even cleaned the thermometer with a sanitizing wipe like she had seen me do. Zara thought it was interesting that Winnie had the lowest temp. She impressed me by announcing Winnie's fever must still be rising. I thought the opposite, but I didn't want to discourage her thinking.

All their temperatures would probably come down soon. *Lethargic, temperature, vomiting.* You learn a lot of skills as a nurse, but diagnosing was usually above my pay grade. I surveyed the kids. All the other girls looked flushed, but Winnie looked pink. I went over to her and considered her face and arms.

"Winnie, can I touch your face?" I asked her.

"Can I touch *your* face?"

I laughed. "Sure."

I put the back of my hand to her cheek, and she copied me.

"You've got a nice face. But you don't have a beard like Daddy," she said. "He doesn't have one now, but he used to."

"I can't grow a very good one."

"Maybe you should get a beard like tattoos. These, but on your face." She pointed to the flowers on my forearm.

"Maybe I will. Okay, did everyone get a freezer pop?" I stood. They all nodded. "I'm going to send your uncle in here to put on a movie for you."

"No horsin' around. Rest, okay?" Al said.

"Okay," the girls said.

"What do you think?" Al asked as soon as we were out the door.

"Have any of them had chicken pox?"

"No, but they had shots."

"Has Teach?"

"Has *Teach*? I'm sure—we all had 'em."

"When?"

"Well, we got it at the same time. Gage brought it home when he was six, so I would've been four."

"So, they would've missed him."

"Oh shit! Is that what you think it is?"

"Maybe, or something similar. I think you should call their doctor back."

Teach was sitting on one of the stools at the kitchen island. I looked at him. "You ever had chicken pox?"

He sucked the chocolate and vanilla ice cream bar before answering. "Naw. That what it is? Chicken pox?" he asked, looking at his arms. They were black with ink.

"Maybe. Or some other virus. It impacts everyone differently, which may be why only some of the kids have it right now. But I can't say."

While Teach and I were talking, I took his temp again, and it was about the same. I handed him a pack of adult fever reducers. I had some for the kids, but I wanted to talk with Al before giving them anything. Teach took the pills with a swallow of ice cream.

"Well, the doc says to keep 'em comfortable till morning, then she can see them. I told her about everything you said," Al announced.

I handed him the packets of medicine, and he and Teach went to settle the kids. Taking liberties, I went to the fridge and opened two beers.

"They seem better, not well but not as dire," Al said, trotting into the room. His shoulders relaxed, and he almost moaned when he saw the beer.

We sat at the kitchen island on the stools. The room was bright with cool, clear light, the fixture over the island a modern, stainless steel contraption. The walls were a warm yellow, almost buttery, and it made Al's hair shine when he took his hat off. It had grown a little floppy and fell across his forehead. He set his arm on the counter and took a long pull of beer. Our knees touched as he drank.

"Thank you," he said.

"It's no big."

"It is to me. And I'm sorry about canceling."

"Fuck off," I said.

He grinned. "I mean it! You didn't have to do this."

I shrugged. I would help any child in need no matter who their father was, but because it was Al, I could feel the added desire to show off, impress him. This wasn't a date, but it felt like something along those lines. *Would Al come over and help me with Lila if I needed it?*

"What're you thinkin'?" he asked after a minute. He looked tired.

I didn't want to answer. So I said, "This." I took the thermometer and swiped his forehead with it.

"I feel fine."

"And this would agree," I said, reading a healthy 98.7. "But you can't be too sure."

"What about you?"

"Well, if it's what I think, then I won't get sick, and Lila's with my moms this weekend, so disinfect the rest of it and I'm good."

He smiled at me. "Good job avoiding the question."

I felt my face grow warm. His eyes were steady on mine. I didn't do anything to stop him from leaning forward on his stool and kissing me. My whole body reacted with a bright heat that washed over me in a wave before settling into a gentle, lingering warmth.

"So," he said after pulling away and taking another drink. "Since you're here, do you want to hang out for a while?"

I hoped my nod looked lazy instead of desperate.

"What do you want to do?"

"What do you got?"

I watched his mouth while he thought about it. He chewed his lip slightly, making one side red instead of pink.

"I've got, like, one video game and every streaming service you can think of," he said finally.

"You own one video game? Which?"

I followed him to the living room, where he set up the game. It was a dungeon crawl where the objective was to kill some demonic big-bad at the end of a thousand nearly identical levels.

"What were you actually thinkin' about?" he asked me after a while.

I considered avoiding the question, but *avoiding* him wasn't the point. Getting to know him was, and I couldn't expect to get far if I didn't let him know me too. I realized how many intimate moments I had been party to in recent weeks. Not just a few kisses and humping each other in the garage, but in his life too. I saw the raw fear on his face when Dani told him his father was in the hospital, and the stress of learning how to care for Coach and the panic with his kids.

"Um," I started, trying to kill a minotaur and talk at the same time. "I don't remember specifically, but I've been thinking about my dad lately."

"Oh yeah?"

"Yeah. Being around your dad made me think of him. I don't have a lot of older guys in my life. I just haven't been able to let the idea go."

"How do you feel about that?"

"I don't know yet. Right now, it's thoughts that are just happening."

Al's character came around the corner after he cleared the cell he was in and killed the minotaur I had been working on, earning him the kill. I glared at him. He gave me a forced neutral glance. *Okay, so it's a contest now.* I steeled my resolve to beat him at his own game, ignoring the fact that we were supposed to be a team.

"Do you want to know him?" he asked. "Your dad?"

"I don't know. I think I used to once. *I did* know him once. He was around for about seven years, then he left. Now, I guess I'm just surprised how little I've thought about him since."

"Fair enough."

I didn't take my eyes off the screen, but I could feel him shift. His body came closer to mine on his couch. We didn't have a whole lot of space to avoid each other. The couch was small with the two of us on it. I was aware of the doubts I had about him—his time didn't seem to be any less restrictive. Being on the couch, though, him only a centimeter or two away, felt a little more like I thought dating him would.

"What?" I said, not having heard his question.

"I said there must be a lot of feelings there."

"Gross. Probably. I can't name them—*shit*!" I groaned as my character was mauled by a werewolf.

"You gotta block, bro!" I waited until he was too close to a zombie-bear and slapped the controller out of his hand. He stared at me for a second before getting the controller. His character didn't die, but his health bar did start to blink, indicating it was time for a health potion. I had to wait for my guy to respawn, so I went for another beer. I brought Al one too. My guy came back, and we played for a few minutes, bumping each other's elbows trying to mess the other up. He was still kicking my ass by way of body count, but I was gaining.

"Fuck this, damnit." *Sure, Lucas, this is going really well.*

"Why'd you pick an archer if you keep runnin' into the battle?" Al asked. His character was walking around picking up all the loot. Mine was limping around behind his.

"I liked his jacket."

He laughed.

His phone rang and he answered. "Hey, love. No, they're better. Lucas came and helped. Yeah, he's right here."

Al looked at me and, for a second, I worried I had miscalculated. I didn't know the boundaries Al and Dani had. Ky and I had an understanding about some things that come with being poly. I knew what would be an issue for her. Playing video games on the couch wasn't one of them. My pulse jumped as I wondered if it would be for Dani.

"She wants me to put her on speaker," he said. I waved to show I didn't care. He put the phone on his broad shoulder, balancing the device between us.

"You're on," he said to her.

"Hey, handsome," she said, her voice not at all hostile or unhappy.

"Hey, beautiful," I said assuming I was *handsome.*

"Okay," Al grumbled.

"How are my babies?"

"Al and Teach are fine. Teach has a fever. But Al's good. Oh, your girls are doing great too."

She laughed.

"All right, thanks," Al muttered. He stood and handed me the phone. "I'm gonna go check on 'em."

"I...but," I said, trying to stop him, pointing to the huge devil curb-stomping his own army trying to get to us.

"What do you think is up with the kids?" Dani asked.

"I'm gonna die," I called after Al. The devil roared.

"Just run away, that's what I do," she said. I followed her advice as Al's abandoned avatar was swallowed by hell's mob. "Lucas, the girls."

"Oh, shit. Well, I took all their temperatures."

Dani asked a few rapid-fire questions about the kids, then she picked up where we had left off talking about dynamic versus static stretching. Al retrieved his character and took us to a town to buy more health and trade in all his loot for gold. Eventually she hung up. Al didn't wait. He picked up the conversation as if she had never interrupted and I just vibed, talking about whatever came to mind.

I went home after midnight, making sure Ky got her twenty bucks' worth. She was asleep when I came in, so I just joined her. It wasn't until I was about to fall asleep that night that I realized Al hadn't rescheduled our date. Luckily, I didn't have to think about what that meant. I just drifted off instead.

CHAPTER SEVEN

Alexander

As it turned out, the kids had fifth, as common as any other childhood disease. Teach did as well, and he was completely annoyed. That also meant they were out of school for a while. Teach was home with them, and so was Coach, since he was too old and too vaccinated to catch it. The rest of the kids were staying with Bets.

I tried to reschedule with Lucas for the next Friday, but he was taking Ky out. It was hard to text with him. Most of what I sent went unanswered for most of the day, and even when I called him in the evenings, the conversation never turned toward our dates. It felt like maybe he was avoiding me.

I was very distracted by Friday, the same Friday he didn't want to go out with me. The same one Ky got to go out on. Not that I was jealous of his wife. I wasn't. She was great, and it was no problem for him to take her on a date instead of going out with me. Jealousy didn't even play into it. *The Gunner can't bluff his way out of this one.*

"Mr. Jefferson," the voice on the phone said.

I blinked. My office came back into focus. "Yes, Mrs. Reed, I'm sorry, what were you sayin'?"

"I'm talking about the land behind my house," she said.

"Yes, I know, Mr. Jacob's field." It took everything I had not to sigh.

"That's what I'm trying to tell you. He keeps tearing up my field. I need you to come out here and flag the property lines so I can fight his destruction of my property."

I pulled my hat brim, taking it off and tossing it on the desk. Every three weeks or so, Mrs. Reed called to try and talk me into appraising Mr. Jacob's field as land she owned. I tried to explain Mr. Jacob had earned it by paying off his father's debt to her father, one of the only examples of sharecropping in the area that I think went the way it was supposed to. But she never listened. Or she had dementia and forgot we already talked about this. I couldn't tell which.

"Mrs. Reed—" My personal phone buzzed with a text from Lucas. *Got time for lunch? I'm downstairs.*

I looked out the window behind me, and there he was on the street looking at his phone.

"Mrs. Reed, I've got to go. I'll call you later. Take care." I hung up without waiting for her to say anything, and I trotted down the stairs.

"Hey," I said, holding the door open. "What're you doin' here?"

"I was at the gym and needed food. I figured you'd be here."

"Come on in."

He followed me up to my office. The office was two stories. We met customers on the first floor but kept the private desks on the second. Paul was out of town for the next few weeks and Teach was still recovering, so it was just Lucas and me. I felt suddenly nervous.

"Nice digs," he said, setting a bag of Chinese takeout on the desk.

"This restaurant isn't in Painted Waters."

"True."

"So, you went to the gym, drove to Valdosta to get food, then drove back?"

He laughed. "Not quite. I was at the hospital in Valdosta this morning to talk with a coordinator, then I went to Beast."

"Good Lord," I sighed, sitting at my desk.

"Yup, Dani is a monster," he said, rolling his shoulder as if trying to work out a knot. Or maybe it was just the memory. Beast was an intense gym, and she was their top personal trainer.

"Tell me about it. I used to work out with her, but I learned better."

"Anyway, she recommended this Chinese place and suggested I'd probably find you here."

God bless Dani. I watched Lucas flop into Paul's chair. I waved him over and cleared shit off my desk as I waited for him.

"It's good food," I tried to assure him.

He grinned and rolled up to the other side of the desk.

"Where you takin' Ky tonight?" I asked. Was I trying to test myself? Maybe. Was I passing? The skeptical look on his face made me think I wasn't.

He squinted but answered, "She likes Grace's, so that's probably where we'll end up."

I nodded. "Who doesn't like Grace's?"

He pulled out the folded paper boxes of food and placed them on the table. "I figured we could share since I wasn't sure what was good. Dani made a few suggestions, but fuck if I can tell what's what."

I nodded and helped him empty the bag. "Why'd you look at me like that?"

"Like what?"

"When I asked about Ky."

He squinted again.

"Don't want to tell me?" I asked as lightly as I could.

"It's not that I don't. I guess I don't really know what you want to know. You know?"

"Huh?"

"Like, Ky and I talk about you because she wants to know. But I also know the stuff she *doesn't* want to know about. She has her limits when it comes to information about metas, but I don't really know where the overlaps are, if that makes sense."

"I get that. I want to know. I enjoyed hangin' out with her at dinner and I'm not tryin' to avoid gettin' to know Ky. I get if you want to keep it more parallel, though. Just let me know."

I paused to think about how to say more. I felt like I had known him for years, like he was so ingrained in my life it never occurred to me I might not be as ingrained in his. I knew other poly people who didn't have a relationship with their metamours, nor did they expect one. I couldn't keep people away from Dani even if I wanted to. She was too charismatic. I couldn't tell with Lucas, so I waited for him to tell me.

"Either that tastes like crap or you're thinking too hard," Lucas said. To confirm it for himself, he reached over and picked up some of the meat with his chopsticks. "It's pretty good, so what's with the face?"

"I was thinkin'."

"I noticed." He was sitting facing the window behind me, and the sun was bright on his face, his skin warm and magnificent. His smile was perfect.

"What's Ky do for a livin'? Like, I know she's a scientist, but specifically? I wasn't really listenin' the other night." I decided to just keep going as I was.

He chewed slowly and stared. "That's what you were thinking so hard about?"

"No, I was thinkin' about what you said about disclosing

expectations about information on our partner's other partners. I'm not really sure what more to say about that and was tryin' to think of somethin', but then I realized I didn't know exactly what Ky does for work."

"Dr. Kyoko Laverty-Okamoto is a soil scientist for the state of Georgia," Lucas said. "Her last paper was about the variation of soil nutrition under different crop rotation practices."

"Wow, that sounds like a read."

"Yeah, it's funny sometimes how niche her field seems, but how valuable it is."

"Hell, who knows the value of land better than this guy," I said, pointing to myself.

He nearly dropped his chopsticks. "Oh shit, is my type *ground* type?"

I laughed. "As opposed to *fighting*?"

He grinned and looked a little impressed that I knew anything about Pokémon. He said, "I don't fight. I mostly pick up heavy stuff and move it around."

"So, what's she workin' on now?"

He considered me for a second before he answered. "What do you know about biosolids?"

I gulped. And spent the next half hour regretting having asked. Not that I regretted listening to him talk about Ky. That was pretty charming. No, I just regretted learning what biosolids were. The conversation flowed naturally from there into other topics, like how they met, what it was like to go to an HBCU, and how he ended up in Painted Waters. He asked me things too, but I didn't pay much attention to what I said. We had just finished making fun of the fortunes in our cookies when the bell at town hall told us it was one in the afternoon.

"I maybe should get going?" Lucas said, "You probably have a lot to do."

He stood and started packing the trash back in the bag the food had come in. I didn't want him to leave, so I came around the desk and put a hand on his shoulder. Then I pulled him into a hug. Despite having kissed and come together, I don't think we had hugged properly.

"Thanks for lunch," I said. Lucas just nodded into my shoulder. He put his hands around my waist and pulled me just a bit tighter.

"Please? Dinner…movie…somethin'?" I asked.

He pulled back and looked at me. "Next week? Saturday?"

"Yeah, perfect," I said. I didn't know what was already on my calendar for Saturday, but I was canceling it. I noticed the concern under his contented expression. "I know it seems like a lot of missed opportunities, but I still believe in this."

I traced the Incredible Hulk on his chest. It was my shirt. He hadn't actually cut the sleeves off it like he threatened, and I think it meant something that he wore it today, even knowing he would see Dani at the gym.

He rolled his eyes, but I had earned my kiss anyway. I felt something slightly more desperate in each kiss we shared. It was starting to feel like any day now I would start kissing him and find myself unable to stop, attached to him forever. I wanted that. I could feel the thrum of his pulse under my hands on his neck, and I could almost taste the same want for more on his lips. I kissed him harder, deeper, his mouth opening, following the trajectory of my thoughts.

"What in God's name are you doing?"

Lucas and I jumped apart. I had to turn around to see who it was, but the horrified look on Lucas's face as he stared over my shoulder was enough to let me know it was worse than I could imagine.

"Betsy?" I said, facing her.

"Oh no, no, I will not abide this," she was saying. She looked ready to kill. "How dare you? Both of you. You have beautiful wives and beautiful children—"

"Bets," I said putting myself between her and Lucas. "It's not what you think."

"The hell it ain't," she screamed.

As she talked, she pulled her hoop earrings out and kicked off her heels. She fumbled only slightly getting her suit jacket off. Honestly, I would have rather she pulled a gun, which I knew she carried. She marched up to me and tried a right hook, which I caught on my shoulder.

"Ow, no, fuck, seriously listen," I begged, shielding my face.

"I can't believe you'd do somethin' like this, Alexander. That woman deserves so much better. I thought you were better—"

I took a left jab to my ribs.

"Christ, Bets, we aren't cheatin'." I backed up until I was practically climbing my desk to get away.

"They know! Our wives know," Lucas said from somewhere behind me.

Betsy finished rapid-fire punching my shoulder. Then she took a breath.

"Yeah, they know. I swear, I can explain," I said.

"What?" she said, her astonishment exaggerated by her breathlessness.

"We're both in *open* marriages. They know, Bets. Jesus Christ."

Betsy took a step back from me and turned in a confused circle. I backed off my desk and found Lucas crouching under it.

"All right," she said, putting her hands on her hips in a way that looked like our mother, not that I would ever say that to her. She paced away a few steps. "You have one minute to explain before I start makin' phone calls."

"Dani and I've always had an open marriage. She dates a few other people. Lucas and I only recently started this. It's called polyamory. She knows he's here, what we do. She knows."

"Ky too. Well, Ky doesn't date anyone, but she knows about him," Lucas said. He was still half hidden behind the desk.

"What are you, some sort of wife swappers?"

"Do we look like *wives*?"

She squinted, marched back across the room, and landed a perfect left cross on my already bruised arm. She was just about as tall as I was and maybe slightly stronger. It hurt.

"What the fuck, ow."

"That's for scaring me. I swear I was ready to have you both stoned to death in the street like biblical whores," she said, taking a deep breath.

"Would it be bad if I left? I think I shit myself," Lucas said, daring to stand.

"No—yeah, I got this. I'll text you later," I said.

Betsy watched him leave, which he did faster than anything. When he was gone, she went to the couch and collapsed on it, not ungracefully, but clearly exhausted. In her attempt to kill me, her polka-dot blouse had come out from her pencil skirt, and her hair had come loose from the weird puffy bun she wore. She looked like a suburban wine mom back from mimosas.

"I'm sorry, Bets," I said, crossing to her.

"Is this real, Al? You really seeing Lucas?"

"Yeah, I swear it."

"Why didn't you ever say anything?"

"I was plannin' on it, but I don't even know what we are yet in relationship terms."

"Naw, not just about him, but about the whole thing. You said you and Danielle were always open?"

I nodded and slowly explained it all to her.

"Welp, I guess I can't blame you for not sayin' anythin' after all this time. Our family ain't been the best at non-traditional lifestyles, or however the kids are sayin' it."

I felt like that was an opening for what I thought should have been a more important conversation.

"Bets, why aren't you surprised that…Well, you don't seem surprised to have caught your brother kissin' a guy."

She sighed, sat up, and looked wistfully at a photo on the wall. "If I had a nickel for every time I caught my brother kissin' a boy…"

She stood and went to the photo. It was a fake door hiding what used to be a safe. Our grandfather kept a stash of whiskey in there. She fetched it and poured us both a shot in some of the paper cups that came with the water dispenser.

"You'd be rich?"

"Naw, I'd have two nickels, but it's interesting that it's happened twice. Honestly, I always thought it'd be you. After seeing how the Frank and Orion thing impacted you, we all kind of thought it'd be you. Even Wynona caught on. She's the one who asked Coach to talk to Orion to try and get Frank away from him. When that didn't work, she tried to get Coach to make him quit the team. She didn't want him infecting you."

"No way," I said, even though it sounded exactly like something she would do. Betsy Ross shot back her whisky like an old pro, and I shot mine back like someone who'd never had whiskey before.

Bets talked through my coughing. "Yup, when she left, I thought it was honestly out of sight out of mind, but then Teach came out. Coach didn't know what to do, so he called Wynona, and she's the one who had him sent to her."

"I thought he wanted to go."

"Not at all, and I didn't want to send him, but then I didn't know what I could do." Her eyes got very dark, and she looked on the verge of tears. "Well, I did some reading online about homosexuals. The whole time he was gone, Wy never let me talk to him even though I called nearly every day. She was probably just bein' hateful because I refused to talk to her beyond asking to talk to him."

She did cry then and looked into her cup. I waited.

"Lord, I remember that day he called like it was yesterday. He'd been there for about a year. I was watching the girls we had around, Gage's four and my two. Daniel was out of town. I was stayin' home full-time, pregnant to the teeth with Mag. When I answered, Teach was sobbing so hard I almost couldn't understand him. He said she was gonna send him to a camp."

"Oh my God. What?" I said. I'd never heard any of this. I had been at college at the time and had a kid on the way. I was so caught up in my own life, I never thought about what it meant for Teach to be with Wynona.

Betsy looked at me and quickly wiped her face. "Yup, she was awful to him. She had some preacher comin' out to the house at least twice a week, and then he was forced to go to therapy at the church. Every time he tried to run, the sheriff would just take him back. He had to wait until she was showering to call me, hiding in the shed out behind her house."

"Holy shit."

"Right! Anyway, I listened to my poor, beautiful brother cry on the phone for an hour. Then he had to go because she was yelling for him. I tried callin' back, but there was no answer. Then I thought about gettin' the girls into the car and drivin' up there myself, but I knew that wouldn't work."

"Why didn't you call me?"

Betsy's answer was probably too generous. "You had school, and Dani. Besides, who knows what she would've done to you if you'd gone over there. She thought you were half the problem anyway."

"What'd you do? I know Coach went to get him, but I thought he called Coach."

She shook her head, blond hair flowing over her shoulders. "Naw, I called Coach. He was still at the school, but I said I needed him at the house. He was there for me in under ten minutes."

"But he doesn't like gay people any more than Wy."

"I don't believe that. I might've thought that then, but something's changed in him. Maybe it's what I said. Maybe somethin' Teach said. Maybe it just took Wynona leavin', gettin' out of his head long enough for him to be reasonable."

"What'd you say to him?"

"I told him to go get Teach. He said no at first, then I explained about the camp, and he said maybe Teach needed it. I lost it. The girls were all so small and were sleepin' around the living room, and I took up Lizzy and I put her right in his arms. I said, 'Daddy, you love that little girl, don't you? You love her and you love all of them and you love me?'

"He didn't answer even though I knew it was a yes. So, I demanded he tell me when he started to love us. I didn't let him answer. I said, 'I already know. I watched you fall in love with each of your grandkids the moment we put them in your arms. And the same with me and Gage and Al and Teach. I remember the look on your face when you first held Teach. You didn't know anything about us then. You didn't know our favorite color or our favorite food or if we'd play sports or look more like Wynona or if we'd be liberals or nothin'. You didn't know a damn thing about us, but you loved us and you love them even though you don't know anythin' about them.'

"So, I said, 'Daddy, if you already love us, why should knowin' us change that love? Why wouldn't it make you just love us more? Teach was gay the day you held him even if you didn't know it, even if he didn't know it, and you loved him. We all love him best.'"

She took a breath and continued. "He told me sometimes it ain't about love, sometimes it's about behavior. I told him that was a big pile of horseshit. I told him it wasn't about behavior because it was the same things any of the rest of us did, kissing and fucking and such. I told him no sir, it was about love. I had been reading, so I said, 'I read that one in six women are lesbians.' Then I pointed at his six sleeping grandbabies, and I said, 'That means probably one of them. When we know, are you goin' to let Wynona torture her too? It isn't wrong. Anything or anyone that produces love—kind and good love—isn't wrong.'"

"Damn." I hadn't moved an inch while she spoke, and when the spell broke at the sound of my own voice, I realized I was crying. I wiped my face with my hands and shrugged just to relieve some stress. "You said all that?"

"I'd never been so angry in my life."

"And he agreed? Right then and there?"

"He never said a word. He just handed me back my baby, kissed my forehead, then drove nine hours to Tennessee to get our brother. He's never said anythin' about that day. But I can tell he thinks about things more."

"You think I should tell him? About me?"

She rubbed her neck tiredly. "I don't know, kiddo, but I do know you should be a little more careful than kissing in your office. What if I'd been Gage or some other redneck that takes it personally when two men kiss?"

"Gage." I didn't think he'd be able to change.

She shrugged. "He'll get his due. I think his Kate is goin' to give him a run for his money."

I agreed. Kate was the most precocious and rebellious of all fifteen girls.

"Betsy," I said. She looked at me. I didn't know how to say what I was feeling, so I hugged her instead.

"All right now, cut it out. I only stopped by because I have a customer wantin' to purchase some land near Boston."

"Okay." I let her go. She stood and went to get her shoes and earrings. I stood too. "You know Dani is goin' to get a real kick out of knowin' you'd beat my ass if I ever cheated on her."

She snapped her fingers. "Sisters before misters."

"You're *my* sister."

CHAPTER EIGHT

Lucas

"I don't see him yet."

Both Ky and Lila were staring out the windows. Ky had a pair of binoculars and Lila was holding her tiny hands to her eyes, miming her mother.

"Stop that, you're going to creep out the neighbors," I said. We did it a lot. The binoculars never left the windowsill.

"If they aren't used to it by now," Ky said, concentrating.

"There's a bird, Ky-ky," Lila said, tapping the glass.

Ky made a show of looking at it. "You're right, kid, it's a... warbler."

I shook my head, amused at the weird habits our daughter was getting. I tried not to look at the clock again. Al had insisted on coming here even though I planned to drive us to dinner. I told him 7:00 and it was 6:58.

"I honestly expected him to show up half an hour early," I said.

"I was thinking he'd be late. I don't know what you see, but I see an overworked, tired dad-son with too much on his plate," Ky said. "People like that aren't early."

I rolled my eyes. He was trying his best. Or at least I told myself he was so I didn't have to think too hard about my own feelings. It seemed crazy to feel neglected when you just barely started to date someone.

"Oh shit, you said white truck, right?" Ky cried. She tried to get closer and ended up jamming the binoculars against the glass.

"Yeah," I said, rushing toward her.

"Oh shit, your boy is fine." The way she said *fine* made my pulse jump. I agreed, but it meant a lot coming from her since up until that moment, she'd only referred to him as Khaki Daddy. I slid alongside her in the window, crushing blinds out of the way.

"Oh shit," I said.

Slowly I took the binoculars from her. She resisted but eventually gave them to me. Watching him lock the truck and cross the street, I realized I'd only seen him ready for work or hanging around his house. He'd put in some effort for this date. He was wearing black jeans and a dark patterned long-sleeved shirt. It was blue and looked almost like water, in a subtle, high-end way. He didn't have a hat for once, and he looked one hundred percent the all-American heartthrob. Plus, he had flowers. I focused my binoculars on his thick thighs in his tight jeans.

"What were the rules about dating him too?" Ky said, fanning herself.

I adjusted the binoculars, the image going hazy as he moved closer. He looked up, maybe sensing us, maybe just looking around. Ky and I jumped back from the window. Lila waved.

"That's Victory's dad," Lila said. She was in the same day care as Al's daughter. I hadn't really put together that they'd know each other.

"Yeah, he is." Then I said to Ky, "Do I need to change?"

"No, you look very handsome." She picked lint off the sweater I had on.

"Is Victory coming to play?" Lila asked.

Ky answered her. "Nope, kid, it's a mommy-daughter night. Lou and Mr. Jefferson are going to do dude stuff."

"I want to do dude stuff," Lila said.

"When you're older," Ky and I told her together.

I froze when the doorbell rang.

"I'll get it," Lila said, running.

"You really think I look okay?"

"Are you nervous?"

I blinked. "Am I?"

She laughed.

"Good day to you, sir," Lila said, bowing.

"Good day to you, madam. Is your dad here?"

"Lou, it's for you," Lila said, skipping back into the living room and leaving Al to fend for himself in the doorway.

"Hey," I said.

He looked me over and smiled. "Hey."

"Hey," Ky said, scooping up Lila and coming to the door.

Al blinked and held up the flowers. "Hey, I…uh…have these. I… this is the thing you do when you go on a…"

He floundered when his eyes landed on Ky and Lila. I thought it was charming and was about to say as much, but Lila beat me to it.

"The alive ones are the best," Lila said, holding her hands out for the flowers.

Al looked at me, and I shrugged. He handed them over. She squirmed away from her mother and crossed to the kitchen table. We watched as she pulled the fall decorations out of the skull vase and stuck the flowers in, plastic film and all.

"Well, that solves that." Al laughed.

"Y'all better get going. Lila and I are due for the movie soon," Ky said.

"Wait. I just—" Al cleared his throat and fished something out of his pocket. He unfolded a packet of papers and asked, "How worried should I be about the understudied titration rate of common pharmaceuticals in biosolid-treated soil?"

"Very," Ky said cryptically. Then she gave me a look and a kiss on the cheek. She turned toward the kitchen and walked away.

"Is she serious?" Al asked me, still confused.

"No, she's impressed and doesn't want you to know it. What are you doing with that, anyway?" I took the copy of Ky's paper from him, setting it down on the coffee table.

"Teach found it. I told him what biosolids was. Those things, the papers I mean, are like forty dollars," he said, truly stunned.

"Let's go."

I stopped him out in the hall and took his hand. It was a brief contact, but it stirred up the embers inside me. I leaned in, pulling him slightly, to capture his mouth in a kiss. He hummed a little, surprised.

"The flowers were sweet. I like 'em," I said.

He ran a hand over his hair. "You're welcome."

"You look great."

"You look great," he answered back.

"Get out of the fucking hallway," Ky shouted through the door.

We went out to the back of the building and got into my truck. We were following a restaurant suggestion from Rose. Her sister-in-law's husband recommended a place an hour away, not that I minded. It gave us a chance to do something we hadn't really gotten to do. We were finally getting alone time together.

"How was your day?" I said as I pulled the truck onto the main road out of town.

"It was a day. The girls are doing a lot better, and so is Teach. Dani said the conference she was at generated enough interest in Beast that she got a few calls about her sister program from some gyms up north."

"That's great. What about you, though?" I could feel his eyes on me as I bounced us over the train tracks on the edge of town, driving a little faster than I probably should. "You talked about your kids, your brother, and your wife. How are you?"

He thought about it. "Shit, um…I'm good. I told you about how good things went with Bets."

He had. Most evenings he'd call me around eight and we'd talk for a few minutes. Usually, he asked questions. Friday night after Betsy caught us, he called and told me the whole story about Teach and his mother. It made me love Betsy even more.

"I did end up talkin' to him about it. He said he never cared if I came out to our parents. He didn't think it would've made a difference. I've had a lot of guilt about that. I didn't know the language for it, not until recently, then I just never did anythin' with the thoughts. It was like enough piled up each day that we never talked about it, then it just became part of the scenery."

"Do you feel less guilty?"

"I don't think so."

"You don't think so?"

He propped his other arm on the ledge of the window and ran his hand under his chin. His arm didn't move any closer or any farther from me. Did he notice? Did he want me to touch it, touch *him?* Hold his hand? That was a thought. *I* was thinking about his hand, but was he thinking about mine?

"Then again, it's pointless to feel guilty when the person you feel like you owe says forget about it," he said, sounding for a moment like a Southern preacher. "Anyway, of all the things I've been carryin' around, that was nearly the last of my past that haunted me. I apologized to Frank and Orion summer before last when Frank was still livin' with Rose, and that had been a part of all this."

"This?"

"What're the kids callin' it? Internalized homophobia—biphobia really."

"Shit. Sure, I get that."

"Yeah?"

"Sure, it's hard to have unrealized internalized homophobia with lesbian mothers who believe in the power of therapy. But I've recently discovered some new internal shit I didn't know was there."

He side-eyed me. "The stuff about dads?"

"Yeah. I've been thinking about it almost nonstop."

"Want to talk about it?"

"Um…"

"You don't have to, you know," Al said.

Then he did it. He brushed the back of my hand with his. I understood it was meant to be a gesture of comfort, but the feeling vibrated through my body. I snagged his fingers before he moved away. It was less of a hand hold and more my hand on top of his, palm to back, fingers laced. Any other position really wouldn't work with our thick-ass arms. But Christ, I loved the pressure of his hand, the grip he had on me.

"I know I don't have to. I just also don't have much to say. It's like, I'm still collecting the facts, so nothing to report. You know what I mean? I guess I mostly keep wondering why he left the way he did. I feel like I'm missing something. I don't know."

He squeezed my fingers slightly, drawing my attention back to his hand. It was warm and big and hard. I remembered his hands on my face and chest, running up my back. And before my thoughts could take a diving leap into the gutter, my phone rang. Because it was attached to the Bluetooth in the truck, I looked at the dash. It was Silvy.

"I'm sorry," I said, reaching across my body to hit the answer button on the steering wheel rather than let Al's hand go. "Hey, Mom, you're on speaker."

"Hey ya, Lou. Hi, Ky," Silvy said.

I groaned. "Um…not Ky, it's Al."

We heard some high-pitched whispering on the other end of the line, and I hoped I didn't look as embarrassed as I felt.

"Hi, Alexander, I'm Lucas's ma." I felt only the slightest betrayal at Silvy for giving the phone to Jojo, who sounded like she was working hard to contain her excitement.

"Hello, Mrs.…?"

"Now, call me Jojo. Do you prefer Al? I know that's what Lou calls you, but I just want to know."

"Al's fine," he said, his voice light.

"What're you boys up to tonight?"

"Ma, you're supposed to be on a trip, what did Silvy need?"

Jojo scoffed. "I know, I just wanted to say hi to your boyfriend."

It took a lot of energy to not hang up.

"Here's Silvy. Bye, Al."

"Bye," Al said.

"Hey, so what're you guys up to?" Silvy asked. She was also restraining her excitement, but I knew it was for very different reasons.

"What is it?" I groaned.

"What do you mean?"

"Mom."

"Fine, but I really don't want to interrupt."

"Well," I said, trying to move it along. She usually called for one of three reasons: the first was food she wanted to share, the second was to pick up Lila, and the third was when she needed help in the workshop. "You got a sale?"

"I did, but I can try to tell them not tonight," Silvy said.

"What does that mean?" Al asked, trying to whisper.

"It means," I said, in my normal tone, feeling our date, yet another date, slip through my fingers. "Silvy makes furniture for a living, and her work is so good it sells for thousands—"

"Don't start that," Silvy tried to interrupt.

"But sometimes buyers are pushy and demand off-hours shipping."

"Congrats on the sale," Al cheered, annoyingly and cutely seeing the good in the situation. I couldn't help but feel a slight prickle about him not seeming to notice that if we agreed to Silvy's requests, we probably wouldn't make it to the restaurant. Our date would just be another solution to family needs. Then again, what right did I have? We were both fathers and sons and husbands. It might be unfair to feel like I was being cheated out of time with him, but I did feel it.

"Thank you, Al. Lou, it'll be quick, you don't even have to take it anywhere, just load it up and send 'em on their way," she said.

"What is *it*?" I asked. She didn't answer. "Jesus, it's the dining room set, isn't it?"

"That doesn't sound too bad," Al said.

"The table alone weighs four hundred pounds."

Al's eyebrows shot up to his hairline, and he looked at his free hand as if it would tell him what he was capable of lifting.

"Well," Silvy said. "That's nothing for big guys like you. Besides, you can use the lift."

"We're on our way to dinner." I hoped I didn't sound as whiny out loud as I thought I sounded in my head.

"I'll have Paul's delivered to the house."

"Pizza Paul's?" Al asked eagerly.

I said something like "hold on," then I put the call on mute. I didn't say anything right away. Inside me was a full-on war. My sense of duty to my parents told me to just do it, but there was some unfamiliar part of me that demanded the date. Now was not the time to unpack that, but I also couldn't ignore it.

"Lou," Al said softly. His words were coupled with a squeeze of my fingers. I didn't answer. "I get it. Help your parents," he said. His hand slipped away from mine.

His understanding was as frustrating to me as it was endearing. Of course he understood that part of it. It was the interruptions and shortened moments together that he didn't seem to notice. Not that I fully understood it. I had no idea what to call that other feeling. I risked glancing at him.

He smiled at me and rubbed his hands together in excitement. "I really like Pizza Paul's."

That broke me. Curse him and his beautiful face. I took a deep breath and turned the call back on. "When will your clients be there?"

"Maybe now," she said, then she glossed that over by asking what we wanted on the pizza.

I told her to just get the usual, and she prodded Al for an answer until he finally said, "The Pizza Paul trio." I turned the truck around and headed over.

❖

We didn't say anything on the fifteen-minute drive. I thumbed on a playlist on my phone and let the music take over the vibe. Al seemed happy enough, singing along. I was impressed he knew the artist, D.J. Roads, who was Black and gay and not at the top of the charts as far as country music went. He didn't sing loud, but I could hear him. And I liked it. But I also hated it. I was stuck between being absolutely irritated and completely smitten. Didn't he want a date? Like, a real date? Didn't he want this to be something other than two dads/handymen/nurses/delivery boys who kissed sometimes? Was there more or was that it?

"Hey," he said. This time his fingers brushed over my knuckles and up my arm.

"Hey."

"You okay?"

I nodded. "Yeah, this means a lot for Ma and Silvy. I just had other plans."

"There's still room for other plans. We hoist a table, eat some 'za, then hit a bar or bowling—it's cosmic bowling night down at the Bowl-a-thon."

I snorted a laugh. "Fair enough. But that place looks like it hosts Klan meetings on the weekdays, so if I say *run*, you run."

He laughed, then grimaced. "Right, maybe not."

The buyer was already at the house—a woman and two men, one who looked like her husband and one who looked like a son. While I showed Al how to help with the table and tried to get the husband to drive his trailer in line with the lift, the woman explained she needed the table now because it was a wedding gift for her daughter, and they were leaving in the morning. She talked while Al and I loaded chairs and strapped everything down. She shook my hand twice and made her husband and son shake my hand too before shaking it a third time. By the time we were waving them out of the yard, I almost didn't want to talk to Al just to have some silence.

"You know," Al said, "I never really got the saying 'talk the ears off corn' till now."

I smiled.

"Hey, it wasn't that bad. Four hundred pounds is nothing." He clapped me on the shoulder.

"Yeah, I thought you'd struggle more. The way Dani tells it, you haven't been in a gym in years."

He turned to stare at me, tightening the grip on my shoulder. "You sayin' I don't lift…bro?"

I nodded and crossed my arms. He stared for one more heartbeat, then faster than I would have ever suspected, he got an arm around my legs and threw me over his shoulder like I was nothing.

"God damn, Al, put me down. You're going to hurt one of us."

"No, I'm not. I can do this all day. Built like an ox, baby," he said with a laugh.

And just to show off, he did a squat without any sign of weakness. I remembered the muscly power he exuded when he was on top of me, holding me against the doors of his garage. His belly gave him a hot sitcom dad vibe, but I liked knowing how much power lurked under his nice-guy appearance. I tried to squirm away, but his grip was steady and all I did was earn some warm laughter. We both stopped when we heard the doorbell. He had carried me almost all the way back from the workshop.

"Pizza's here," he cheered.

"Put me down, Al."

He pretended not to hear. I did the only thing I could think of. I took the back of his jeans in both hands and pulled. He yelped and half set, half dropped me down. I laughed, catching myself. I trotted to get the door as he picked his wedgie in the yard. The driver was some teenager who handed me the pizzas without looking up from his phone. He didn't even wait for a tip. I put the food on the dining room table.

"Woo, I'm excited," Al said, sliding the back door closed behind him. He looked at me, and his smile did something to my stomach. "I can't tell you how long it's been since I had a pizza that was more than just cheese. Seven kids, all who don't like pizza toppings. It's criminal."

He opened a box. I decided to get a drink before I thought too hard about the feelings his smile gave me. It wasn't like I was trying to resist him. But my mood from the truck was threatening to come back now that the job was done. I didn't want it to spoil the rest of the night. Beer would help.

I opened the fridge, but it was empty of alcohol. I groaned. "Well, you have your choice of water or whatever veggies my mom put in a blender yesterday—oh, there's tea."

"Water's great."

I grabbed two bottles and stood to go back to him. Then I froze. His back was to me. He was rubbing absently at the ass of his jeans. It looked less like scratching and more like thinking. His shirt stuck to him where he sweated, even though it was winter and even though the house was cooler than it should have been. The way the shirt material draped and clung emphasized his wide shoulders and thick back muscles.

Every part of me woke up to the physical idea of him. It was too bad we were here. *Hold the phone.* That was a thought. And I looked around my parents' house like I'd never seen it. There was no one here. No kids, no wives, no metamours, no parents. Not even a snowball's chance in hell his sister would show up out of the blue. What *was* here, though, was at least two guest rooms. It felt like the revelation of the century. Him or me, one of us wasn't leaving this house un-fucked. Well, if he consented. I put the unopened waters down on the counter and strolled over to Al.

"Hey," I said. He turned, a pizza slice halfway in his mouth. I smiled. "Do you think you could hold off eating for a little longer? I have one more thing for you to do."

He hadn't bit down on the slice; it was just hanging in his open mouth as he looked at me. He nodded and set the slice back in the box, wiping his mouth with his sleeve.

"Name it," he said, giving me another stupid handsome smile.

I stepped into his space. "Oh, you already know my name."

His eyes went wide as the innuendo landed. I was close enough now to lean on him. He practically fell back against the table, surprised, but his hands held me. His breathing shortened and his face flushed, clearly giving away his excitement. He looked around the room and grinned. "Table seems sturdy enough, but we should probably move the pizza."

"Good to know you're willing to do it in the dining room. There's a guest room."

He pressed forward, not to push me away but to press into me. He cupped my face with his hands and kissed me. It was suggestive and slow. I was his, and he was all that was holding me up. *Shit*, I thought, *am I falling for this guy?*

"Lead the way," he whispered against my lips.

I let myself have a few more seconds with his mouth before I backed away and started toward the stairs. Then another idea occurred to me. "Oh shit, I just realized I don't have condoms. I guess it doesn't have to be penetrative."

"Yo, I brought some," he said proudly. I watched him fish two condoms and condom-sized packs of lube out of a pocket.

"You had those in your pocket the whole time? What if they'd busted?" I was as surprised as I was relieved.

He blushed slightly. "I didn't think about it."

"Wait a minute." I gestured to the whole of my parents' house. "This wasn't planned. So, when did you *plan* to use those?"

He didn't back down or get embarrassed. Instead, he looked at me with proud, clear eagerness. "Maybe I googled every hotel between the restaurant and home."

"Really?"

He turned his confident, lusty expression into charming casualness. "I mean, yeah."

He walked over to me, stopping on the first stair, leaning against the rail. He smelled so great.

"That wasn't necessarily how I wanted it to happen, but I figured it'd be fun anyway. It'd give us a place to be together without worryin' who might show up. Privacy is a rare commodity in my world."

I knew how small towns worked. Even I couldn't go anywhere in Painted Waters without being Rose's nurse. I wondered... "How would you have wanted it?"

He looked around. "Like this, I guess, in a place more intimate, less temporary."

And I fucking believed him. No, I more than believed him, I loved him for it. He had said it with the same perfectly serious tone he had explained wanting to date me, the same way he asked me to give him any time at all right before his sister interrupted us. I understood right then that for all my worries and for all the failed logistics, he really did want to be with me in a way that wasn't temporary.

"You okay?"

I kissed him. I was already so gone for him. I knew every moment from that one meant moving forward was toward love. At that point it wasn't *if*, but *when*.

"That was really cheesy," I said just to rib him.

"Call me Gouda."

"Oh no." I groaned.

"Why not? I'm *Gouda* in bed."

"You're un-Brie-lievable." I crossed my arms and waited for him to be impressed.

"Oh, I like that. I always knew cheese puns were sexy."

"I guess if I'd known you were already thinking of sex, I would've come more prepared." I laughed and started up the stairs. He followed. I hoped he understood.

"I am."

"What do you mean?"

"I'm prepared. I *prepared*."

I tripped on the last step, caught myself, and turned to face him. He grinned. He had never been more attractive than in that moment.

"You are?" I asked.

He put his hands in his pockets and slowly leaned in to kiss me. My whole body warmed to that kiss, burning under the surface like lava. If I got any warmer, I'd probably start to produce light. No other part of him was touching me except his mouth, tongue, and lips, but that was all he needed. He had me right where he wanted me. *Who literally goes weak in the knees?*

"Which room?" he asked. His grin was very smug, like he knew the impact he was having. I would've had to be really clueless to believe he hadn't noticed how hard I already was. I felt almost giddy. He seemed to be the opposite. He was confident, collected, and *prepared* to take my dick.

"You okay?"

"You keep asking me that," I said in what was almost a gasp.

I hadn't realized my eyes were still closed, so I opened them. His eyes, brown and warm and phenomenal, met mine.

"I wasn't expecting anything physical, so I'm surprised, I guess."

"You want to stop?" he asked.

"Do I look like I want to stop?" I was genuinely wondering. I felt like a panting dog cartoon whose eyes bugged out when the hottie walked by.

He grinned and filled even more of my space. His legs were slightly longer. I remembered them between mine, slightly too thick and strong, holding me up, holding me in place. His cock rubbed against mine as I swayed a little. The lava under my skin bubbled. He slipped his arm around my back and pulled me into him, crushing my dick against his.

"You seem like you could come right here on the stairs," he said, his voice smooth.

"I'd rather come on you."

He laughed. "Well, which room, then?"

I didn't answer, just turned down the hall to the last door on the left. Al kissed me and backed me against the wall just inside the chilly room before I could even get the light on. I let him press into me, bringing my hands up to either side of his face. I could feel his thick, hard cock on my thigh and knew all my molten want was reciprocated. He wanted me enough to have his way with me standing half in the doorway.

I knew there was one of those old-timey half couch things along the wall. He let me turn us, focused on my mouth, his tongue rolling over mine then backing off to just a ghost touch of lips, some crazy give and take that was everything fucking amazing about the way he kissed. With all that going on, I backed us up until my calf caught the edge of the couch thing, and we both dropped onto it with a grunt.

"I'm surprised that held," he said breathlessly. He let me up so I could get more comfortable, then crawled up me to press me into it.

"It was one of the first things Silvy did. She made it out of a single log, so we could probably get five more guys on here."

"Who do you know?" he teased, kissing my neck.

I relaxed, kissing whatever of his skin came my way, letting him have whatever part of me he wanted. I traced my hands down his back and under his shirt. I didn't get to undress him last time. He let me pull the fabric over his head, then followed my lead and slipped his hands under my shirt, not removing it, just feeling around. I kissed his broad shoulders and his thick arms. When I pressed up into him, he growled low in my ear.

"How do you want to do this?" he asked.

"As far as I'm concerned, you can stay up there."

"Oh, I see, I bring the condoms, prepare, *and* have to do all the work?"

I shrugged, which made him laugh.

He sat up slightly, one knee on the couch next to my hip and one foot on the floor. "Do you want anythin' else, or just get to it?"

The only light was coming from the door, silhouetting him, edged in warm yellow. I traced my hands up his thighs, up his stomach, over his pecs, nipples, and down his arms. His muscles flexed. I could tell he was trying not to flinch. I was probably tickling him. I took an evaluation of my current state.

"Survey says probably wouldn't last through anything else."

He nodded. Annoyingly, but also wonderfully, he stood and started to undo his pants. I wanted in on that, so I sat up and pulled him toward me. I took over for him, his hands falling to his sides.

"See, not all the work," I said, pulling the leather belt out of the loops.

He just grunted. I wished I had turned the light on. I loved the fullness of his body, the imposing shape of him but the gentle nature of his soul. I undid the fly of his jeans and pulled them lower on his hips. I liked the contrast of the black jeans and briefs on his white skin. He looked like he wanted to touch me.

"You can touch wherever you want," I said, pulling him closer. I lost interest in his hands on my shoulders and arms fairly quickly. Somehow, he managed to get my shirt off. I traced his thick thighs around to his firm ass and pressed my face against his stomach. He made some happy sound and rocked toward me.

"So far so good?" I asked, curling my fingers into the waistband of his briefs.

"Are you kiddin'?"

I grinned and pulled the fabric away. His dick—free, hard, and practically eye level—was tempting, but I purposefully ignored it, opting to kiss a trail from stomach to inner thigh. I made sure his cock brushed against my hand or face, but I gave it no more attention than that.

"Fuck," he whispered.

I could tell he was trying to be patient, waiting to see what I would do. I wondered how far I could tease him before his polite veneer started to crack.

"Put your foot up," I said as I leaned back.

"What?" He sounded both confused and irritated, but I pretended not to notice.

"Give me your foot."

He put his booted foot on the edge of the couch, and I started pulling the laces. He watched me with an intensity that was borderline audible.

"What're you looking at?"

He smirked. "The biggest tease I know."

"Thought I was the biggest flirt you knew," I said, pulling his shoe off and gesturing for the other one.

"I guess you're a triple threat."

"What's the third?" I said, working on the other boot.

"Stupidly charming."

Boots gone, I shifted so that my knee was no longer between his legs. His pants slipped to the floor. I figured he could manage the rest from there at some point. Pulling him by the ass back toward me, I immediately slipped his dick into my mouth.

"Christ," he said as he grabbed my shoulders to steady himself.

Head is a lot of things for a lot of people, but it usually turns my crank. My mouth is probably the most sensitive part of me. Al smelled like some mix of floral soap and deodorant. He tasted like salt and groaned with a depth that vibrated every place we made contact. I probably could have gotten off on just the way he kissed. I liked the way he used my mouth, explored, and caressed. Now it was just some other part of him, but it had the same effect. It was like eating a good meal. I sucked.

"This feels fuckin' amazing," he said.

I had a few more things I wanted to explore. Everything in the vicinity of his cock was fairly slick with spit, including my hand. I licked my fingers anyway. I slipped them between his legs and caressed his hole. That seemed to jolt him into a higher gear because he started thrusting in small ways, chasing the sensation of my fingers against him but not wanting to leave my mouth.

"Damn, that's, that's gonna make this really short," he gasped.

I slipped away slowly and looked up at him. I watched him watch me as I sat back on the couch and pulled my pants and briefs down to my upper thighs. I wasn't in the mood to fight with my own shoes to get my pants off, so I just left them. He didn't seem to mind. He was back on top of me, covering me with his body. The body heat he generated was almost obscene.

"You're so fucking hot," he said.

I considered saying something. I wasn't much of a talker, at least not in words. I opened my mouth to try, but he took that as a request for a kiss. I moaned into it, his tongue deep, his body caging me under him. Sandwiched between us, his dick rubbed against mine as he moved, pressing into me when he breathed. And that felt perfect.

"Dude, if you're going to get on it, it better be soon," I half moaned.

He laughed and sat back. "*Dude?*"

I didn't answer. I watched him reach for his pants on the floor to get a condom, the light and shadow playing across his muscular back. He tore it and a pack of lube open. I figured he could see me pretty well, given the way the light fell into the room. I tried not to think too hard about what I must look like.

His eyes barely left mine as he rolled the condom on my dick and added lube, moving fast and dexterously. He straddled me but had to keep one foot on the floor, otherwise we wouldn't fit on the couch thing. I also had to shift down a little, being slightly too tall.

I lost track of watching as I started to sink into him. Fucking hell. His movements were methodical, slow ins and outs to acclimate to my presence inside him. But I was about to fucking lose it.

"This feels great," he said, his voice low and blissful. There were other words, but I couldn't keep them in my head. I made some ridiculous sound in agreement.

It felt like forever and no time at all before he was fully seated on my lap. I expected him to lean over me, kiss me, and finish us both off in record time. Instead, he traced the lines of my body, my muscles. I could feel every time he flexed, and every shift felt like an electrical pulse.

"Who's teasing now?" I said.

His grin was almost sinister. "I was just admiring the view."

"Admire and fuck at the same time."

He laughed. But finally came down for a kiss. I almost couldn't kiss him back. The warmth and friction of him slowly starting to ride my dick was sending me toward orgasm at a distracting speed.

He said something against my lips and panted, but I understood nothing. No words at all could penetrate my laser focus on where his body took me. It wasn't until he caressed my face and I opened my eyes in response that I heard anything he said.

Is this okay? That's what he was asking. I was baffled by the question. This was so much more than okay. "Unbelievable," I said.

I slid my arms around his back to bring him closer. I regretted not letting him lie down so I could trap him under me and make him feel as attractive and wanted as I felt. I suddenly didn't care if I got off or not. I wanted to see him lose himself in this. I could see the pleasure on his face, but I wanted to make it powerful, meaningful for him, like it was for me. I slipped my hand down between us and covered his cock, pressing it against my lower stomach. He moaned, almost losing his footing. I steadied his hips with my free hand.

"Shit, I like that," he said.

"Do you have any more lube?" I asked. It was surprising how clear my thinking was now that my goal was to watch him come apart on my dick.

"Um…" He struggled for a second to find the packet, but he handed it to me. I made him sit up slightly as I applied a strip of lube along his dick. Then I tossed the packet aside and covered his cock again.

"Fuck me," I said.

His grin was carnal. He braced his hand against my chest and began to fuck me again, regaining speed. The space around his dick became atmospheric as the lube warmed between my hand and stomach. I felt like I could watch him do that for hours.

"Fuck, that's crazy good," he said.

He leaned over me again, his huge hands on either side of my face. I couldn't hold back my smile as I watched him disappear, the concern and focus on his face drifting behind a haze of pure pleasure. His pace started to accelerate, and it started to draw my focus back south. The drag of his dick on my stomach was a perfect match to the pull of his hole on my cock.

"I…God, I'm so close," he said, and I think he meant it as a warning.

I could tell. His muscles tightened, the hand next to my head became a fist, and the veins in his arms raised. His body flexed around my dick, pulling my orgasm closer. And his eyes were shut tight.

I wanted to feel as much of him as I could when it happened, so I pulled him down with my free hand and kissed him, invasively and freely. And that sent him over the edge, body clenching, cum warming my stomach, a stifled scream of pleasure vibrating in my chest. Because I wasn't focused on it, my orgasm exploded from me, surprising and hot like a flash grenade. There were a few moments of silence. Well, relative silence with nothing except breathing. Then he sat back and made a face at me.

"What?" I asked, worried.

His smile broke through. He said, "That was so good. Like, so good I'm low-key mad about it. I kind of want to fight you. You ever feel like that, like when someone gets you such a good gift you wanna tackle 'em?"

"You want to arm wrestle or something?" I said, not knowing what else to do but laugh. I understood the feeling, though. It was a flex, being able to make someone come harder, better than they expected.

"Yeah, I do." Instead of trying, he leaned over and kissed me. That kiss was a problem. It felt different than his other kisses. It felt like that damned L-word that kept popping up for me.

"How about pizza instead?" I said, sounding vulnerable to myself.

"Wait, are you good? Did you come? You're so fuckin' quiet, I can't really tell."

I giggled. "Yeah, I did—I'm good."

I wanted to tell him I came in a way I never had before. I wanted to tell him I had fallen in love with Ky during sex too, only with her I felt like crying, like I was home. But this was different. With him, I wanted to fall over laughing, I felt like a kid on a roller coaster coming back toward the loading zone, wondering when I would be able to get to go again. I didn't say any of that. Relieved, we stared at each other for a heartbeat.

"I thought you were going to get the pizza," I said, feeling like if he stared at me any longer, I might actually say it.

"Oh, I have to—okay, got it, Pillow Prince. I guess I can feed you too."

"Good, bring ranch."

That actually did make him fight me. Laughing, he wrestled me to the floor, pinning me with my arm behind my back. Not that it was hard with my pants around my thighs. I cried uncle. And he let me go. We cleaned up first, then sat at the dining room table and ate cool but not quite cold pizza.

I reminisced about the way he kissed.

"Hey," I said, as I was thinking about his tongue in my mouth, "did you use to have a tongue piercing?"

He stuck his tongue out as if he could see it. "Yeah, I did. How'd you know?"

"I can feel the scar. Ky has one like it."

He rubbed his tongue with his finger. "Oh yeah?"

"Yeah, she took it out after about two years. She kept swallowing—"

"Swallowing the gear, same. I used to get stressed about never really seeing it come out the other end, you know what I mean."

I snorted. "So, ground and steel type, then?"

He smiled. "I guess. Are Ky and I that similar?"

"No, not really. I feel like I like different things about you, despite the similarities. I don't know if that makes sense, like it's not even masc or fem things but for some reason it's different."

"I think I get it."

"What's different about it for you? You identify as bi, right?"

He shrugged. "Yeah, I guess, but it was never a guy-girl thing or an in-between or neither thing. I think I like attitude, I guess, that and anyone who thinks lifting weights is a good way to spend a few hours. Bi is just the label that made the most sense."

"What if I stop working out, though?"

He flashed me a peace sign without hesitation. "Deuces, bro."

I flipped him off. We ate and cleaned up the boxes. Al made sure to leave behind no evidence of our having fucked in the guest room. His voice got very Southern when he said something about having done things in the home of people he had yet to meet in person. I tried not to think about introducing him to my moms. That sounded like real relationship stuff. And the more I thought about this as a real relationship, the more lost to him I felt.

CHAPTER NINE

Alexander

I got out of the van and joined the rest of the parents milling on the sidewalk, the Thursday afternoon crowd a little thinner than most other days. Teach and Coach followed, mixing in. I scanned the people looking for a parent or staff member I might know. When I caught sight of Lucas, my heart jumped. Even though he was never hard to spot, I was surprised to see him.

"Lou," I shouted, putting a hand up.

He grinned and trotted over when he spotted me. That grin went straight to my guts. His messages since Saturday had been terse, and maybe it was making me nervous. But that smile made me wonder if it was all in my head. It was starting to get hard not seeing him or hearing him on a daily basis. I knew our nontraditional situation would have to remain nontraditional. But learning love in a monogamous setting made it hard to interpret the feeling any other way. I wanted him *every day*. We met a few strides away from Coach and Teach. My first instinct was to hug him, but I knew any touch between us would automatically be less than platonic looking. I didn't do anything but smile like a fool. *The Gunner needs to find some chill or else mistakes will get made.*

"Hey, Al. What's up, Jeffersons," he said, waving around. "Mr. Jefferson."

Coach just harrumphed and flapped his coat a little. Teach waved.

"What're ya doing here?" I asked. "I thought Lila was still in preschool."

"She is." He held up the folder in his hands. "I have an interview."

"Oh yeah? As what?" I asked.

He grinned. "Cheer coach, obviously."

Teach laughed and even Dad smiled.

"Ha. That's great. Good luck. Would love to see you do a high kick." I rolled my eyes.

He nudged me and whispered, "I know at least one of us is flexible enough."

I felt that one in a not-safe-for-work place.

"What're you really here for?" I asked, trying not to give away how much I liked his teasing.

"Really, though, school nurse. Mrs. Brunswick is retiring. They need someone at least through the end of the year. And since my patients keep improving…"

"Damn, that's good. She's older than the South," I said.

"She was the nurse when *I* was in middle school," Coach said.

"That's good for you, though." I smiled at Lucas. I remembered him saying he was bored. This school must have been on a fault line considering how much damage these kids took on the regular. Then again, maybe that's just how elementary and middle schools were. The bell rang and children started to pour out of the building.

"Why didn't you tell me?" The question was out before I realized I'd said it.

He looked genuinely confused. "I don't know. I guess I forgot about it until the hospital coordinator called me this morning."

"I really do mean congratulations. Sorry, that was weird—"

He waved me off, but his expression shifted slightly. "I should probably—"

"Wait." I pulled him a step or two away from Coach and Teach. *To catch up the folks just tuning in, our guy Al "the Gunner" Jefferson and his latest match Lucas "the Tank" Laverty gave us one hell of a show last week. Word on the street is negotiations for the next one have taken a turn. While this wouldn't be the first time the Gunner has been shot down, this was definitely out of left field. Will we get to see these two ever play again?*

"What is it?" he asked.

I nearly whispered. "Nothin'. I just like lookin' at ya. I feel like I haven't seen you in weeks."

"It's been five days," Lucas said patiently, scanning the crowd before he said, "I missed you too."

"You never answered about next week."

"Okay, yeah, I know. I will. I just had a lot on my mind."

The gravity of his words made the whole world tilt a little to the left. The pickup area of my kids' school suddenly felt like the exact wrong place to talk about this. Maybe my read on the tone of his messages wasn't so far off. Did he not want this? He did just say he missed me. When his eyes met mine, I sensed a question. Right now was not the time.

"Fair enough. Can I—" I was drowned out by the high-pitched screaming of a herd of girls.

"Grandpa, Teach, hi, Daddy, hi, Uncle Al!" All of them had bundles of papers, thrusting them at Coach all at once.

"What's all this?" Coach asked.

"Art for Turkey Day," someone answered.

"Well, let's see some of it." It was always alarming to see my dad with kids. He was weirdly good with them; he always had been. Even when being a total ass, he was still something else.

"What were you going to say?" Lucas asked.

"Right, uh…I'll call you?"

I said this half listening to the girls explain their drawings. Apparently, for the holiday they had to draw someone they were thankful for. Most drew pictures of their parents, and they very diplomatically took turns handing them to Coach for evaluation. Teach got one, and Zara passed over a picture of me and Dani.

"Yeah, that's a good idea. I'll be done with this in an hour or so," Lucas continued.

"Okay, I'll—"

I never finished the sentence. It was Margret's turn to show Coach her drawing.

"And who is this?" Coach asked.

"That's Uncle Al's boyfriend."

Lucas and I both turned. Teach, standing behind my dad, was shocked enough to almost drop his phone. I hadn't come that close to shitting myself in years. I wasn't much of a religious man, but God had a hand in that moment because Teach, Lucas, and I were all looking stupefied, but Coach didn't look at all impacted by her announcement.

"Oh yeah? Why'd ya draw him?" Coach asked. Since Margret was the last to show her grandfather her picture, most of the other kids had moved on, swinging from the doors of the van or chatting with their classmates. They probably hadn't even heard her.

"He cured us when we were sick, and he cured you. And I like that," Margret said. She was trying to get a candy bar out of her coat pocket, but it was jammed in sideways. That beautiful child had effectively thrown me and Lucas to the wolves, and she was worried about a Milky Way.

"Here," Coach said, helping her get it out.

"I won it in the Turkey Chase," she screamed, wielding it like a sword.

"Attagirl, but no eating it till after dinner," Coach said. He was standing again. And was still holding the drawing. We could see it now, the brown and blue crayon scribbles representing Lucas in his scrubs.

"I need it back," Margret said.

"Oh sure." Coach handed it back to her. There was nothing in his voice—no tone, no judgment, no rage. "Maggie, who told you he was Uncle Al's boyfriend?"

That was a question we all had.

"Mommy told Daddy," she said with a shrug, marching over to Lucas.

"Here, you want it?" she said, handing it to him. "It's you."

His eyes were on Coach, but he snapped out of it and took the picture from her. Next to me he made a to-do about the picture and thanked her. I watched Coach, who was watching Margret. She hugged Lucas and ran off.

I waited, my heart in my shoes. I remembered when Fin had come out to the soccer team—well, it was some guys who just played soccer, not an official team yet. That was right before high school, long before I put two and two together and figured out what being gay really meant. My parents knew, though. Wynona was always sending him home early with some excuse, like we had to go to the store or pick up takeout or something. Coach then would give me hour-long lectures about how *gay* was behavior for other people, lesser people. Betsy Ross had confirmed all of it, so it made some strange sense Margret had been the one to rat us out. Like mother like daughter.

I couldn't even begin to guess at what Coach would do. With all the kids back at the van, we all had no reason to stand around. I couldn't get my legs to move. Coach put his hands back in his pockets. His expression was back to that of a reserved, strategic coach.

"If the girls know, Gage is gonna know sooner or later," Coach said. It sounded like he meant it as a warning. Then he turned and walked away.

I was about to say something to Lucas, but he looked stunned. He spoke before I could.

"I have to get to the interview."

"Okay, I'll call," I said.

He walked away, looking at the drawing Margret had done.

"The fuck just happened?" I breathed.

Teach looked as confused as the rest of us.

"Bro, you looked like you were gonna shit your pants," his roommate Arturo said through the phone. Teach must have been on FaceTime with him. I walked closer to Teach and watched Coach help the kids into the van.

"I considered it," I said, looking at the phone.

"Aye, I meant him," Arturo teased, pointing at Teach.

Teach flipped him off. "Eighty-five-percent sure I did."

I laughed and started for the van.

The mood among the adults should have warranted a silent, awkward ride home, but the girls kept it from being that. They screamed and laughed and cried, and it was as it always was. My eyes kept drifting toward my phone. I don't know what I expected it to do. I think I was waiting for Lucas. I didn't want to believe things were rocky or whatever. Things had barely started with us. Hadn't he had fun on our date?

Then again, the cat was out of the bag now. I'd have to be insane to believe Coach was okay with this. He liked Lucas; I could see that much. But to be okay with this? And given what Betsy had said—

"Going the long way home?" Coach asked from shotgun. I blinked. I had passed the turn to the house.

"Sorry, I was on autopilot."

"I noticed."

His voice was as colorful as the gray winter outside the car. I didn't dare look at him. I just took the van around the block. The kids practically climbed each other to get out, running inside in a flurry of hair and backpacks. Some of the younger girls ran to the door to meet their sisters. I could see Dani in the living room, shooing them. Teach grabbed the discarded hats and coats and backpacks. I tried to help him.

"Let's go see about the mail," Coach said.

I looked at him. He was bundled to the teeth, looking older in his denim hat and wool-lined denim coat. He was staring down the drive to the mailbox. That meant we were going to have a talk.

"Okay."

He didn't wait for me. I looked at Teach. He shrugged and started toward the house. The house was on the rural side of town, with an orchard and forest surrounding acres of backyard. I followed Dad, locking the van behind me. He didn't stop at the mailbox.

"Coach," I said after a long silence.

"You know why we named your brother John Adams?" Coach said, his voice materializing as cold breath. He turned into the street and started away from town, toward the farms.

"You and Wynona always said you wanted everyone to have strong American names."

"Well, that's what your mother wanted. I wanted to name my first boy Elton."

"What?"

"But your mother thought people would *associate* him with Elton John. So I picked a different name."

"Oh." I snorted, trying to picture my big, redneck brother as an Elton, but then I caught on. "*You* didn't have a problem with people associating him with Elton John? Just Mom?"

"It never occurred to me, but the pastor down at the church agreed it probably wasn't the best start to a good Christian life, so I let it go."

"Huh."

"Do you know what I wanted to name you?"

"Liberace?"

My father laughed. When he was in a good humor, he looked like Teach. He looked like someone who was supposed to be happy but never got the chance.

"Naw, nothing so hard to spell. I suggested Kareem."

"I bet Mom loved that."

"Yup. She loved it so much, she chose Robert E. Lee."

"Yikes."

He just nodded.

"Wait, Dad, you're serious? You always seemed so…"

"Racist?"

"Yeah."

He shrugged. "Can't deny he was the greatest basketball player who ever lived. Besides, I can't say I wasn't."

I didn't understand. "Coach."

"Now, I was thinking about when I was young. I wanted to teach English. I went to college, and my dad wanted me to study business. You know all that."

Right. That was half the reason my grandfather and his brother left the family business to me and Paul. That and I loved the work. But my dad had never wanted it, and neither had his only cousin.

"Well. He kept telling me people would feel a way about it, but I ignored him. But the more people I told, the more they kept asking me if teaching wasn't a woman's job."

"Good Lord," I said.

"I kept telling people they didn't know anything, that it was the seventies and eighties and people could do whatever they wanted."

"Right."

"Well, I guess it was around 1989 when I forgot that."

"What happened?"

"Thou art my father, thou my author, thou my being gav'st me; whom should I obey but thee, whom follow?"

"What part of the Bible is that from?"

"It's not. It's from *Paradise Lost* by Milton."

I looked at him.

"In short, your brother was born and Wynona moved us back here from Atlanta because my mother was going to help with him. Wynona was never much of a mother, and being left alone with a baby scared her. But coming back here was a re-education. I was told fathers had to be certain things for sons. Like my father had been. Lead them down the right path and so on."

"So you thought the right path was racism and bigotry," I asked, my voice conveying some of my disgust.

"Well, back then they called it the path of righteousness and social decorum." His tone didn't falter.

"So..."

"So I tried my best to walk that path. I had never been a father, so I turned to the only person I could to teach me."

"I never knew Grandad to be as hateful as Wynona was."

"He kept to himself about much of it when he noticed me and your mother started having problems."

"Oh."

"That was about the time you were born."

"I'm the source of you and Wy's problems?"

He looked at me sincerely. "No, *we're* the source of our problems, but you...you sort of forced us all to look around. You challenged me and your grandfather and your mother."

"I did?"

"People think Teach is the black sheep, but I know it was you first. Teach is more of a goat."

"What'd I do?"

"You pointed to everything different about the way we all understood the world to be. You lived right here in the present and pointed at all the things we were still trying to hold on to but had already changed around us."

"No way."

"You did. Your grandfather would say something about male teachers, and you would go on and on about all the male teachers at your school or point them out in movies. And you would talk about how cool your friends of color were—"

"Friends of color, since when—"

"And your mother would say something about welfare or being lazy and you would talk about their parents and how hard they worked."

"I did all that?"

"One day you came home and told us you wanted to play soccer. Your grandfather would've rather you played baseball, and I wanted you to play basketball, but you insisted. Then I made the mistake of joking about how soccer was full of queers."

"You said soccer players were all…" I couldn't bring myself to say it.

"Well, do you remember what you did after that?"

I shook my head.

"Every time you learned about a new player, you'd tell me if he had a wife or not. You'd also tell us who was the first American Black player and first out player and so on and so on."

I snorted. "You should've kept me off the internet."

"The point I'm trying to make, son, is I realized the world around us was different, changing. Living day to day, small things accumulate, and it's rare for people to take stock of those things. You seemed to understand this at four and ten and fifteen. You were the first person in our lives to point out the speed of slow changes. The way the world slowly becomes some other place and then bam, all at once, it's different."

"Like noticin' how big the girls are only when you try to pick one of 'em up or send 'em to their first day of school, but it feels like yesterday they were just startin' to crawl."

"Exactly."

There was a thick silence for a few seconds, broken only by our breath and the sound of leaves crunching under our shoes.

"So, Coach, what's this got to do with today?"

"When the line started to blur between the fans and the players, sometimes things can get ugly. Kareem said that in 2005. Once I noticed the world was some other thing, I knew my teachings weren't going to get either of us very far. I didn't know who you were becoming, so I couldn't lead you. So I stopped thinking like the biblical shepherd and started thinking like a coach. I could teach you some of the fundamentals, but it was up to you to play the game. I think my father caught on late in life, but your mother never got on board."

"Why me? You had three other kids."

He sighed. "Betsy Ross was lucky enough to be like my mother. She did what she wanted for her own reasons. It was like she was born responsible and kindhearted and intelligent. Teach is like me, and he'll learn to build on everything I've done against him. He has a better head on his shoulders, though. I saw things a little slower than I should've with him. We've said what we needed to say."

"And Gage?"

"I think Gage is lost, so he wraps himself up in someone else. For a time, it was that ex-wife of his. Unfortunately, he was a mama's boy through and through, and most of her teachings stuck."

I nodded. "Dad."

He hummed.

"Why have we never talked like this before?"

"There's no play clock for life, son."

"You know, this is a long way to go to say you don't mind me datin' a guy."

"Having one of your nieces spill the beans is a long way to go to say you're dating a guy. I can say this, though. Teach is a better showman."

"Fair. Are you okay with me and him?"

He stopped. "Welp, I always knew you were interested in men and women. You talked a little too much about some of those soccer players."

I groaned.

"And I didn't figure out I was okay with it until your sister got on my case about Teach."

"Yeah. She told me."

"And Lucas is a good guy."

I smiled.

"Now, that being done, are you cheating on your wife?"

I nearly fell over on the street laughing. By now we were a ways down the road, surrounded by orchard. My cackling echoed through the trees. He let me laugh. I had to hold on to my knees and cough before I could get it together.

"No, Coach. Dani knows. It's called polyamory."

He shook his head and turned to head back to the house. "In my day, we called it swinging."

"Man, it's pretty funny," I said, chuckling.

"I can see that."

"No, Bets caught us in my office a few weeks back and she nearly beat the piss out of me thinkin' I was cheatin' on Dani. I just…it's funny that was her first concern and it was your second."

He didn't say anything. He just nodded. We started back toward the house.

"What's poly-moly?" he asked.

"Um…okay…what do you know about biosolids?"

He squinted at me. I explained how polyamory worked, at least for me and Dani. I told him about Lucas and Kyoko and Lila. He didn't ask any other questions, but he didn't interrupt either.

"Well, that sounds fine," he said as we approached the house.

"That sounds fine?" I asked, incredulous.

"Make sure you wipe your shoes, the lane back there was muddy," he said.

I stopped on the stairs and looked at my feet.

"If I didn't know better, I'd accuse you of being sarcastic," I told him. But I wiped my feet anyway. I caught his smile as he let himself into the house.

"Tell Dani I'll be in in a minute. I need to make a call."

"Let me know if he gets that job," Coach called.

I smiled. It was past the time we'd agreed on, but not by much. I listened anxiously to the first few rings. I was just starting to worry I'd have to call back and look really desperate, but he finally picked up.

"Sorry, I mean hi."

"Hi."

We spoke next at the same time.

"How was it with your dad?"

"How was the interview?"

Then a silly silence ensued as we waited for the other to speak.

"I want—"

"You can—"

"Damn it, Al, just tell me about your dad," he said, his sentence ending in a slight laugh.

I took a breath and relayed what Coach had said.

"That's really great," he said, but he didn't sound relieved.

"What's the matter?"

"What do you mean?"

"What do you mean what do I mean? You just sound...I don't know what emotion that is, but it's not happy."

"Yeah, no, I'm okay. I just have a lot on my mind."

"Care to share?"

"Um, I think I got the job."

"And that's a good thing?"

"Yeah. It'll be different."

"So, what's botherin' you is not the job?"

"No."

"Is it me?"

He didn't answer right away.

"It's me?"

"No, not you but, like, I think the limits of things are just starting to weigh on me a little."

"What do you mean?"

"I mean every date we've tried to have gets interrupted."

"Oh."

"And I know life is like that, but it feels like maybe things aren't meant to happen this way."

"But *we* are happenin'. Life is happenin' *and* so are we, right? Sure, there's been chaos, but we've managed."

"Right," Lucas agreed.

He didn't sound convinced.

"Listen, have dinner with me tomorrow night. We can talk about it in person then."

"Can't tomorrow."

"Okay, so when?"

He took a breath. "Sunday?"

"Okay, deal. I'll arrange to have someone watch the kids, and I can meet you at a restaurant. Just name one."

"Yeah, of course. Um, let's just do Grace's since it's easy."

This whole phone call had me feeling like I was treading water. His choice of Grace's, though, made me feel like I was starting to sink.

"Lucas, I want this," I said.

"I know. I want it too."

I didn't want to hang up. I wondered if I should insist we talk about it then so I could figure out what was scaring him off and fix it.

"Lucas."

"Al, I'm fine. I just think about it too hard sometimes."

"Okay, well, I need to head inside."

"Bye, Al, Sunday at…?"

"Seven," I said. I had a sudden lump in my throat, and I couldn't trust myself. I was overcome with the urge to finish the call with "I love you." I never expected that.

"Bye."

"Bye."

I went inside. Later, getting into bed, I told Dani about everything that had happened at the school and between Coach and me. I even told her how weird Lucas was being. I had come home from that date on a relative high, and now I was worried. She said it was probably just new relationship jitters. I prayed that it was. It took me a few hours to fall asleep.

CHAPTER TEN

Lucas

As I drove to the school, I couldn't help but wonder who'd pick up the Jefferson girls. It wasn't that I didn't want to see Al, but I knew he'd notice my mood, and I couldn't explain it. I couldn't name the feelings behind it even for myself. But trying to plan dates with him had been a catalyst for some sort of funk.

I *did* want to see him. I had gone to that party with the hopes of finding someone I could form a relationship with, someone who could occupy some more of the space in my life, and he did that and then some. *So, what the fuck, bro?* I blinked and shut off the truck. I had been on autopilot all the way to Valdosta. I was at the school to meet Mrs. Brunswick to onboard, then the position of school nurse was mine.

"Okay, kids…right. Filter, filter, filter."

I went up to the sprawling single-story school. It was a big circular shape with five wings branching off. At the center was the cafeteria, which shared a wall with the gym. The whole structure wore the front office like the knot on a tie. It was painted an inexplicable sun-dried red that matched the Trojan mascot. I stood on the red crest of a helmet painted on the ground and pressed the buzzer to page the office.

"Hello," one of the secretaries answered.

"Lucas Laverty, I'm here—"

"Ooh! Our new nurse. Yes, come on in."

The door clicked, and I went in. I'd worn scrubs and a light sweater, not knowing what else would be appropriate. The secretary who let me in came around her desk to talk to me. A few more women stood in the doorways of their offices.

"Mrs. Patterson told us you'd been brought on. I'm Mary Lincoln," she said, shaking my hand. "Just Mary, if you please."

"Nice to meet you, Mary. That's an interesting name. I know a guy called Thomas Jefferson."

Her eyes brightened. "God, I know Teach, who doesn't? He used to call me Todd for fun. I went to school with him."

"Right, I should've known."

She giggled, tossed her brown hair over her shoulder, and pulled her librarian-ish cardigan around her. "Well, it's not like he and I were friends. My mama always thought he was going to be a criminal."

"Turns out he's just a skateboarder."

"Right you are. Well, let me have you meet some of the other gals that make up ye olde henhouse."

She started walking toward the back offices, holding the little gate open for me to cross through. "With a rooster in our midst, I guess we'll just be a regular old coop now."

I laughed out of politeness, but really, I was groaning. I was in a small enough circle with enough gender-aware or gender-neutral people that I forgot jokes like that existed.

"You remember Mrs. Jones? We all call her Tracy. And that's Polly North, and our new librarian, Alice."

"Hello," I said, waving. I followed Mary into the nurse's office. She patted a chair for me to sit on. It was funny engaging with her. She was shorter than me by nearly a foot and probably weighed less than one of my legs. But you could tell she was one of the personalities at the school.

"Mrs. Brunswick will be right back. We had a little one throw up in gym today, so she had to march on down there and take a look at him."

"Oh, okay."

Mary left the room, but I could hear most of the conversation going on in the "henhouse." *At least she didn't call me a cock.* I took out my phone so I could send an update to the group chat Dani had dropped Ky, Al, and me into. We used it mostly to send memes—well, *they* all sent memes. I rarely sent anything. I had a hard time knowing what to put in the group chat or what to send to Al separately.

"Who was it this time?" one of the other women asked Mary. I tuned back into her conversation.

"If it wasn't that little Nation child, it wouldn't be Friday. God bless him," Mary said, snorting.

I almost dropped my phone. I turned in the chair, but I couldn't see anyone through the open door. *Nation.* That was my bio-dad's last name. Somewhere inside me, an alarm went off. How common was that last name? Why would it be here in Valdosta of all places?

"That poor boy, he's thinner than a sheet of paper and weaker than a wet noodle. I wouldn't think the child ate if I didn't see him out that window every day," whoever Mary was talking to said.

My heart clenched at the idea of an ill child. But I couldn't get my head to come around. I was still stuck on the kid's name. I wondered if I could ask about him or his family. It was probably against HIPAA or FERPA or both. Then again, I was now the school nurse, and if a kid barfed enough that the staff knew just by the day of the week, I could probably get away with asking.

I didn't get the chance. As I rose, Mrs. Brunswick stepped into my line of sight. She was a squat Latina with white hair and squinted eyes. She looked like a Disney grandmother.

"Well, hello, Mr. Laverty," she said sweetly.

"Please, Lucas is fine," I said, offering her my hand.

She just patted it like it was the top of a dog's head. "Well, then, Lucas, I'm Bea. I was given a list of things I need to go over with you. Just give me one minute to find it."

I sat, charmed and amused, as it took her twenty minutes to locate the list someone had taped to her computer. It was hard to focus on the rest of the meeting. I couldn't let it go. *Nation.* Why was that name here, why now? Why did it disrupt me as much as it did? Probably a lot of people were called Nation. Whatever the reason, it gave me a sinking feeling.

I was let out with the kids when the bell rang. Bea shooed me away with the list in my hands and some sort of school orientation book written in the mid-nineties. I would probably just google "school nurse" later.

I followed the flow of children out into the crowd of parents, but Al wasn't there. Neither was Teach nor Coach. I recognized the Jefferson girls easily enough, and some waved to me. I waved to Daniel Casillas, Betsy's husband, when I spotted him. He looked like every other construction worker, but he'd been nice enough the few times I'd worked with him at Al's place. He looked like he expected me to come talk to him. I didn't. I had no room in my head for Daniel Casillas and whatever code I was breaking. Let him think I was rude, I didn't care. I called my parents as I marched back to my truck.

"Mom," I said when Silvy answered, barely letting her say hello.

"Yeah, Lou, how's it going?"

"There's a kid at the school I work at." I paused long enough to fish my keys out of my scrubs.

"No kidding? Who would've thought?"

I sighed but moved on. "Mom, their last name is Nation."

She was silent for a lot longer than I would have expected. Then she surprised me by saying, "Well, I suppose that'd make sense."

"What? Why would that make sense?"

"Lou, don't you remember?" she asked. Her end of the line got quieter. She must have turned off some drill or saw or sander.

"I don't. Remember what?"

I could tell my voice was shifting. I sounded almost angry. I *was* angry. I was angry I was having feelings I couldn't explain or direct at someone. Silvy wasn't to blame for my feelings about my father or the Nations. Al wasn't to blame for my confusion about dating. I wasn't to blame, either. I didn't know where to direct my feelings.

"Maybe you should come on over," she said. All I could hear in her voice was sadness. I took a deep breath and pulled the truck into the long line of cars waiting their turn to get out of the lot.

"Yeah, okay, let me call Ky and tell her."

"Have her come over. Jojo was thinking fried chicken for dinner anyway."

Jojo really had no chill when it came to frying chicken, and Silvy would usually drive some over to the house so she wouldn't be forced to eat it all. I knew so many details about my moms. I didn't have details for DeAndrew Nation. My anger fizzled in the wake of love for my parents. And more importantly, I knew it impacted them a lot when I asked about my father. I took a deep breath so my tone would be lighter, more loving, for Silvy's sake.

"See you soon," I said. Then I told her I loved her and called Ky.

I couldn't really bring myself to tell Ky the details when she asked, even though I could tell she knew something was wrong. By the time she'd answered, I was out of the line of parents and was watching the school shrink in my rearview. I thought that if I opened my mouth to have to explain, I might keep driving and see how far a half a tank of gas could get me out of my own life. The only words I could find were "Please meet me at Mom's." She said she and Lila would be there. I hung up. But the phone went off a few seconds later, and the truck announced the text was from Al. I had the truck read it to me.

Hey, hope your first official day as school nurse went well. Tell me about it later when you call.

Fuck him and his fucking nice-ass texts. I groaned into the steering wheel. I loved it. I loved that he was a shirt-off-his-back type. I knew if I told him something was happening, some weird thing about a kid with my father's last name, he'd come to my parents' place too. And for some reason, that pissed me off. Maybe I was just tired of everything being an emergency with him. I blinked and remembered to stop at a stop sign just in time to avoid a truck with a horse trailer. I drove the rest of the way with the windows down, hoping the freezing November air would snap my thoughts into place.

The house was already full of the smell of frying food. Fried chicken was one of the only unhealthy things that remained on Jojo's list. She got her chicken locally sourced from a butcher across the border in Florida. Silvy complained that Jojo just had a crush on the butcher. Jojo would wave her off but never denied it.

"Hello," I shouted.

"Hey, Lou, come on in."

I followed her voice and the smells to the kitchen. I was surprised to find her by herself. She was standing at the counter rolling drumsticks in seasoned flour and eggs. A pile of golden-brown breaded chicken pieces was already on a plate. Based on the other cookware on the stove, I knew there was mashed potatoes, gravy, and corn on the cob.

"Ky should've been here by now," I said, settling onto a stool.

She smiled at me over her shoulder. "They are. They're up in the attic helping Silvy find something. I had them park in the back to make room for you."

I nodded. My anxiety and anger turned into worry and sadness as I watched her cook. I could feel her own unease, even though she smiled and hummed a little.

"How were things at the school?" she asked as she put the last of the chicken in the oil.

I did my best to tell her.

"Sounds like a good fit."

I was going to answer, but Lila came running into the kitchen with a big floppy hat on her head.

"Gran, look at my new hat," she told Jojo. When she spotted me, she screamed and demanded I pick her up.

"Hey, kiddo," I said.

"Lou, I have a new hat!"

"Yeah, looks like a third cousin's wedding hat to me," I said, referencing the horrible wedding we all attended a few years ago.

"It's a better hat than it was a marriage," Jojo said under her breath.

"Lou," Silvy called.

"Coming," I answered, carrying Lila into the dining room. Ky hopped over and kissed me on the lips. She held up one of my old jean jackets. I hadn't been able to fit into it since middle school. She was so small, it probably fit her perfectly.

"Can I have this?" she asked.

"Sure. I don't even know why they're carting this stuff around, but if there's money in it, I want it."

She frowned and pulled a crumpled five from her back pocket.

"Sweet," I said, taking the bill. "Thanks, past me."

"This is also courtesy of past you," Silvy said, patting a shoebox. "You want to eat first, or you want me to tell you what's in it?"

I stared at her. Her laugh was both understanding and sad. Whatever was in that box hurt her, and it'd probably hurt me too. She sat at the head of the table and kicked out the chair next to her. "Come have a seat."

Ky told Lila they needed to help frost some cupcakes, so they both went into the kitchen. I watched them leave before I sat down with Silvy.

She slid the box to me. "You were really close with DeAndrew. I guess maybe we let you get a little too close for your own good. He'd visit all the time, and every time you got to see him, it was like Christmas. Even if he just went around the corner, when he was back, no one else existed.

"You knew he was your father at some point. He'd told us he didn't want to be a father, but because he was in our life, he was in yours. You even asked him to move in with us once. Anyway, he moved away when you were six. You called him every day, but he eventually told us not to let you call anymore. We didn't have the heart sometimes and you would call, but he wouldn't answer. Then you begged us to let you write him. I talked to him on the phone a few times after he moved. He just insisted you were ours and that he never meant to get so involved. But you wouldn't stop, so we gave you his address. When you were eight, you wrote him a ten-page letter. You dictated the whole thing to me."

She paused and looked at me. I blinked at her. "You were pretty young," she said, "so I'm not too surprised you don't remember some of this. But I never would've thought you'd forget the letter you got back."

"I got a letter back?"

"Yeah. I can't believe after all this…When you finished reading it, you said you were never going to think about him again. So maybe that's just what happened. 'Cept until now, of course." She studied me.

"What do you mean by 'after all this'?"

"Some of the things we told you about him. Well, I just assumed they stuck since we ended up here."

"Mom, I don't know what you're talking about."

She shook her head. "Here, just give this a once-through. I'm gonna try and get one of those cupcakes away from your daughter."

She pushed the box toward me slightly and stood. I watched her leave before I pulled it closer. I could see through the door to the kitchen. Jojo and Silvy were helping Lila mix frosting into Easter egg colors while Ky slowly ate an unfrosted chocolate cupcake. The perfect scene. But I was so far from it.

I looked down. The only semblance of a father in my life was in that box. My mind flashed to a memory of Al, holding two screaming brown-haired girls on his shoulders while two blondes clung to his legs, his work polo coming untucked in the struggle. Logically, he should have been the farthest thing from my mind. But he wasn't. I had the urge to snap him a picture of the battered, dusty shoebox and clue him into this side of my life. I didn't.

The box was old. I remembered the shoes that had once been in it. They were jet black with neon green thread. They'd made me feel like a superhero. It didn't take long before I grew out of them, but it did take me a while to throw them out since I loved them so much. That box had been a on a journey of its own. It had survived several moves with my moms. They had to deliberately pack it so it would end up here, now.

Shit or get off the pot. I carefully lifted the lid. The array of things inside seemed vaguely familiar. I reached in and grabbed the first thing

I saw. The paper was rolled up in a ball, but I opened it carefully so it didn't tear. It was directions, handwritten by an eight-year-old.

"Minneapolis," I read. We had lived there until I was eleven, then we moved to Michigan. I had liked the north, even though I hated wearing coats in the winter. The directions followed the interstate nineteen hours south without detour until—

"Valdosta!"

I stood reflexively, as if I were about to run away from the paper, then I sat back down and started pulling stuff out of the shoebox by the handfuls. Another page was a list of colleges my father had been to. There was also a list of just general facts about him.

Business major, painter, played saxophone—

I had tried the saxophone in middle school and couldn't remember why I had started or stopped playing.

Liked bagels with bacon and cream cheese. Marvel. Allergic to bees.

I pulled out a cassette with a handwritten list of bands and songs. At first glance, most of the songs were ones I knew by heart. There was a Baby Ruth wrapper. While it wasn't one of my favorites now, it always reminded me of being a kid.

The last thing in the box was an envelope. The letter inside was addressed to me, written in a hand I didn't recognize. But then suddenly I did. Holding it was like grabbing a lightning bolt. Parts of my brain that I must have shut down decades ago rebooted, and I remembered. I didn't need to open the letter. I already knew what it said. I sat back in the chair, making it groan under my weight.

I put the letter back in the box and pressed the heels of my hands into my eyes. When I was eight, I had written him telling him everything I had been up to since he left. I told him I liked playing kickball, and my best friend was a girl named Dylan, and I liked the same music as him and that if he wanted, I could come visit. The letter he sent back had three sentences on it. I could do the math—three sentences against my ten pages was a slap in the face. I remembered those sentences word for word.

Lucas,
Thank you for the letter.
I can't swing a visit right now.
Do well in school and be good for your mothers.
D.

He hadn't even signed his full name. Rage followed the lightning bolt of understanding. I stood fast enough that the chair didn't have time to slide but instead toppled, clattering to the floor. All the women turned to stare at me, visibly scared. I marched from the house without saying anything.

I paced in the yard between the house and the workshop. I was so hot with anger, I felt like steam should have been rising off my skin. The motion sensor light outside the shop had popped on as soon as I stepped out of the house, and my breath was white and shining as it hung around me in the cold air. My phone buzzed, and I knew it was Al based on the time. I didn't answer. I wanted to throw it into the forest.

How could I have forgotten so much? It was like my brain had just deleted all the files I had on DeAndrew. At eight that had been so easy. You could make anyone who didn't give you what you wanted a villain and forget about them. But now…How could I unlearn this? Did I want to? I was mad that I knew now why DeAndrew's disappearance from my mind had been so clean. I maybe even missed my ignorance.

"Lou?" Silvy stepped out of the house. She had two beers.

"God, Mom, I can't believe—I remember now. I remember pouring my feelings into that letter and hoping like hell he'd want to see me. But he didn't. I wasn't dense. I knew 'I can't swing a visit right now' was code for 'Hey, kid, I'm just not that interested in being your dad, so have a good life.'"

Silvy handed me the beer as I paced closer to her, sipping her own as I paced away. I could feel her eyes on me.

"I must be really fucked up over it, though, right? I went to the same college as the guy, moved to the same town he was from. Talk about internalized trauma."

"The doctor we spoke to about it said it's pretty common for children to want to be like their parents, take on bits of them. He said it was true even for children who didn't have good relationships with their parents. It's not like DeAndrew was a bad guy. He was just a bad parent," Silvy said.

"He's not *my* parent. What doctor?"

"The counselor we took you to after the letter. You didn't come out of your room all weekend. No, he's not your parent, but you wanted him to be. So what if you internalized some things?"

"It's kind of fucked up, Mom. I based my whole personality on some guy I don't even know."

"I don't think so," she said. "First of all, you knew him. And you have a lot of personality from a lot of people. Even from me."

"Like?"

"Bet you can still identify wood like a champ."

"Mom."

"Besides, I knew DeAndrew, remember? And you didn't get the worst parts of him."

"Why'd I go to the same school? Huh, I'm like some ridiculous stalker."

"It's a good school. He studied business because he wanted to be rich. You studied medicine because you want to take care of people."

"I moved everyone here."

"You also studied Valdosta as a kid, looked it up in every atlas at the library. I think maybe you fell in love with South Georgia as you were trying to fall in love with your father. And you read *Fried Green Tomatoes* at an impressionable age. It took us a really long time to talk you out of jumping onto trains. Besides, we all love it here."

I made a farting sound with my mouth and put the bottle back to my lips.

"Lou."

I looked at her and almost lost my footing, surprised by her expression. She was so sad. I could see pain behind her patient eyes. I was angry but not at her, not even a little. She needed to know that. I marched over to her and buried her in a hug. Every time I needed to talk to someone about anything—boys, girls, food, money—it had been Silvy. Sure, Jojo was there in her own way, but Jojo mostly showed her love in food. Silvy could talk. I loved them so much.

"Kiddo, nothing I can say is gonna matter much."

"Everything you say matters, Mom."

"Well, I think...maybe it's just time now. Maybe it's time to finish the journey you started when you wrote that letter. We haven't heard from DeAndrew in years. But if there's a Nation here, there's a high chance they're related. Maybe it's worth asking around. Who knows what difference twenty-ish years can make?"

I grunted.

She sighed. "Come back inside."

"I will, I need to call Al back."

Silvy nodded. I caught her right before she turned away.

"Mom. I love you. You're a great mom. This isn't because of anything you did or couldn't do."

"I know it, but it's nice to hear it." She smiled and her eyes started to shine as tears pooled. "Also, whatever you need to tell Al, you should get that over with too."

"What? I don't have anything to say."

"People can and will make space for you, Lou. Just give 'em a chance."

I groaned and let her go into the house. I didn't bother listening to the voicemail Al left. I pressed the call button.

"Hey, babe," he said almost right away.

The endearment was stunning. I couldn't think for a minute. He had never said that before. I wasn't one for pet names, except for maybe "love" or "bro." Which is not to say it didn't make me feel something, a good something, butterfly something. By the way it made my pulse jump, I liked it from him.

"Sorry I missed your call."

He was slow to answer. "You okay? You sound tired."

"It's been a hell of a night. But I can tell you later. Maybe on Sunday. I'm at my parents', and Ma just got dinner on the table."

"Tell *Jojo* I said hi—"

"Hey, I don't like the way you said that," I warned, not missing the warmth and maybe flirtatiousness in his voice.

"Flirt with my brother, I flirt with your mother." He laughed, and before I could protest, he added, "I look forward to hearin' it, or maybe not forward if it's a bad story. Well, not *not* forward but—"

"Dude, it's fine. I get what you mean."

"Ha, okay. Um, tell Silvy hi too."

The fact that he knew Ma from Mom made me feel a little giddy. I wiped my hand over my mouth, hoping to prevent the dopey smile I felt. "I will."

"Is there anything I can do for you in the meantime?"

I could see this as the perfect chance to open the door to him a little more, but the same thing stopped me as before. I wanted him when there wasn't something to fix. Then again, could beggars be choosers? I couldn't keep demanding his time and turn around and refuse when he offered it, no matter the reason. I was willing to believe I had the wrong idea about time. Maybe time just came when it came. Now might be the time to reach out to my father again. Now might be the time to adjust what I thought spending time with someone meant. I needed to ask Al what he thought it meant. I didn't know how.

"Lou?"

I shrugged even though he wouldn't see it. "Sorry, I have a lot of thoughts. But, naw. I…thanks for calling."

"Of course."

I had the real and urgent desire to say, "I love you." Instead, I said, "Talk to you tomorrow."

"Yeah, sounds great."

"Bye."

"Bye."

CHAPTER ELEVEN

Alexander

I was scrubbing the kitchen floor when someone knocked on the door. I tried to stand and ended up banging my head on the table. I closed my eyes and sighed because a concussion would be the perfect topper to a hard morning. I heard the door open and close, so I looked over the table to see who came in. A giant trucker in a stained suede jacket and dusty jeans walked straight to the fridge.

"It's me," Gage said. He dropped his sweat-stained hat on the counter.

His presence in my house annoyed me. I knew he was just holding up his end of the deal and was coming to help Coach. I should have been grateful. Not that Coach had needed much help over the last few weeks. He had always been a man of routine, and once the breathing machine and the inhalers became part of that routine, he hadn't needed assistance or reminders. Yet a very small seizure last week when Betsy Ross was with him put everyone in a much more diligent mood. Well, *almost* everyone.

I glared at him. "Well, damn. You're only a few hours late."

He belched as he chugged a Coke.

"Really?" I said.

"What's the problem? The nurse said no matter what, the seizures was goin' to happen. 'S not like I could stop it."

I didn't particularly care for the way he said "the nurse."

"*Lucas* also said we aren't here to stop it, we're here to call for help if he needs it."

He rolled his eyes. "Whatever. I'm here now, so you and the nurse can go fuck yourselves."

I was about to retort when Teach came into the room. I was glad he was going to stay through Christmas. I did have to bribe him, but I liked having him home.

"What's up, faggot?" Gage asked, slapping Teach hard on the back.

"My boner," Teach said coolly, giving Gage the finger.

Gage's face soured. "You hangin' around here all night?"

"Hell no," Teach said. He was probably going to hide in town. Dani would be at a fitness open house the gym was hosting. And I would be with Lucas, which meant I would probably be dropping Teach off somewhere. That left the girls in Dad's care and Dad in Gage's.

"What about you?" Gage asked me.

"I mean, it's my house, so it's not really *hangin' around*, but no. I have errands to run."

I considered just flat out saying it. I wondered what Gage would do if I said I was going on a date with Lucas. I watched him talk to Teach, sneering and complaining. Teach's face gave away none of his actual emotions, even though I knew he hated talking with Gage. What would Gage do with the knowledge that he had two queer brothers? I wondered what he would do if he found out Dad was okay with it. As if I conjured him, Coach stepped into the kitchen.

"Sons," he said to the three of us collectively.

"Coach," we all offered.

"Gage, let's go."

"Where?" Gage asked.

Coach didn't say anything, just turned and left.

"Third Sunday," I said.

"Haircut day," Teach and Gage said together. It was almost funny how in that one moment of shared understanding, we could have passed for any other set of siblings.

"The girls're around here somewhere," Gage grumbled, leaving.

I took note of the increased screaming coming from the second floor.

"You okay?" I asked Teach when I was sure Gage was out of the house.

He didn't answer. He just continued to thumb around on his phone.

"Got any idea how to get Sharpie off Spanish tile?" I asked.

He looked at me. "Do I look—"

Then he said, "Okay, Google," and asked the internet. We ended up doing a spontaneous test of all the cleaning products we had in the house. Some of them worked better than others. I think it was the mix of it all that actually worked. I tried getting him to talk more, but he just ended up listening to me rant about Gage and Dad and that babyproofing a house doesn't end when the child is no longer a baby. He didn't engage until I asked him what I should wear on my date. In between breaking up fights between the kids and checking on the youngest few in their play area, Teach and I managed to find me an outfit that, to quote Teach, "didn't make me look like Jake from State Farm." Gage and Coach walked through the door around six with Dani on their heels.

"What're you doin' home?" I asked her as she breezed past us toward our room.

"I forgot my binder that has the stupid schedule and program and everything else for tonight." She gave me a quick kiss before trotting away. I went into the kitchen to compliment Coach on his haircut. He'd been getting the same cut every month since the early 2000s, but he would pout if no one said anything.

"Hey, Coach. Looking sharp," I said. He was standing in the kitchen by the fridge watching Gage crush some of the peanuts we kept on the counter. Shells crumbled everywhere as Gage snacked.

"Why, thank you, son."

He handed me a mug of coffee before popping another one under the machine, turning away from Gage to put more grounds in the refillable cup.

"You going somewhere?" he asked, looking me over.

"Uh, yeah."

"And where would that be?"

At some point in his old age, my father had gotten nosy. He half smirked as if he knew what I was thinking. I opened my mouth, but Dani poked her head into the kitchen.

"Hon, I'm leaving."

"Love you, good luck," I said.

"Can I hitch a ride?" Teach asked her. He was holding his skateboard and had on a coat three or four sizes too big. It matched his extra-large, extra-long T-shirt and made his legs look bird-ish in his skinny jeans.

"Get the lead out," Dani said, throwing a thumb over her shoulder.

Everyone froze for a heartbeat when the doorbell rang. We all looked at each other wondering who it could be, especially since they didn't come in after ringing. All of us turned, but none of us could see down the hall to the front.

"I got it," girls screamed, stampeding down the stairs.

"No, you *don't*. Y'all go play and mind your business," Dani shouted.

I lost sight of Dani in a flash of brown ponytail. I listened to her shooing the girls away and I added sugar to the coffee. We all listened to the door open. I heard her say hello and ask who it was.

"Why, I'm Wynona, Jeffery's wife."

I didn't realize the coffee cup was out of my hand until the bright clatter of it smashing on the floor filled the room. For the next ten minutes, the house was a flurry of chaos. Coach cleaned up the coffee and the broken mug. Gage practically tossed Dani to the ground as he went to hug Wynona, and I nearly shoved them both out the door, telling Wynona she needed to leave. After a small scuffle between me and Gage and a few sentences comprised solely of the word *fuck*, I found myself sitting across the kitchen table from Wynona. Dani and Teach had disappeared to God knew where, probably to herd away the girls, who had come running to watch the commotion. Coach sat next to me, and Gage next to Wynona. If we'd had guns and it had been 1881, it would have been an Old West–style standoff worthy of the O.K. Corral.

No one said anything for a minute. Wynona primped, pulling a small mirror and several makeup tools out of her bag. Gage stared at her like a golden retriever, and Coach might as well have been a cardboard cutout. I was so mad I probably could have bent steel. *Well, sports fans, our MVP is in the pickle of a lifetime. No way in, no way out. What's he going to do?*

"I should just call the cops," I said, my mouth out in front of my thoughts.

"Now," Wynona said, her tone playful, as if I were six years old.

"Son," Coach said as a reprimand, but his eyes flashed an expression I have come to learn was agreement.

"Don't be a dick," Gage said.

"Why are you here?" I demanded.

Wynona took her sweet time moving unnoticeable pieces of hair out of her face and fluffing her eyelashes, or whatever that gesture was called.

"Wynona," I said. I really didn't know how much more I could take before I turned the kitchen into a WWE arena.

"I've come to check on you, Jeffery."

"Hoped he was dead?" I growled, thinking about Betsy Ross telling us about a call from Wynona's lawyer to Coach's a few weeks back.

She rolled her eyes. Wynona Jefferson had the vibe of a fairy tale stepmother at a modern PTA meeting. Her blond hair was piled on her head in the biggest mess of curls and hair spray. She wasn't any taller than Coach, both being five nine at the tallest, but it was obvious where I got my build from. She was mostly shoulders and chest in her fancy power suit. It was dark outside the windows behind her. Her presence turned our kitchen from a country dream into something out of an exorcism. I half expected the windows to blow in at any moment.

"Well, if someone around here would answer my calls every now and again, I wouldn't have to stop in."

"Nine-hour drive's a long way to go to *stop in*," I said.

She didn't even flinch. "I was in the neighborhood."

"Like hell you were."

"Christ, Al, don't talk to Mom like that," Gage hissed at me.

"Why didn't you call *him*? He seems happy enough to talk to you."

She waved me and Gage off with one flick of her braceleted wrist. "Oh, you know your brother's never been able to keep track of so many details."

That made me laugh. Gage at least seemed to understand he was being insulted. His grin faltered. I wondered if she ever contacted him. As much as he loved her, she had never given him the time of day. She used to actually tell him to his face that by the time *he* got interesting, she'd had the daughter she wanted. And she pretty much treated him like that was true, despite how much he tried to please her. She was flat out wrong about him most of the time. He was a right piece of shit, but he was also raising five girls on his own and helping his father— I blinked. *Do I hate Wynona so much I'm willing to defend Gage?*

"Hello," Dani said, coming in the room. My adrenaline started to pump a little faster at the sound of her voice.

I stood and went over to her. She gave me her I'm-here-for-you look. "What about work?"

She shook her head and whispered, "Teach is helpin' me scan it all to the gym. I told them I had an emergency."

"They need you."

"I'm one of five owners. If the place couldn't run without me, I wouldn't be doing very good business."

"And who is this beautiful lady?" Wynona said, her voice like scraping glass.

Dani patted my hands as we both faced Wynona. "Kelley Danielle Jefferson," I said, "this is Wynona Jefferson."

Dani went around the table and offered Wynona her hand. "I've heard so much about you."

"And I nothing about you," Wynona said. "But I guess a boy is bound to talk about his mama quite a lot. I do know you own a gym. My, you look great. I personally never thought that women with a lot of muscle carried it very well, but…you seem to manage."

Dani slipped her hand out of Wynona's the way someone would stop holding expired meat.

"Isn't that a thought?" Dani said, retreating to my side of the table.

"What a lovely home you have," Wynona said. She leaned on the table. "Will I get to meet my granddaughters?"

"If you want. They're all Democrats, though," I said just to irritate her.

We all jumped a little at the sound of the front door being slammed open. Dani winked at me. "I called your sister."

Dani was on her way to get the girls as Betsy and Daniel stepped in.

"Well, speak of the devil and she doth appear," Betsy said, crossing her arms over her chest.

"Why, Betsy Ross," Wynona said as if Betsy showing up out of nowhere wasn't a surprise. "You were thinking of me?"

"I always think of you when I sage my house. That's how you get rid of demons."

"Jesus Christ, Betsy," Gage said.

Wynona didn't flinch, though. She just scrunched her nose in a way that might have passed for amused rather than insulted.

"Hi, Betsy," Coach said, coming to give my sister a kiss on the cheek.

"Hey, Coach. Nice haircut."

"You do look very sharp today, Jeffrey," Wynona said.

"What are you doin' here?" Bets asked.

"As I was telling Alexander, I came to see how your father is."

"Don't worry, *Mom*, you can take the gravediggers off speed dial."

Wynona laughed. "My goodness, why do you all think I want him dead?"

"I don't think that," Gage said, but she ignored him.

Betsy squinted at her. "Naw, you were probably hopin' he wouldn't be in his right mind and would sign those damned papers. Or worse. I got a call from Coach's lawyer about your snoopin' around."

Wynona sighed, pretending to be defeated. But she didn't deny it.

I looked at Coach. Just then, Dani cleared her throat as she led twelve girls into the room, Tess in her arms. Betsy hadn't brought her kids. I saw Teach slip in and drop behind the crowd to stand near Daniel by the fridge.

Gage's girls greeted her, but none of them approached her.

"Hello, girls. My, y'all've gotten so big."

I turned to my kids. "Girls, this is Wynona Jefferson. She's my mother."

None of the girls moved. They looked at me instead. Even two-year-old Tessalee watched me as if I were going to cue her. I told Wynona each of their names and ages. She greeted them in turn, saying something benign and generic. There were moments of silence as she considered each child. And they all considered her back. It was Xander, my six-year-old, bravest of my children, who stepped out front to address my mother directly. She was dressed in overalls, and her short, sandy hair sat on her head more like a helmet than a bob. She squinted at my mother, then stuck her hand out, waiting for Wynona to shake it.

"Nice to meet you," Xander said.

"Charming."

I could tell Wynona didn't actually find it charming.

Then Xander turned to me and Dani and announced, "She's pretty for a witch."

I laughed, which set most of the girls to giggling. Dani tried to swat my arm and scold Xander at the same time. Betsy Ross high-fived my kid. Gage got on my case, Betsy got on his, then Wynona started to say something. Right behind my head, a high, impossibly loud whistle broke the chaos. The entire room turned to Coach.

"I think we've had enough of that," he said. He looked at his grandchildren. "Go play, girls."

They all ran screaming from the room.

"Now," Coach said, looking at Wynona, "I think you can see I'm fine, so you're welcome to leave."

She glared at him, but her voice maintained a chipper clip. "Why is everyone treating me like a criminal? I just came to check on you."

"State your actual business or get out," Coach said.

"This isn't your house."

"It *is* his house," I said.

"Come on, Coach," Gage whined.

"I never did anything to you, Jeffrey. I cleaned your house, I made your dinners, I bore your children—"

"Wynona, this isn't something we need to get into," Coach said.

"I don't deserve to be treated like this."

"I think you do. You've been out of their lives since they were teenagers. Even if I was dead, there wouldn't be any reason for you to come back here. If this really is about the divorce—"

Wynona groaned dramatically. "My God, isn't anyone happy to see me?"

"I am, Mom. They're just being bitchy," Gage said.

"Don't confuse us with your ex-wife," Betsy snapped.

Teach made the mistake of laughing. Wynona hadn't noticed him until then. Her mask of polite disgust turned into dense loathing when she realized who he was.

"Good God, Jeffery, is that Thomas?" She leaned her whole body across the table as if that would help her see him.

In a moment of confusion, Coach actually looked over his shoulder.

"Look what he's done to himself. I told you. I told you letting him interact with those degenerates would turn him ungodly. He looks like Satan himself."

"He's fine," Coach said.

"You better mind who you talk about in this house," I said, stepping closer to the table.

"Don't you threaten me, Alexander. This," she said, gesturing at Teach like he was a dumpster, "is half your fault."

"Excuse me?"

She looked at me and squared her shoulders. "You brought homosexuals into his life, gave him unholy ideas—"

I laughed and looked at Teach. "Unholy ideas…about who? Fin? And here I thought I was the only one."

The air got sucked out of the room, like losing cabin pressure on a plane. Teach raised his eyebrows at me, the grin on his face one of unconditional support. He was safe now, with me and Betsy and Coach and Dani and Daniel standing between him and a world of hate. Now he wasn't the only queer in the house who would have to stare down Wynona's self-righteous bigotry. I had finally said something damning out loud to her. She and Gage were staring at me, open mouthed.

"Are…are you serious?" Wynona asked, thrown off by my comment.

I sat down, feeling suddenly at peace. "I guess you were always right about me."

Gage looked at me like he was looking through a window caked in years of dust and dirt. His expression cleared suddenly, and he snapped his fingers. "The nurse."

I looked at him, surprised.

"I fuckin' knew it, I knew that guy was a queer," he said, happier that he'd gotten it right than offended at the implications.

"Watch it," I said.

"A nurse?" Wynona asked.

"Some Black fella," Gage said. His tone was even, factual. At this point Gage had no language other than his usual semi-racist shit, just without the hate.

"Gage," I said anyway.

"I'm sorry, he is." He put his hands up trying to show he didn't mean anything by it.

"John Adams, please," Wynona snapped. "This isn't about you."

Gage closed his mouth and slumped back in his chair.

In the silence, Wynona looked from me to Teach to Dani and back to me. "But you're married."

"Don't have to be single to like dick."

To my surprise, Coach laughed.

That really turned the dial up on Wynona's fury. She turned on him. "You knew about this?"

Coach shrugged. "Only recently."

Wynona was red with emotion. "I can't. How…this is unacceptable. How can you let your sons behave this way? That…heathen over there was one thing—"

She pointed again at Teach.

"Okay, I've heard enough," Betsy Ross said. She balled her hands into fists and started toward Wynona. "Maybe with my foot up your ass you'll finally get your head out of it."

"Betsy," Gage said, stepping between them.

Betsy walloped Gage right in the chest with no hesitation. "John Adams, if you weren't the father of some of my favorite nieces, I'd beat you silly."

"Christ Almighty, Bets, stop," Gage said. "It ain't worth it."

Wynona wasn't the least bit worried about Betsy. She stared at me. "Alexander, how could you stray so far?"

"How many dick jokes do you want me to make tonight, Wy?"

"And how could you let them?" Wynona said to Coach.

"The greatest among you must become like the youngest, and the leader like the servant," Coach said wistfully.

"Ugh, you and your blasted quotes. All right, Jeffery, who is that, huh? Milton? John F. Kennedy? You know, if you hadn't filled our house with so many unchristian teachings, these kids probably would've turned out better."

Coach nodded and sipped his nearly forgotten coffee. "My dear, that was from the book of Luke."

That was a kill shot. She looked at Coach and he stared back. Then she looked at me, then Betsy, and then our spouses, probably seeing only the same general contempt for her. The look she gave Gage was desperate, but he just stared at the floor, half holding Betsy off, half holding himself up. She didn't look at Teach. She was outnumbered.

"Well, I don't know what you all have against me," she said, her voice low. She looked back at Coach. "All I did was come to see how you were."

"Thank you, Wynona. I can't imagine what it cost you, save maybe the love of your children."

"And what, they love *you*?"

He stood and gestured for the door. "Now, that's where you and I have never seen eye to eye. They don't have to love me. I love them regardless. I'll walk you out."

Wynona didn't say another word. She grabbed her bag off the table and stormed from the room. Coach followed her to the door. There was silence in the kitchen in the wake of them leaving.

"I don't know what was more surprising," Daniel said, his gentle voice barely breaking the structure of the tension. "Al coming out or Coach saying the word 'love.'"

We didn't answer him. Everyone deflated, though. Betsy surprised me by hugging Gage. And I went around to Teach. He gave me a bright smile and a fist bump. Dani put her arms around my waist from behind.

I heard my phone vibrate over by the coffeepot. I turned toward it, catching sight of the time on the microwave. Every emotion I was feeling at that moment concerning my parents was dwarfed by the sense of dread that came over me.

"Fuck me," I groaned as I snatched up the phone.

"What?" Dani asked.

"I stood up Lucas," I said, sliding the phone on. Three missed calls and a text.

I didn't really hear what was said, I just walked past everyone and onto the porch, hitting call return as I went.

CHAPTER TWELVE

Lucas

I looked around the diner, which was also a bar. It wasn't crowded since it was a Sunday night. Some kid played keyboards on the stage, filling the space with random lo-fi. The music contrasted with the Southern bar, but made both better in a weird way. I finished off my beer.

"Can I get you another, baby?" Ms. Wilhelmina Grace asked. She was the owner of the restaurant, an older Black woman who gave the impression of eternal understanding. She'd been hovering near my table since Al missed the ten-minute mark. After a half hour, she brought me a slice of apple cobbler with ice cream. I hadn't asked for it.

"No, ma'am," I sighed.

I couldn't believe I was waiting for him, but I wasn't in a hurry to get back home since I'd planned to be out most of the night. Besides, I didn't want the beer I'd ordered to go to waste. It wasn't like I hadn't sat at Grace's by myself before. I gave him half an hour's worth of benefit of the doubt before I called. I tried a few times, then I gave up. If it hadn't been for Ms. Wilhelmina's apple cobbler, I would have left. But I was still there when he called. He said he'd had an emergency and he could be there in fifteen.

Ms. Wilhelmina was still looking at me. "Wanna talk about it?" she asked.

"No, ma'am."

She laughed. "Child, if you keep ma'aming me, I'm gonna take my cobbler back."

I smiled. She had been the owner of the place for as long as anyone could remember. It was just outside Painted Waters on the highway heading toward Valdosta. Like most of everything in that part of Georgia, it seemed stuck in time, halfway between yesterday and never. It might have even been here before Valdosta.

"Hey, Ms. Wilhelmina?"

"Mr. Lucas?" She stood there carefully placing dishes in a bin. I knew she had arthritis now, but while it slowed her down, it didn't stop her.

"Did you ever know someone called DeAndrew Nation?"

She thought about it. "I knew a Raymond Nation and he had a handful of kids. Now, Ray and I once got into a fight over the price of potatoes, and he figured that meant to stay away from here. So I ain't seen a Nation in some years."

"Who doesn't come here?"

She grinned. "Someone who knows better than to piss off a woman with a meat grinder."

I liked her story, but it didn't help much. "That's all you know?"

"Sorry, sugar."

I scooped up more of the ice cream turning my cobbler into soup.

"Oh," she said, bumping my side gently with her hip. "I think someone's looking for you."

I turned and caught Al scanning the room. As if he could feel me looking at him, he turned toward me and our eyes met. His face brightened, then fell. I looked back at the cobbler.

"Lucas, God, I'm so sorry. Somethin' insane happened, and I lost track of time," Al said, sliding onto the bench across from me. He looked like he was fishing for something more to say, but he couldn't find anything.

I looked at him. It was a crime how fucking good looking he was. He had on a green sweater that made his eyes shine like polished wood. His hair was combed back. His sandy stubble enhanced the angles of his jaw. God, I loved looking at him. But he also looked absolutely drained.

"What happened?" I asked. I heard my voice go soft. *Fuck me.* I really did care about him. About his problems.

He hesitated. "Lucas, I…are you mad? Or upset? Well, I'm pretty upset about missin' the start of our date, so are you?"

I blinked at him. I was still surprised every time he asked me directly about my emotional investment in a situation. I couldn't really answer. Besides, this date was going like the others. *Another emergency.* I still wanted to enjoy some of it, though.

"Later. Al, what happened?"

He looked at me like he wanted to push, but he didn't. A waiter came over and put two burgers, a large basket of fries, and two beers down on the table. Neither of us said anything. I picked at the fries while Al took a swig of the beer and a few breaths.

"Wynona showed up at the house."

Okay, that was genuinely an emergency. "Holy shit. What? Why?"

I asked enough questions to get the whole story from him. He told it like it had happened years ago and not just minutes. I could see the impact of it on his face, the way his hands clenched the beer. He was so much stronger and so much more vulnerable than anyone would notice without spending a few months staring at his face like I had.

"Bro, your mom's a bitch," I said, finishing off the fries.

He sighed and half collapsed on the table, his elbow and fist propping up his head. "I know."

"Nice that your whole family was able to stand up to her," I said.

He nodded thoughtfully.

"Why hasn't Coach divorced her?" I knew her demands were a lot, but I had to wonder how bad since they were doing this a decade or more later.

"She wanted full custody of us kids, which was really just Teach, and she wanted the house, to name the top issues." Al lifted his shoulders and held them there. It made him look smaller. "But there's no more house. I can't imagine what she'd want now. It has to be somethin'. Dad's pension maybe?"

"Well, he should just sue her."

Al looked at me. "Can he do that?"

"I don't know. I guess what I mean is, he should file a different divorce claim because she's not even lived in the state in years. He has ground to stand on. Then the lawyers can figure it out."

"I guess we never thought about it that way."

He smiled at me, and that warm display of lips and teeth got the earth moving again, the lava heat rising a little in my chest.

"What about you? You said Friday somethin' was goin' on at the school."

It made sense for the conversation to go like this. When we were together, I felt exactly like I wanted to feel with him. I hadn't known what I was looking for when I got with him at that party, but I had trusted his idea of dating. *The problem is we aren't really dating.*

He sat up and looked at me. "You seem to be havin' some thoughts over there. Penny?"

I considered it for a second. I wondered how many more moments like this we could carve out for each other around all the other random shit in our lives.

"Is…is this going the way you thought it would?"

He blinked at me. "I'd planned to be on time."

"I don't mean just tonight. Is this really what you had in mind when you said *dating*?"

"I…Lucas, what're you askin'?"

Over the course of talking with me about events at his house, some light had returned to his absurdly warm, oak-colored eyes. As he waited for me to answer, sadness crept into his expression even though I could tell he was trying to remain neutral.

I wiped my hands and tried to collect my thoughts. "I'm having a hard time feeling like this is dating. It's not how I know how to do it. I've been wondering if you're too busy to really do this. And the fact that we can't seem to have a real date seems to make the point."

"I…we…we have dates."

"When?"

I could see him going down the list of all the time we spent together—his father ending up in the hospital, his kids getting sick, his sister and my parents interrupting.

"I've had a great time every time we've been together," he said. "Haven't you?"

"Of course. I just wouldn't call it dating."

"What would you call it then?"

"I don't know. Friendship?"

A hurt crossed his face. "You see me as just a friend?"

"No, Al…I don't. My feelings are stronger than that."

"But you don't think we're datin'." His expression was shifting to anger, and I could tell that I wasn't getting my point across.

"I'm just saying it doesn't really seem like it to me."

"What looks like datin', then?"

"Having time, like—*making* time for each other."

"I make time for you, Lucas."

I pointed. "Then something happens."

"None of that's my fault—our fault." His voice was sharp, insistent.

I had yet to see Al lose his temper. I had heard him yell in play and to get someone's attention, but not yet in anger. Frustration was visible on his face. And there was something else there. Hurt maybe. I hadn't intended to hurt him. I was just so fucking unsure.

"I know, Al. Fuck, this conversation wasn't supposed to be like this."

"Maybe I'm not understanding," he said.

I could tell he almost said it against his will. It had to be hard. Ky had called Al emotionally intelligent, and I could imagine that was exhausting, especially after the night he'd had. He looked like he didn't want to temper his anger or hear my thoughts. I couldn't blame him.

"Maybe we should talk about this later," I said.

He blinked at me. "Lucas, come on. It sounds to me like you want to break up with me. Or break this off. I don't think that's somethin' I can table."

I blinked. Was that what I was saying? It wasn't what I wanted. I wanted to be with him. I was on the verge of being in love with him if I wasn't already. What the fuck was I supposed to say? I could only think to be straightforward.

"Al, I don't want to break up. I just don't know how to do this. I want to be with you. There just doesn't seem to be room right now."

His face turned to stone. "That's...God, Lucas, that sure as hell sounds like a breakup."

I tossed my hands up. I felt something inside me roll over, like getting to that point in a horror story and not wanting to turn the page because the killer was there. Somehow everything I said was leading to disaster.

"Al, I—*fuck me.* That's not what I'm trying to do."

"How do we move forward, then?"

"That's the part I don't know."

He sighed. There was a long silence. The kid playing the lo-fi stood, bowed, and waved goodbye to the crowd. A waiter came and cleared our plates. I watched Al think. I watched him breathe, his face steely and distant.

For every minute I spent in his presence, I wanted another. But maybe that was asking too much. I guess that's what I was trying to say. Either he had offered something he couldn't give, or I wanted something that was too much to ask. It was probably unfair to ask for time without interruption. No one got time without interruption. Even when Lila was with my parents, Ky and I were being interrupted by a million things. I guess the difference was that Ky and I had more opportunity for time generally. We lived together.

Was that what I wanted? To live with Al? Maybe in a way. Maybe I wanted for him to have his life, for me to have mine, and then somewhere was the one we worked on together. I didn't know how to fit it together, though.

"Lucas," Al said.

"I'm sorry. I was thinking."

"Care to share?"

"I just know that I like our friendship," I said.

He looked at me, nodding. "I do too."

I tried to smile. It wasn't enough. People didn't get to kiss their friends. Or fuck them. Al had made it clear at the start he wasn't looking for a hookup buddy. And I wasn't either. But I was absolutely lost as to what to say.

"Maybe after some time," I said. It seemed like a reasonable concession. If now wasn't exactly right, then maybe later. It was possible. The holidays were always problematic, and his life might settle down. And my new job, while adding to the chaos, wasn't going to last forever. Maybe the summer.

"Sure, Lucas. Look, I'm...I'm gonna take off," he said. His voice was mostly air with a hint of sadness at the end.

"Really?"

"Yeah, I don't really like my broken heart being on display."

I had to think about that. "Al...I..."

I watched him stand and take his wallet out of his back pocket. He tossed a few bills on the table. He gave me a sad smile, a pat on the shoulder, and left the bar. I looked around, confused as hell. *Broken heart?* Sure, I was sad we weren't exactly dating right now, but we weren't out of each other's lives.

"Well, if it matters, that was the nicest breakup I ever heard," the waitress said. She was a skinny Black woman with white box braids collected in a loose braid over one shoulder. She sifted the money. "And he picked up the tab with tip. Sheesh."

"I really hadn't intended to break up with him."

She sucked her teeth and walked away. "Sounded like it to me."

Shit. I thought about chasing after him. Maybe if I tried to explain it again some other way. But I really couldn't think of a better way. So I didn't get up. I sat staring at the empty spot that had once contained Al.

Then someone dropped into that space. I looked at the soft, all-knowing face of Rose Ness. She put out her hands, and I placed mine in them.

"Want to talk?" she asked.

"Not really."

She nodded. "Want to listen?"

I laughed and sucked back what might have been tears. "Okay."

She patted my hand. "I know you probably haven't been watching on your own, but last week on *The Bachelor*…"

I shook my head. I had been half forced, half willing to watch that show with her every week it aired while I worked for her. Admittedly I got into it. She caught me up on the latest drama. I tried not to think about losing Al.

CHAPTER THIRTEEN

Lucas

I slammed the hole punch and slipped the stack of pages into the binder of students who needed daily or weekly medical assistance. The school had two kids with type 1 diabetes and several asthmatics. Nurse Bea had kept the records old school. She had photocopied the old forms so often they were almost impossible to read. I found some updated versions online and printed a bunch. I would make a spreadsheet of them someday, but I really didn't have the attention span for anything more complicated than hole punching.

It had been less than twenty-four hours. Rose sat with me at Grace's for an hour before I shuffled to the truck and drove home. Ky asked what was up and insisted I tell her everything. I didn't go into detail about the incident with his mother, but I did explain enough so she'd understand what Al had been through. Then I tried to explain what I had tried to tell him. Ky listened, and I felt like she understood me. But she didn't have much advice on what to do with Al, not that I was really looking for advice. I hated to think it, but maybe this was how it would work out best.

I groaned to myself as I hole-punched more pages. How had it gotten so far from what I actually wanted to say? I shouldn't have said anything at all. *I'm such a dick.* The guy had just spilled his guts about his horrible mother showing up out of nowhere and there I was asking for attention. I was already getting a lot of attention. He had called every day and we hung out; so what if it felt like I was second to some things? There were just some things a boyfriend needed to be second to, like a wife and kids and parents and work. Right?

"My Lord, we might have to upgrade the quality of that desk if you're gonna keep pounding that hole punch like that," Mary said.

"Sorry. I'm gentler than I look."

She gave me obvious bedroom eyes. "I bet you are."

"Okay, what's up?"

She jolted out of her daydream. "Right. It's DeAndrew Nation."

My blood froze in my veins and I couldn't move. I probably looked stupid holding a stack of papers in one hand and the hole punch in the other. Mary didn't seem to notice.

"He threw up again, this time in math class."

I stood, my body responding to the emergency even though the name DeAndrew Nation was ping-ponging around in my brain. How could it be the same? How could the only people I have ever known to have the last name Nation both have the first name DeAndrew? Maybe I had heard it wrong. Then again, I knew the Nations here were probably *the Nations*. How close was this child to him?

"Where is—what was his name again?"

She grinned warmly and put her hands on her hips. "DeAndrew. He's a fifth grader over in Mrs. Wallace's class. She sent him and another student to the boys' room right across from her before she called down here. We sent Charlie, the janitor, to go clean it."

I started down the hall. Yup, she really had said DeAndrew Nation. *Just like my father.* What if this DeAndrew was my father's kid? What if I had a brother? But he never wanted kids. What if that had changed? What if he had wanted this kid and not me?

I blinked and took a breath before going into the bathroom. I was doing a good job of hurting my own feelings. In the child-sized bathroom, a small, thin kid with warm brown skin was leaning against the wall holding a backpack.

"Hi, I'm Nurse Lucas. What's your name?"

"Gabe."

"Hey, Gabe, is DeAndrew here?"

Gabe just pointed to the stall. I could see two crusty sneakers under the partition. By the looks of it, DeAndrew was just standing in there leaning against the wall.

"DeAndrew?" I said, knocking.

"Don't call me that!"

"What do you want to be called?"

"Drew."

"Right, Drew. Come out and come down to the nurse's office with me."

"Why? I'm fine. Mrs. Bea used to just send me back to class."

"That's fine if you want to go back. Me...I'd rather lie down in the nurse's office for a minute. Chew some gum. But, hey, if you want to get back to fractions or whatever, that's on you."

The door to the stall opened. "You're gonna let me have gum?"

"Only for a minute and only in the nurse's office. Can't let you walk around the rest of the day with funky breath."

"Drew's breath always funky." Gabe laughed, handing the backpack to Drew.

"I'd rather have my funky breath than your busted face," Drew said. "You look like my grandpa's toes."

Gabe cackled and tossed an arm around Drew.

"You have to go back to class," I told Gabe.

"What? Come on, I got barf on my Nikes," Gabe groaned, pointing at his shoes.

"That's cap, bro," Drew said, "I've seen Nikes, and those ain't it. Your granny got those at Walmart."

They both hollered with laughter and continued to roast each other as we left the bathroom. He was a small kid, small even for ten. His buddy, Gabe, had three inches and probably fifteen more pounds on him. Drew was a much darker brown than me, with wide features and shaved hair. I couldn't see myself in him. Then again, it wasn't like I was sure we were related.

We dropped Gabe off at the classroom, then walked in silence to the office. He led the way, stomping down the hall, annoyed. He hopped onto the couch and put his bag next to him.

"What kind of gum?" he asked.

"Here, your choice." I handed him four assorted packs and went to the cabinet. He made a series of incomprehensible youth sounds that I assumed was slang and picked cinnamon, of all things.

"Why'd you barf, my guy?"

I could hear him shuffling around on the couch, but I didn't look over. I was rifling through Mrs. Bea's files looking for Drew's. Her filing system was almost as incoherent as his slang had been.

"Well?" I said when he didn't answer.

"I don't know. Mr. Parker makes us run, and sometimes that makes me sick. I'm sick of runnin', man."

"What else happens?"

"What you mean?"

"Do you get dizzy or short of breath or...?"

"Naw."

"How do you feel right now?"

"Tired, bro. Let me sleep here."

There was about thirty minutes left in his math class, then they'd finish the day in homeroom and walk out to the pickup zone. I could always walk him out. "Maybe. Let me take your temp first."

"For what?"

"It's my job. It's Mr. Parker's job to get you to run, it's mine to take your temp." I crossed to the desk with his folder. I had found it shoved into a drawer labeled *Chronic*. Chronic what, who knew. I opened it and read as I prepped gloves and a thermometer.

"That's a butt one?" he asked, eyeing me cautiously.

Any adult patient asking me that would have gotten a relatively smart-ass answer. For this, kid I just shook my head.

"No, I'm just gonna scan your face," I said. "Your mom's name is Latisha?"

His bravado faltered, and his eyes went wide. "You gonna call her?"

I knew I had to. His folder gave permission for a basic level of care, so I'd do all the steps allowed me. But I still had to report any child coming in to see the nurse. "Not yet."

"Yeah, that's her," he said.

I swiped his head. Then I checked his eyes and ears.

"Will she be picking you up today?" I asked.

"I don't know."

"When she doesn't, who does?"

"Someone. Sometimes my granny, sometimes my uncle."

"What are their names?"

"What's it matter?"

I looked Drew in the face. It didn't. Mostly it was generic conversation to get through the exam with the least amount of discomfort.

"Well, you seem fine," I announced mostly for myself.

"So, can I sleep here?" he asked.

"Sure."

He grinned, and in the haste of moving, his backpack fell off the couch and spilled on the floor. A cell phone, some Sharpies, and some food fell out. I picked up the phone, and he scrambled to get the food back in the bag. I wasn't supposed to see it. It was an apple, carrot sticks, and half a burrito. On first glance, it looked like bits of a home meal, the carrot sticks and burrito tucked into Ziploc bags. But I also knew they had served those exact items for lunch in the cafeteria. He looked at me, pulling the backpack to him. It was the look of a kid thinking I was about to take his food away.

Instead, I handed him the phone back. "You have a phone at your age? I didn't get my first phone until I was fifteen."

He grinned, his mood reversing back to happy. "Loser."

"Watch it, or else I'll send you back to math."

His response was to flop back on the couch and dramatically pretend to be asleep.

"Spit out the gum," I said.

He laughed, rolled to toss it in the can, and he was asleep in less than three minutes. I messaged his math and homeroom teachers.

As I escorted Drew out to the pickup area, I didn't worry about seeing Al. Betsy always picked up the girls on Monday. Even though I was thinking of the Jeffersons, I was more interested in Latisha. I watched, wondering what I would say. I didn't get a chance, though. The person who came for Drew was a short, dark-skinned man. Drew thanked me and ran to where the man was talking with the pickup coordinator. The kids not getting on the bus had to check in with the pickup coordinators, and the person picking them up had to be on an approved list. The man must have been approved, though there was no more family resemblance between that man and Drew than between me and Drew. I watched them drive away.

"How was your first day?" Ky asked as I came into the kitchen. She closed her laptop slightly and looked at me over the top of it.

"It was good. Where's Lila?"

"Your moms said they would grab her from day care while I finish the revision. They want us to go over there for dinner. Also, Rose called saying her son and his partner will be in town soon and invited us over to her place for dinner later in the month."

"Maybe moms could come here. I'm not really interested in getting back in the truck."

"I'm sure they would, and that's fine by me. And Rose?" Ky asked.

Because of Ky's schedule, she needed to have events on the calendar as early as possible. That made me think of Al and his infinite responsibilities.

"I don't know about Rose. I'll call her. Ky, how did we manage it?" I asked, coming to sit by her at the table.

The flowers Al had brought were nearly dead, but Ky and I liked the morbidity of them. They matched the skull they were sitting in, so we silently, mutually agreed not to throw them out. One of my moms would probably do it when they got here. The only flower not horribly withered was a tall rose that had petrified itself, the outer petals drying to a rusty pink.

"Manage what?" Ky asked.

"How did we manage dating? You were a postdoc, and I was a student. Then we got married and had Lila. How did we do it?"

"You know as well as I do."

I shrugged. "I remember a lot of phone calls."

"There was that, but there was other stuff." She looked past me into her own memory. "I told you every weekday from noon to two and every Saturday from seven to ten was yours if you wanted it, and you showed up every day at those times."

Right. "That's kind of unromantic."

She nodded. "To others maybe, but not for us. You liked knowing I reserved that space for you and nothing else. I liked that you were willing to give me so much time for my work."

"Hmm."

She thought about it. "Plus, you're willing to go away for a twenty, and if that doesn't wet a woman's whistle, I don't know what would."

"How about this to wet your whistle—shower with me?"

She looked at the computer, then at me.

"I'll be naked," I added, trying to tempt her.

She smirked. "Naw, keep the scrubs."

I scooped her up out of the chair and carried her into the bathroom.

"Wait, I have to save," she groaned.

CHAPTER FOURTEEN

Alexander

I watched Dad read one of the cases on Paul's desk. Paul took most of December off since no one really wanted their land appraised during the holidays. If anything came up, I could handle it. But since nothing did, I took the time to clean up files. I called it spring cleaning, but no one else thought it was funny. Since it was my day to spend with him and he insisted on helping me put things in order, Coach sat behind Paul's desk ready to work.

We hadn't talked about Wynona showing up last week or anything that had been said that day. I honestly hadn't even said anything about what happened with Lucas. That day had been a lot, but the worst of it was possibly losing Lucas. I'd learned to handle any insane altercation with Wynona, but slowly and rationally being handed back my heart was new. I hadn't reached out to him, not knowing what I would say that didn't sound like flat out begging. But maybe begging was the point. Then again, he hadn't reached out to me, so maybe I was supposed to just leave him alone. *Keep in mind, sports fans, some injuries not only change how you play the game but can take you out of it altogether.*

"Keep that up and you're gonna need to buy carbon credits," Coach said.

I sighed as a reaction, not even meaning it sarcastically.

"Want to talk it over?" he asked.

"Naw, it's—"

"Hey, I think they messed up the food order," Teach shouted, coming up the stairs. He had insisted on tagging along. He was starting to get a little stir-crazy. I knew Georgia was too small for him. But he was putting up with it.

"How?" I said, immediately ready to report it on the food delivery app.

"They sent two extra sausages," Teach said. As he stepped into the office, he shoved some fries into his mouth, two or three falling on the floor.

I stared. "We didn't order *any* sausage."

"I guess we should go then," a very familiar and very welcome voice said.

I stood as my best friend, Franklin "Fin" Ness, and his partner, Orion Starr, came up the stairs.

"Fucking hell, what're y'all doin' here?" I asked, stepping around my desk to hug Fin.

"It's almost Christmas," he said, wrapping his thin, strong arms around me. I hugged him as hard as I could without snapping him in half. He was a tall, lanky redhead. His sport of choice was running, his occupation was medical student, and he lived across the country. I missed him.

"It's so good to see you," I said.

"Better to see you," Fin said.

"Orion, get over here," I said. He was tan skinned, and his long, black hair was piled on the top of his head, enough to get in my face as I hugged him nearly against his will.

"Okay. There, there, big guy," Orion said, laughing.

Fin went over to shake Coach's hand. "Hi, Coach."

"Hey there, son," Coach said. He smiled. I was still surprised by how at ease he had become. I thought moving in with me and Dani was going to be a burden, but it seemed to be the opposite.

"How ya feeling?" Fin asked.

"Right as rain," Coach said. "And how are things going with you?"

We all looked around to see who that "with you" was for. It wasn't Fin. He was looking past Fin at Orion. Orion looked like he ran more in my brother's crowd than Fin's. Fin was wearing a neat button-down with a nerdy sweater vest over it. Orion had on a black band hoodie, his band, which might have been a little too tight on him. And even though he'd tell you he was chubby, he had a lot of muscle. Parts of him shimmered with silver jewelry. If you had asked me six months ago if Coach would openly address Orion, I would have laughed.

"I...uh...good," Orion finally said.

Coach had his hand out to him, and Orion eventually shook it. He nervously adjusted his glasses as he backed away.

"Very good. Last I heard you were studying music?" Coach

continued as if they didn't have a negative past. Then again, Orion had forgiven me for bullying him as much as I had.

"Yup, just that and the band." Orion gestured to the logo on his chest.

"Ah, and that's lucrative?" Coach asked, his tone curious.

"Naw," Orion said.

"A man is a success if he gets up in the morning and goes to bed at night and in between does what he wants to do," Coach said. "That's—"

"Bob Dylan," Orion finished, "I know."

My father smiled and looked at Teach. "Are you going to eat everyone's lunch?"

Teach was still munching fries out of the bag. He looked in the bag like he was considering it, then he shrugged and started to sort out the orders.

"Your father was nice to Orion," Fin whispered to me.

"I know. He's better?"

"A lot's changed around here," he said, looking around the room. He rubbed the back of his neck, and I caught sight of something else new.

"It sure as hell has. What the hell is that?" I screeched, grabbing his hand. He was forced to spin around, ducking under his arm like a bad dancer.

"Oh shit, right," he said, turning a shade of red that matched his hair. "I was gonna tell you. It happened last week."

I gave him his left hand back, the silver band bright. "Congratulations, bro!"

I hugged him. Then I marched over and hugged Orion again.

"Married?" Teach asked, putting my food on my desk.

"Engaged," Orion said. He had on about a thousand rings, but only one that matched Fin's.

"Who asked?" I wanted to know.

"I did," Orion said. I wasn't at all surprised.

"Shit, guys, I might cry." I wiped my eyes. I hadn't been joking. Teach and Coach added their own congratulations.

"Cut it out already," Fin begged. Even though he was usually the center of attention, he hated it. Orion, on the other hand, secretly loved it.

"Best news I've had in a week," I said.

There was a small burst of chaos as I took out my grandfather's whiskey and poured Teach, Fin, and myself a shot. Coach and Orion declined. Coach tossed Orion one of Paul's Cokes, and we all toasted. There was a shuffle as everyone found somewhere to sit. Orion and Teach ended up on the couch, Fin sat on the short filing cabinet by my desk, and Coach remained where he was at Paul's desk.

"What's new around here?" Fin asked.

"Al's been moping around for a week," Teach said. I glared at him. He was right, but I didn't want to talk about it.

"Come to think on it, we haven't heard from Lucas in a while either," Coach said, not looking up from his sandwich.

"Guys..."

"He knows about that?" Fin whispered.

I sighed and said for the sake of the room, "Yes, everyone knows. Not that I want to talk about it."

"Why? We won't judge," Orion said, reaching over to take some of Teach's fries.

"It ain't that. I just...you two just got in town, just got engaged. Can't we talk about that?"

"But I thought it was going well," Fin said as he took half my sandwich. But I didn't say anything. Neither did they. In fact, even though I tried eating my meal, deliberately dipping my sandwich in my soup and not looking around, I could feel four sets of eyes on me. It was dead silent.

"I fuckin' hate you all."

They nearly cheered.

"You better start mindin' your own business before we get the chance to turn on you," I warned Coach. He didn't say anything. He didn't even blink. I turned back to my sandwich. "I swear it's not an interestin' story."

"Then why won't you tell us?" Teach mumbled around a mouthful of burger.

"Yeah," Orion said.

They waited. Generally, they all knew about as much as each other. I didn't have the time or the energy to keep things on the down-low. Dani had asked what had happened, and I brushed her off with a cursory summary.

"Lucas broke up with me," I said finally.

They stared. I blinked.

"Well?" I snapped. I was kind of mad at them. After all that, they didn't even react.

"Well, that doesn't sound right," Fin said.

I looked at him, moving my soup out of reach of his lengthy arms. "What do ya mean?"

"He said 'I'm breaking up with you'?" Fin asked. I didn't answer. He shrugged. "He told Mom last week he was happy, excited about your date. Why would he break up with you?"

"He didn't seem happy when I got there."

"You *were* a few hours late," Coach said.

"That wasn't my fault," I said, "and it was only an hour-ish."

"Grace said it was hard to watch," Fin added.

I looked at him. "You saw Ms. Grace?"

"We had to eat lunch *somewhere*," Fin said.

I snatched back the small bit of sandwich he had left. "If you already ate, what're you eatin' *my* lunch for? And no, he didn't say those words exactly."

"What'd he say exactly?" Fin said.

"He usually says what he means," Orion said.

I groaned and resigned myself to telling them the facts. I kept my brokenheartedness to myself. I didn't feel like going into detail about how the gentle way he smiled at me made me want to flip the table or how his quiet "I like our friendship" made me want to scream.

"Huh," Teach said when I was done telling them. He had finished eating and was rolling around the office on his skateboard, sometimes pushing it with his foot, sometimes walking it by balancing on the side.

"What?" I asked, my head on my desk, all work forgotten.

"It doesn't sound like you broke up to me," he said.

"No way!" Fin cried on my behalf. "He said 'let's be friends.'"

"Naw, I'm with the kid on this one," Orion said. He was holding a yardstick we kept around the office like a guitar, pretending to strum a little.

"What do you think?" Fin asked Coach.

"I'm with AC and DC on this one," Coach said, pointing at Teach and Orion with his forefinger and pinkie. They grinned at each other.

"Well, it'd be nice to know *why* you think that," I said, trying to sound neutral and not enraged they didn't side with me.

"He also said he *didn't* want to break up," Teach pointed out.

"Then he said, 'I like our friendship.'"

"Well, he does."

"He said he didn't think I had time for him."

"Naw," Orion said. "If you're quoting him right, he was just asking if *you* thought *you* had time for him. Sounds like he was just feeling insecure about the time you were able to make for each other."

"Thanks, Dr. Phil," I said.

Fin pointed at Orion. "He makes a point."

"Are you serious?"

"Lucas asked if the relationship was what you thought it was. Maybe that was just a question. When he said he didn't know how to date you if you weren't going on actual dates, maybe he meant he really didn't know," Fin said.

I sighed. "But what does that even mean? How does he not know how to date me if we go on dates?"

"You said your dates get interrupted," Orion said.

"Well, there's a lot more than just those times too. I invited him into my life—into my every day. I ask about his day and want to be a part of it. We hang out and talk all the time and have…been physical. I don't really know how much more relationship-y you can get," I said, standing to pace.

"Well sure, but that's not dating," Teach said.

"What is it, then?"

"I don't know, but…look, you've been out of the gay scene for a minute—"

"I'm not gay."

Teach waved me off, trying to stand on his board sideways. "Either way, some queer circles tend to be pretty specific about what they're doing. If you're going out, then you're just sleeping together. If you're getting to know each other, you're sleeping together but you make it a plan instead of just a booty call. If you're dating, you show up at places together."

"All right, all right, we get the picture. Why would he get stuck on that, though?" I asked.

"This is his first poly relationship," Fin said. He had moved into my chair and was unashamedly finishing my abandoned lunch.

"So?"

"So maybe he's still trying to figure it out."

"Maybe he doesn't know what else he could have," Coach said.

We all turned to him. I felt suddenly like I was at soccer practice. Coach had learned the sport because of me. I had said I wanted to play, and he spent years trying to talk me and Fin out of it. But he couldn't, so in my freshman year of high school, he said he'd coach if I could get a team together. It took so long we missed that first season, but I did it. While I was trying to get people to play, he learned how to coach it. And there he was again. He'd done some research.

"If you said you wanted to date him, then maybe stepping out together is all he feels he has. And if that time is getting interrupted and you don't even notice, then maybe it's not special enough."

Teach laughed and told Coach people didn't say "stepping out together." Orion snapped a finger gun at him in agreement, and Fin grinned at Orion.

"You really think so?" I asked. The thought gutted me.

"Someone coming into the life of a married person would have to wonder what was next at some point," Coach answered.

"He's married too."

"Marriage is a strange thing," he said.

I could see in his eyes a complicated history he'd probably never share. But he would know better than anyone else in the room. Coach, after all, was technically still married. And anyone coming into his life would have to contend with that. I never once thought about him not getting the chance to find someone new because Wynona wouldn't back off. I blinked and considered it.

"Also, you've never really dated either," Fin said. I looked at him. He had to swallow to continue. "You slept around for a while—"

"Fin." I tossed a nod at Coach.

"Sorry."

"Well, I could have guessed, seeing as Zara wasn't exactly planned," Coach said.

"See, that's what I mean," Fin continued. "Then you married Dani after what…a month? The minute someone comes into your life, it's like they're *in it*."

"Was that what I was tryin' to do to Lucas? Like skip dating and go straight into whatever's next? Even though we don't know what's next?" I was feeling dizzy from information.

"Sounds like it," Fin said.

"And he didn't get that 'cause I told him we were dating?"

Teach gave me a thumbs-up to confirm.

"And what we've done hasn't been traditional, so he's not sure what it means?" I looked at Coach. He nodded.

"So, I…"

Orion stood, placing his yardstick down like it was actually an instrument and not some free county fair swag, and came to pat my shoulder. "I think you broke up with yourself, bro."

"Fuck me."

I let the whole conversation with Lucas play out again in my head through the new lens my friends and family created. It all snapped together, his words suddenly making sense with his face and his voice and everything I understood about him. Realizing it, the congealing of it all in my mind, was like jumping into a lake in the dead of winter, shocking and impossibly cold.

"I have to be dumber than a fork at a soup-eating contest," I groaned.

They all sighed and offered me condolences.

"What am I gonna do?"

They all suddenly had nothing to say.

CHAPTER FIFTEEN

Lucas

Hey.

I deleted that and typed *Hello.*

I deleted that too. I hadn't heard from Al in a week and two days. Sure, it wasn't a lot, but that was a year in are-we-broken-up-for-real-or-not time. I still didn't know if I should text him first. But I also couldn't stand to speculate why he wasn't texting me either.

I put the phone in my pocket and started to leave my office at school. It had been a long day. For some reason, several of the middle school girls thought it would be funny to cover all the girl's room toilets with Icy Hot. I spent the day passing out baby wipes that wouldn't really help. I lost count at twenty little girls and a few teachers. Some of the Jefferson girls fell victim. They cheered up as soon as they saw me, though, which felt both nice and heartbreaking.

Either way, the paperwork had been lengthy and annoying. It put me about forty minutes behind the dismissal bell. The only bright side was the traffic from the busses and the parent pickup would be gone. I yawned and cut out the lights to the office.

"Ya headin' out?" Mary asked. She had a phone to her ear but looked to be on hold.

I smiled at her. "Yup. See ya tomorrow."

"Bye, Nurse Lucas," a small, annoyed voice said. I turned to the row of chairs in front of the principal's office.

"Drew?" I said, looking at the small kid in the large chair.

"What up?"

"What are you doing?"

"No one came for me today," he said. His tone let me know that this was a regular thing. I went over and sat with him.

"Don't worry, Miss Mary's callin' my uncle," he said.

"Is that who picked you up most of last week?"

He nodded. I'd been curious about Drew, but I was also concerned about his circumstance. I had tried calling home after the afternoon he spent in my office. No one answered and no one called back. I spotted him a few more times that week. Him and the Jefferson girls were the only children I knew. Well, there was his buddy, Gabe, who insisted on calling me Nurse Gum.

The more I saw Drew, the more complex he became. He arrived in the morning from the far end of the athletic field, as if he had walked to school, but a car always drove away. I watched him at lunch, curious about the items in his backpack. Most days he ate his lunch, some days he saved some. Yesterday I watched him squirrel away almost all of his lunch. He made sure no one was looking when he pulled a fresh Ziploc from his hoodie pocket. He stuffed in his pizza and the applesauce cup. He ate only the green beans and drank the milk. He didn't come to my office, but I heard later from Mr. Parker that he kept having to go to the bathroom. He had hidden away his chicken nuggets today.

I knew it was probably enough evidence to report, but I wasn't ready to do that. Even though it was meant to help, child protective services seemed like a large step. According to the internet, he was either saving some of his lunch because he didn't know where dinner was coming from or he was sharing with someone else somewhere else. Even though I called every day, his mother never answered.

"Hey there," Mary said, coming around the counter. "Looks like your uncle's on his way. He said about ten minutes."

"I'll stay with him, if you want to finish up," I said.

She gave me a grateful look. She had been one of the victims of the Icy Hot prank. It had been really hard to not laugh as she walked around most of the day grabbing her ass. I asked Drew a few random questions about being a kid as we waited. I did manage to learn his mother worked as a bank teller, and he was an only child. The front door buzzer rang almost exactly ten minutes later. I stood as Mary let the uncle in. We could hear him before we could see him. For a full minute, the sound we heard was his hard-soled boots on tile. Most of the teachers wore sneakers or Crocs, so I forgot what business shoes could sound like. He was wearing suit pants and a button-down. His jacket was suede and his hat was for the Atlanta Falcons. He spotted Mary first, then Drew, then me as he looked around the office.

"Where do you want me to sign?" he said, his voice soft compared to the strength of his presence. It was interesting how commanding he sounded without being loud.

"Right here, Mr. Nation," Mary said, flipping a book around toward him. Mr. Nation strode to the counter, produced a pen of his own, and signed. Then he crossed to where Drew was sitting.

"Ready, boss?" he asked.

"Sure. Uncle Chandler, this is Mr. Lucas," Drew said, shouldering his backpack. "He's the school nurse."

"What happened to Mrs. Bea?"

"Dead," Drew said casually.

"No," I said, trying not to laugh. "No, just retired."

"Oh," Drew said, though it obviously didn't matter to him.

Chandler gave me a long look of appraisal. He had to look up to look me in the eye. He didn't seem remotely intimidated despite my towering over him, which intimidated me a little. He did extend his hand.

"Chandler Nation," he said.

"Lucas Laverty."

His expression changed then, a barely-there raising of his eyebrow.

"All right," he said with a nod. He turned so his next comment included Mary. "Thank you for looking after him."

"He's a dream," Mary said.

He looked at the child. "Let's go, Drew. You want to drive?"

"Naw, I want the aux cord," Drew said.

I watched them leave.

"He's such an interesting person," Mary said, her bag on her shoulder and her car keys in her hand.

"Seems it."

"He writes sports articles for a gay magazine, of all things. I didn't know people who lived that way were into sports enough to read about them. But there you go. He's one of those transgenders," she said.

I blinked. Then I tried not to sigh or sound too annoyed. "I think if he wanted people to know, he'd tell them himself."

She looked at me playfully, then she backed down, reading my expression.

"Right, okay, I didn't mean offense. See you tomorrow, Lucas."

I let her leave first, then I followed a second or two behind. Out in the lot I could see Mary pulling her SUV out of its spot. I could also see Chandler on the phone outside his car. Drew was inside, looking down, probably on his phone. I wondered if Chandler could get Drew's mother to answer my calls. As I trotted over, I also wondered if he knew the older DeAndrew.

"Excuse me," I said.

He turned and looked at me and put up a hand, asking me to wait. It was the politest I had ever seen anyone do that.

"Look, I have to go, but this conversation is not over," he said into the phone. "Bye."

I waited for him to turn back to me.

"What can I do for you, Mr. Laverty?" he asked.

"Um. Well, I've been trying to get a hold of Drew's mother about some concerns I have, but I can't seem to reach her. Maybe you can relay the message?"

He blinked and rubbed his temples. "What concerns?"

I sighed. "I'm not allowed to discuss them with you. I can only tell those authorized by—"

"FERPA, I knew that," he said. He put his hands in his pockets and looked into the car where his nephew was singing along to the radio. "Damn it. When would you want to talk to her?"

"Any time. I have time tomorrow even, the afternoon is better."

"If I get her to sign like a form or something letting you talk to me, would you?"

"Sure." I shrugged. "Probs would have to be some legal thing, or I'd need proof you're part of his day-to-day care."

"What, this isn't enough?" He glared at me, gesturing to the car and the parking lot.

"I'm not sure. I'd have to look it up," I said.

I felt like he was some Black Sherlock Holmes. I didn't know what he could see, but it was something.

"All right, Mr. Laverty—"

"Lucas," I said.

He nodded. "All right, Lucas. I'll see you at two thirty tomorrow with paperwork."

"Righto," I said, saluting him. I had never said that in my life, nor was I the saluting type, but he made me nervous. He knew something about me. I could see it in the way he looked at me. It was like a gastroenterologist who could tell you liked anal. I blinked and tried to regroup. "I mean—good, see you then."

He smiled at me and got into his car.

❖

It was both surprising and unsurprising to have Chandler walk into my office at two thirty on the dot and place a form in front of me. I picked it up.

"Good afternoon, Lucas. This is from my lawyer. My sister has signed it and I've had it notarized. A copy has been provided to both the school district superintendent and the principal. This one is for your records."

I closed my mouth. "Damn."

He pulled off his coat and hat and pointed to the door. "Do you want this open or closed?"

I considered Mary and the other hens. They were as gossipy as you would expect. "Closed."

He shut the door and placed himself in the chair I had moved across from my desk. It was usually against the far wall. I liked that he had covered all the bases to be at this meeting. I also had done my part, informing those who I needed to about the meeting.

"Mr. Nation—"

"Chandler." I could tell his mood was better today than yesterday. There was almost a smile on his face, and his dark eyes were welcoming instead of scary.

"Chandler. I'm worried about Drew's eating habits."

He blinked and sat forward in the chair. "Elaborate."

I did.

"Fuck," he said, mostly to himself. "I can't believe—listen, Lucas, I'll be straight with you. My sister is not always on top of things. I guarantee from this day onward he'll have three straight meals."

I wanted to pry, but I knew I didn't need that information. "I guess that's all I can ask for."

"What would be a threshold to report?"

"Um, there's no hard line on these things," I said.

He nodded. He surveyed me, biting the thumbnail on his left hand thoughtfully. "Latisha didn't ever expect to have…she helped raise me and said I'd be the last kid she ever dealt with. Then Drew. But she's not a bad person."

I put my hands up. "I get it. Parents aren't always everything they should be."

Chandler sat forward even more and grinned. "What an interesting choice of words."

"Um…"

"All right, Lucas, I'll ask. You're DeAndrew's son, aren't you?"

I almost stood up from shock. I couldn't look away from Chandler, but I also couldn't say anything.

He laughed like my stunned silence was all the confirmation he needed. "Wow. I never thought I'd see you in person. I knew your name from my brother."

"Brother?"

"DeAndrew Senior is my brother."

"But you're so young."

"I know. We have the same father—and the same birthday, as a matter of fact. He's twenty-five years older than me."

"I can't believe—wait, I'm older than *you*?" I said, trying to work out the math.

Chandler looked so excited he was ready to run laps around the room. "You *are*! So, nephew, what're you doing after work?"

"Nephew? After work?"

Chandler stood and gathered his hat and coat. "I bet you have questions."

"No shit."

I had plans with Lila that afternoon, so Chandler and I made plans for Saturday morning brunch. I wasn't really sure why, but the first person I wanted to tell was Al.

CHAPTER SIXTEEN

Alexander

I consulted the sticky note again. "Couscous?"

Dani had asked me for a million things over the years, but never once for fucking organic couscous. I looked around. In front of me, a third of the way down the water and soda aisles, a thin woman was struggling with the bottles of water on the top shelf. She was standing on the shopping buggy and reaching to the back of the top rack. She was tall enough that if the bottles she wanted were closer to the edge, she wouldn't have had a problem. In a misstep, she lifted one foot in a Hail Mary of a reach and started falling while the buggy rolled off the other way. I was there with an arm under her so fast I impressed myself.

"You okay, ma'am?" I asked, righting her. She turned to look at me, and we both laughed.

"Ma'am, huh, Al?" Kyoko said, straightening the big sweater on her shoulders. She pointed at me. "Look, I'm not *falling* for you, so don't get any polyamorous ideas."

While it was a good line, it stung a little. I smiled anyway. "I won't. I didn't recognize you."

"How many Georgians do you know with green hair?"

I laughed. "You've a hat on."

She touched her head. "Shit, right. Welp, fair enough. I think the gentlemanly thing to do now would be to ask you how you are?"

"Me, oh, I um…I'm well enough," I said, not convincing myself.

She wasn't buying it either. "Okay, sure. And I'm a polar bear."

"Good luck with global warming."

She pointed at me. "I bet it's been a hard week."

I nodded and shifted the basket I was carrying from my left hand to my right. "It was, and it's gotten worse now that I'm here looking for couscous."

She looked around. "You must really be lost. This is the beverage aisle. Here, give me a boost, and I'll help you."

She took my basket and put it in her buggy. I lifted her cheerleader style, and she took the seven or eight bottles of water off the top shelf and dropped them in next to my basket. When there weren't any more, I set her down.

"Right, let's go find your couscous." She started moving before I really had a chance to think. The bottles rolled dramatically as she shoved forward. "So why haven't you called my husband?" she said over her shoulder.

"Well, first of all, I fucked up our dinner the other night."

"Second?"

Her frankness was almost scary. Dani hadn't even been that blunt. After my spur-of-the-moment therapy session with the guys I, at least, had answers. "I don't know how to bridge the gap."

"Pole vault?"

That wasn't a very helpful comment, and I hated that I found it amusing. "You know, your paper on shit would've been a lot better if you'd put in some of these jokes."

She turned to look at me, impressed. "Two insults in one. Who knew you had it in you?"

I almost tripped on my feet following her around a corner. "Oh really? Crap, I wasn't tryin' to be that insulting."

She laughed. "You basically just said my paper was bad, and my jokes belonged in shitty papers."

"Good Lord. I didn't mean it like that."

"Relax. If it matters, I do write them in, but someone always edits them out."

We were silent as she scanned the aisle markers. It was one of the only supermarkets in Valdosta that even hinted at having organic anything. There was a pretty decent crowd, but Ky's buggy driving scared people out of the way. I wondered what Kyoko was doing in Valdosta.

She was an interesting woman. I hadn't gotten to talk to her much in person, but she dropped the weirdest things into the group chat. Dani's new favorite phrase was "Did you see what Ky sent?" Even that chat had fallen silent since that Sunday. It had been hard on Dani even though I knew she and Ky talked in a separate chat.

"In all seriousness," she said, drawing me out of my thoughts, "Lou is just a guy, a bro. All you have to do is talk to him."

"The last time we talked, I put my foot in my mouth."

She grinned. "Who knew you were so flexible?"

"You live and you learn, I guess."

She gave me a punch on the arm.

"I just don't know how to get it back out again," I said.

"Well, maybe you're doing it wrong. Instead of pulling it out, you ever think you should just swallow?"

"You really want to suggest that I swallow?" She stopped the buggy and gave me a very serious stare. "Well, it ain't like I know what that's supposed to mean."

"Maybe instead of trying to take it back, you just push on forward. Last time you talked to him, you put your foot in it, but think of how many times you talked to him and didn't."

"I don't know. It seemed like an important moment, weighted or somethin'."

She waved that off with a vague gesture toward the butcher counter. She looked at my list, then she turned down the dry products aisle. I was sort of over getting advice, even though hers was probably the best since she knew Lucas better than anyone. I wondered if Lucas would ever go to Dani for advice about me.

"Is this really fair, though? It seems a little like cheatin'."

"I already told you no. Calm your polyamorous ass down."

I groaned. "No, I didn't mean it like that. Talkin' to you about Lucas like this seems like an unfair advantage. It seems like pine tar in baseball."

She paused midstep to think, then walked on. "I don't know what that means, but I was counting on this advantage around his birthday. Ya boi is hard to shop for."

I sighed.

"So, you better get your shit together by then. Quit striking out or fouling up or whatever. Besides, I never understood the point of having a partner with another partner if you couldn't commiserate with that person every now and then. Poor Lucas, I joke that his metamour is my work and, well, you can only get so much information from soil samples."

"Yeesh, tell me about it. I don't know how to answer his question, though. I don't really know how to date."

She really turned on me then. She stopped the buggy in the way of an old lady trying to get Shake 'n Bake. "You mean to tell me you can't figure out a way to just make time for him?"

I carefully moved the buggy and helped the lady. "Ky, I'm sure I can. I'm tryin' to, it just hasn't worked out yet. What even is romance?"

Ky abandoned the buggy completely and walked to the bags of rice and beans and stuff. She squatted to stare at the bottom row.

"If spreadsheets and psychological thrillers aren't your idea of romance, then I can't help you."

I rubbed my face to try and relieve some tension. I couldn't really give him the quality time he wanted. I considered my small basket in the buggy: flowers for Dani, and the rest of the fixin's for dinner.

"Lou, on the other hand, loves regular romantic shit. Not from me because I'm bad at it. But he also tends to get stuck on the idea of roles, you know. Once something gets labeled, he gets even more confused if actions don't align with his expectations. It's not that he's not open-minded to different modes of operation, but he has to be talked through that stuff sometimes. We still talk about his expectations for a wife. I think that's why he wants a boyfriend sometimes, because he loves that romantic shit so much. Boyfriends traditionally give the flowers and chocolates and cards and sing serenades—"

"He wants to be serenaded?" I exclaimed. Then I thought about it. "I guess Orion is in town. He can play the guitar and could probably teach me a song or two."

Ky came back laughing. "Wow, okay, you're struggling to figure out how to just call the guy and yet you think you're ready to stand outside his apartment and sing to him."

"I was spitballin'."

She handed me the couscous and looked in the basket. "You need chicken?"

"Um, if that's what's next," I said, looking at the sticky note she seemed to have memorized. "Though I really can take it from here if you have somethin' to get to. I can do it."

"I bet you can, but I'm getting a kick out of this. I love grocery shopping with a list. The order of it gives me a thrill."

"All right, sure."

I followed her out of the aisle. I guess if he needed reassurance, that could just be words. And Ky did just say "card." What's more affirming than a good old-fashioned lovey card? Lovey. I hadn't thought about being in love with him since Sunday. Sure, I felt it, but I hadn't given the thought much ground. If he thought boyfriends were supposed to give cards and flowers and I could be that kind of boyfriend, maybe there was a way forward.

"Earth to Al." Ky waved a hand in my face.

"This is Al," I said, shaking my head to focus.

She patted my back. "People could see the smoke from your brain working so hard through the whole store."

I laughed.

"Al, the shit you were doing was working. So you don't really have to reinvent the wheel here. He's been gaga-eyed for weeks over your eight p.m. on the dot calls."

My face warmed. "Gaga-eyed? He mostly looks at me suspiciously."

"Yeah, that's the look."

"Well, what I was doin' before obviously wasn't enough. I've really been tryin' to figure out how to recut my evenings so our schedules align like he wants...needs."

"He's out of school at three. That seems like a lot of evening."

"I'm not out of work until five."

She tossed out her arms as to encompass the whole meat section of the store. "You're the damn boss, Khaki Man. Let yourself out at three a few days a week to have, like, the senior citizen special down at Grace's."

I stopped walking. It was single-handedly the most fascinating sentence anyone had uttered all week. And for a number of reasons. Her suggestion was the easiest damned solution in the history of solving problems. I was almost mad at her for it. "God damn, that's fuckin' genius. Would he go for that?"

"It worked for me. Don't tell him this because I don't want him to get any fancy romancy notions, but when we first got together, I'd always start a big data analysis around noon. And those bitches used to take two hours or so to run. Instead of working while the program was running, I told my boss I'd work from my apartment because the program made the office computers too slow. Then I'd spend the two hours with Lucas."

"Aw, why didn't you tell him that?"

She giggled. "I'm saving it. It's my wild card should we ever have a fight that requires receipts."

It was my turn to be impressed. "That's...wow."

"Ruthless, I know. Now that that's out of the way, you can work out your problems with our bae," she said. She gestured to the chicken. "How much chicken do seven little girls and four adults eat?"

"A lot, but I have another question."

"Okay," she said. She adjusted her sweater again.

"Khaki Man?"

She grinned. "Lucas won't let me call you Khaki Daddy anymore."

I laughed so hard I drew a crowd. We parted ways after we grabbed carrots for me and a butternut squash for her. When she was out of sight, I doubled back and spent a little too long finding a card. Dani didn't notice I was late picking her up. She was having a push-up contest with one of her new trainers, a young kid fresh out of college. She was at seventy and he was at sixty-four. I told her I would meet her in the truck after she won. I wrote a small note and sealed the card.

"Don't overthink it," I said.

CHAPTER SEVENTEEN

Lucas

I was at the gym when my phone rang. I pressed the button on my headphones to answer.

"Hello," I said, wiping my sweaty face on my shirt.

"Hey."

I froze, shirt over my nose with one hand, fifty pounds of iron in the other. That greeting sent a shock wave through my body like a meteorite striking Earth. I looked at the huge clock on the wall of the gym. It was about the time he usually called. But he hadn't for a week. Or was it over a week? What day was it? What year?

"Lucas?" Al asked tentatively.

"Oh, yeah…hey, I'm here."

"I wanted—gee, it's good to hear your voice."

"Oh yeah?" I put the weight down and gathered my wits.

There was a soft breath. I could picture him messing with his hat.

"Yeah. It's not that I didn't want to call, I just didn't know what to say. I still don't, really, but I want to figure it out. It sounds a little loud there, are you busy?"

"I'm at the gym." It didn't answer his question even if it was true. I would have stopped, if he'd asked. I would have put the weights up and met him wherever he wanted if he named a place. My throat tightened a little when he didn't ask me to do that.

"That's cool. I, um…want to see you. If you want to see me. When are you free next?"

"Tomorrow?" I said before I could stop myself.

"Perfect. Text me the details when you're done with your workout."

"Okay."

"Okay. I can let you get back to it. And check your mail when you get home."

"What?"

"Check your mail when you get home." He added a hasty bye, then he was gone.

I looked at the phone. Was that a code for something? I didn't realize until I was sitting there with my phone in my hand looking like a sweaty fool that I had honestly thought he was done with me. But I guess this meant he wasn't. There were a million questions, but he had been so casual, and it was so amazingly familiar to hear from him, that I couldn't think of a single one. I couldn't even move.

"Bad news?" a woman asked, pulling her headphones away from her ear to hear my answer.

"No, I just…there's a delivery waiting for me, I wasn't expecting anything."

"Fun?" she asked.

I felt suddenly shy. "Yeah, a surprise."

She grinned and went back to her workout. Before I left, I gave her one of Dani's business cards. She'd probably be more comfortable at a different gym. Thinking about Dani only added more fuel to the fire inside me that had sparked when I heard Al's voice on the line. I replayed that phone conversation as I cleaned up and drove home.

I sat in the truck for a few minutes. I hadn't even been gone that long. I had spent the afternoon after work with Lila, playing a game she called magic tricks. She'd try to stump me by hiding coins under cups or playing cards in my pockets while I had my eyes closed. Ky had been at her rented office all day, then she went to the store, and we traded being the magician's assistant so I could go to the gym. She said she had an interesting story for me when I got home. I hadn't even been gone forty minutes. I guess I had an interesting story for her too.

I got out of the truck and went around to the front where our mailbox was—the metal kind that hung in a tower of boxes on the side of the entry. I lifted the lid and put my hand in. I don't know what I expected, but it wasn't the high-gloss feel of fancy paper. The green envelope I pulled out was blank.

"Why would he get me a card?" I said to the mailbox. It didn't have any more answers than I did. It was too dark on the street to read it properly, so I stepped into the stairwell up to our apartment hallway. We kept the light on in case of emergencies. I thumbed the envelope open and pulled out the card.

The front had a cartoon of a medieval-looking academic holding scrolls with obvious constellations on them. He was talking to an assistant in some library. The speech bubble said, "I said tracking stars, not trekking stars." Mucking about in the background was the original crew of the starship *Enterprise*. I laughed out of surprise. I opened the card. It said, *When you can't beam yourself out of your mistakes, resort to the ancient earth custom: an apology.*

Beneath that Al had written a small note.

> *I'm sorry. I think I understand now what you were saying on Sunday. Give me a chance to prove it? I know a card isn't enough, but I'll make the rest up to you later. I spent way too much time picking this, so I hope it at least made you laugh. I thought about getting a more romantic one, but there are just some things you should hear for the first time in person.*
> *I miss you,*
> *Al*

I read the whole card again. It was funny. But what did he mean by "some things you should hear for the first time in person"? I was still looking at the card when I opened the door to the house.

"Lou, you're back. Mommy and I can do our show for you."

I smiled at Lila and looked at the clock. "Do you think you can do the show in your pajamas?"

She frowned. "I don't want to go to bed."

"I know and you don't have to, yet. But get ready anyway."

"Hey, bae," Ky said, coming to the living room. "Crowded?"

"No, I heard from Al and couldn't focus." I put my bag down by the couch and walked over to her. I kissed her, feeling grounded in her familiar, stable love.

"Woot, that's a good thing, right?" She held my face.

"Yeah, of course, but why now?"

We had to pause our conversation to help Lila start her bedtime routine. But then we sat at the kitchen table and Ky poured me a cup of tea.

"About Al, well, that's what I was gonna tell you. I ran into him while I was shopping in Valdosta." She laughed at my alarmed expression and explained what they had talked about.

"So, this was your idea?" I asked more to know than to accuse. It sounded accusatory, though. "You suggested the card?"

"What card?"

I got the card off the coffee table and handed it to her.

"Oh, my fucking heart. What a doll. This is…so…gross," she cooed dreamily as she read it.

"I know, right? I love it."

"Of course you do. And no, he did this on his own." She handed it back.

"Why?"

"He's in love with you, silly."

I almost spat out my tea. "How'd you get that from this?"

"Well, he practically told me at the store, and he said he didn't get you a romantic one because he said you should hear some things in person first."

"I don't know what he means."

"Romantic cards all say 'I love you' in them."

I gulped and blinked at her. She tossed her hands up and got up from the table. She kept talking, but I didn't listen. I looked at the card. Now that she pointed it out, I couldn't unsee it. But could he really? I thought about the way it felt to be with him: in the car, his hand touching mine, watching him care for his children, fucking him—

"I think I love him too," I told her quietly.

She waved me off as if I had just told her it was dark outside. "Lou, that's not even the point I was trying to make."

"I wasn't listening," I said.

She sighed.

I decided to move on. "Hey, would you mind it if I took a few hours tomorrow to meet up with Al? I was thinking after the meeting with Chandler."

"You're so funny."

"Why?"

"Only you'd connect with a long-lost uncle and call it a meeting."

"Well, I'm *meeting* him. Is that okay with you?"

She looked at me like she was following all the steps of a recipe in her head to make sure she had the right ingredients. "Do you want me to meet you at Rose's?"

"Oh shit, I forgot about that. Naw, I can come home."

"Love, it's fine. I don't mind. Lila and I can pick up some flowers."

"Let's bring wine or something. Plenty of other people will bring flowers."

"Even better for me. Lila and I can meet you at the party."

I kissed her, trying to communicate how my life would not make sense without her.

"Ahem," Lila said from behind us. "I've been waiting forever."

"Let's do it, then," Ky said.

"Give me a minute," I said, "I'm gonna clean up out here."

Lila looked at me with more impatience than a four-year-old should have, and Ky followed her out of the room laughing. I cleaned up the tea, put the card back in its envelope, and took it to my room. I stuffed it in a box I had for that sort of thing. Then I texted Al the proposed plan, asking him to meet me at the Winter Park. On Saturdays during the holiday season there was an ice-skating rink and a food truck. Not that we would do any of those things, but I liked the ambience. His message back was instant and affirmative.

The whole night, everything from Lila's magic, to Ky's support, to Al's card had left me feeling goofy. If I was a cartoon character, I would have been floating around with little heart eyes.

I got to the diner before Chandler the next morning, but my anxiety had me out of control. I almost knocked over a waitress on my way in, and then I spilled coffee creamer into the little dish they kept the sugar packets in, ruining them all. I apologized while the same waitress I'd run into cleaned it up. I wondered what she would say if I tipped her before the meal.

Chandler came in about ten minutes later, on time to the second like he had been to the meeting at school. I was jealous of his poise. He was dressed down today, wearing a large hoodie for the Pittsburgh Penguins, of all teams. I waved at him. He waved back and turned his ball cap backward as he slid into the booth.

"Well, good morning, nephew."

"You seem happy," I said.

"Hey, can't be business all the time. Besides, I've been wondering about you my whole life. I feel like I've found Bigfoot."

"Watch it," I said with a laugh. "Your feet are as big as mine. You're like a fucking hobbit."

"Yeah, I got lucky."

The waitress took our orders, then we sat and stared at each other. It was like we were both struck with the same sudden realization that we had an unalterable connection to the complete stranger opposite us. I wondered how much Chandler looked like him. I had forced him out of my mind so often that I was having a hard time solidifying a memory.

"You look like him," Chandler said, surprisingly in tune with me.

"I do?"

He nodded. "Yeah, it's a little creepy. Looking at light-skinned DeAndrew."

"I'm creepy?"

He grinned. "Sure, but only because…Well, it's a long story."

"I've got time."

"No way. Tell me about yourself."

"How'd you know it was me?" I asked.

He looked at me like I had asked the silliest question in the world. "Private investigator."

That was unexpected. "Really?"

"Hell no. I knew your moms' names and googled y'all. I'd been hearing about DeAndrew's long-lost kid for years, and all he ever told me was you were *their* kid. When I was ten, he gave me their names and I've snooped around since. You were my first big story."

"Welp, uncle, who's creepy now?"

He wasn't fazed. "No, I've always known that somewhere there was a guy with my brother's genes. D just never wanted us to reach out. Then things seemed too far away. We both got too old or something."

"I get that. It never even occurred to me as a kid to try and figure out if DeAndrew had brothers or sisters or parents."

"Don't worry. With a twenty-five-year age gap between him and me, he barely knows I'm his brother anyway. And you're his son. Crazy. What's your life even like? You work at the school, sure, but what else? How are you even here?"

Something unlocked inside me, and the sum of my whole life flowed out of my mouth and onto the table for this stranger to examine. He was gracious and interested, though, asking questions that gave away his profession. And I answered every single one. Deep down, I'd always wanted this conversation—me and some older male figure having a heart-to-heart. The fact that Chandler was younger than me didn't matter.

"Absolutely riveting," Chandler said when my story had caught up to the last few weeks. "I'd love to meet your wife and…boyfriend?"

"Her, sure. Him, well, it's complicated."

"Oof, I know what that means," Chandler said, leaning on the table.

At some point a waitress had brought food and we had eaten, and now there were empty plates. I started stacking the cutlery and flatware into neat piles for the waitress to take away.

"What's that mean?"

"It means what it means. Tell me about it. Who better than to get advice from than a kindly old uncle?"

I laughed shyly but told him anyway because I had told him damn near everything else. I explained about mine and Al's weird breakup and the silence over the last week. It was only a little embarrassing to tell him about the card and only slightly more embarrassing to tell him about the meetup later.

"Sounds like growing pains to me. You got a lot of pieces you want to fall into place right away, but sometimes it only happens one by one. You got to move 'em around, look at 'em, see where they go."

"That's not really advice. That's some shitty fortune cookie shit."

He shrugged. "Fine, the advice is give him the benefit of the doubt. Being partners isn't always flowers and rainbows."

"Partners?" I said. I had never considered the title. Even Ky was my wife and not partner, despite our respective queerness. But Al? I wondered. "What's the difference between a partner and a boyfriend?"

"The difference is whatever you need it to be."

"Bro, *what*? That doesn't…Why bother having both terms, then?"

"Not all synonyms are synonyms," he answered quickly as if he already had that answer prepared.

"That's not how synonyms work," I nearly shouted. "Look, just because you're using complete sentences doesn't mean you're making sense."

He looked off toward the center of the diner where people milled about doing diner things. I looked out there too, half expecting to see the answer walk up to him.

"When I first started transitioning, people used to ask me what the difference is between being a straight woman and a gay man. And I would always say syntax." He looked at me carefully, gauging my reaction. I didn't know really what my face was doing, but he kept going. "The distinctions between life this way or life that way are sometimes only as good as the words you use to describe them. A cabin in the woods has a whole different mood and meaning than a shack in the forest even if, at the end of the day, you have a ten-by-ten box in a bunch of trees. Now sure, there are meanings that people assign to words. That's the point of words. But other times you have to look at all the other stuff beyond meaning. Like I'm a man and you're a man, but we probably define that differently. So, if this guy is someone you love and want in your life, but you can't marry, even though you're so much a part of his day-to-day that you might as well be married, then maybe partner works better than boyfriend even if it's not quite husband."

I considered it. I really didn't have any way of verbalizing my understanding of what my relationship with Al was. Which I think *made* Chandler's point more than not. I could picture a cabin in the woods and I could picture a shack in the forest and I could picture a man like him and a man like me and a man like Al. And even though the words got us close, we really did need whatever else there was to take us the rest of the way to understanding.

"And then I said, 'Turn on the oven? Shouldn't I buy it dinner first?'" Chandler said.

"What? I missed the first part of that."

"Naw, that's just something I say to get people's attention. There's no first part."

"Uncle, I think that was some pretty solid advice."

He raised his coffee mug for a toast.

"Now tell me about your life," I said.

I learned he'd been a sports journalist for three years but only at his current magazine for less than six months. He came home to Valdosta between stories. He kept an apartment here, which I thought was impressive, but he had inherited it from DeAndrew, so not really.

"Inherited?" I asked, my mouth going dry at the end of the word.

Chandler put his hands up. "Oh no, he's not dead."

I exhaled, relieved. I didn't think I could handle hearing this distant cryptid of a relative called *Dad* had died.

"How'd you get his apartment, then?"

Chandler took off his hat. "He couldn't take care of it. Can't even take care of himself most days."

"Sick?" I asked, thinking of hospitals.

Chandler shook his head. "About five years ago, he was in a car accident. He lives in an assisted living facility in Virginia. His mother had been in Virginia since she found out about me. D came back to Valdosta when I was six-ish and the news of our father's other family broke. Of my half siblings, D is the only one who really wanted a relationship with me. There's Latisha, who is his full and my half sister, and then there's Ben, my full brother. Anyway, D lived in Valdosta for about ten years, then he wanted to travel. But a car T-boned him somewhere in Florida. He has brain damage and memory loss."

Maybe I would have rather heard he was dead. Five years ago… assisted living…brain damage. I let all of those words bounce around in my brain like an old-school screen saver. It was almost as if the feeling was too alien to understand. "Oh shit."

"Did…did you ever want to see him again?" Chandler asked.

I stirred my cold coffee. "I did, more when I was a kid. I would now, though."

I tried to meet Chandler's eyes but ended up looking into my coffee cup. I wasn't embarrassed about wanting to see DeAndrew still. I was embarrassed because it still felt as childish as it had been when I first sent that letter. At that moment a waitress came and refilled the coffee, probably thinking my staring was me wanting more.

"You could. I could arrange for you to see him."

I looked up. "Really?"

Chandler nodded once. "Yeah, sure, if you want to make a trip up to Virginia, but it's not likely he'd know you."

I nodded. I let his warning sink in. I knew what patients with long-term disabilities and memory loss could be like. I had cared for a few over the years. But still, if I didn't go see him, I would always wonder. It wasn't like I wanted anything from him anyway. I didn't. Except to stand across from him once, just once, as adults, as fathers. I had to know what that felt like.

"I want to see him."

"Really? When?"

We talked it over, and I looked at my schedule. We finally picked the next weekend, the last full weekend before Christmas. I could swing three days in Virginia, not including the drive. I still had to clear it with Ky, but I knew her schedule well enough. The government work usually slacked off in the winter since it was too cold to get samples, so she mostly wrote and analyzed, which meant she would be home. Or she could go with me.

Chandler and I spent another hour together bouncing around various subjects. We fought over who got to pay the bill, and we ended up overpaying and overtipping. He said he'd text me later in the week because, in his words, "I don't plan on losing my nephew again. I won't look twice." Then I watched from my truck as he drove off in a small, eco-friendly car, different from the one he'd driven to the school.

I called Ky as soon as I lost sight of him. I told her everything Chandler and I had talked about. She listened excitedly. As I started to drive, I told her about Chandler's offer to take me to meet DeAndrew.

"Wow, love. Are you ready for that?" she asked with equal parts excitement and caution.

"How could anyone be? Would you want to go with me?"

"I'd go to the ends of the world with you," she said. She was silent after that, but I could hear the gears in her brain cranking around.

"But?"

"Buuuttt." The word was long, buying her that one second more to finish thinking. "What if you asked Al?"

That was so surprising, I almost missed a stop sign and collided with a plumbing van. Why would she say that? She'd already said she'd go, so it wasn't like she was suggesting him to get herself out of it.

"Why?" I asked.

Something on her side of the phone clinked, a water bottle maybe. I looked toward the office space she rented. From where I was idling at the stop sign, I could see the corner of the building she was sitting in, writing. Lila was with her, probably showing Kyoko's officemates her magic tricks.

"I was just thinking he's probably closer to this in terms of personal experience than I am."

"You think?" I took my foot off the brake and slowly rolled in between the people toward the park. I could've gone around the block and parked at my house. But I was already late, and there were spaces near the food truck. *Al is closer to it than she is.* "How so?"

"First of all, he's a father."

"So what? You're a *mother*."

"Well, that's obviously not the same. If it were, would you even be on this journey? You've always said you wondered what your father was like, not what your paternal gene source was like. Even if all it took to be a parent was to make peanut butter and jelly sandwiches and we both made one every other day, I still wouldn't be a *father*."

That was a fair enough point. "But you have a father."

"So what? My parents have been married for twenty-nine years and they've never been happier or more in love. It's nauseating."

Also a good point.

"I'd say my parents are more like Jojo and Silvy. Al, though, has an estranged parent. I've never had to wonder why my own genetic source, mother or father, didn't want me. But I bet he has."

If I nodded any more, I would be a bobblehead. I tried to justify not agreeing with her reasoning. "I don't know…he's…we're…"

"You're there to figure out what you are. Listen, I'll go with you. Lila and I will move in with the guy, if that's what you need. But you're a father, Al's a father, and you're assessing DeAndrew as a father. What do I know about that? I guess I could google it."

I let the truck roll too far into the parking spot, and the front wheels bounced off the cement marker. "Fuck, I can't even tell you how many times I've googled fatherhood."

"Same, well, not fatherhood. The only thing Google turned up that I ever resonated with was a study about the nursing habits of wild boars."

We laughed.

"Hey, I have to go," she said. "But you don't have to ask him if you don't want to. You don't have to do anything I'm suggesting. I'm there with you no matter what. But think about it. You might get a little more out of it if he was there."

"I love you."

"I love you too. See you later."

The golden hues of the Christmas lights weren't strong enough to fully chase away the gray of winter, but they were strong enough to gild the edges of people and trees and park benches. Al was sitting at a picnic table, his blond hair as warm as the lights. He had two coffees.

Every time I saw him, it was Mount Vesuvius in my chest. He hadn't spotted the truck yet. He smiled dreamily at the ice skaters and sipped his coffee, the medium paper cup small in his huge hands. The way Ky phrased it—he was a father, I was a father—echoed Chandler talking about the different ways men could be men. I could see what they meant even more now. All the meaning packed into the word *love* would probably take a whole novel to explain, but I loved him. And I would ask him to come to Virginia to see DeAndrew. I hadn't felt that hopeful or nervous in years. I got out of the truck and started for him.

CHAPTER EIGHTEEN

Alexander

"What's a guy like you doing in a place like this?"

I jumped. I knew the voice, though. I turned around, smiling.

"Evening," I said, standing up to greet Lucas.

Since I didn't know if I was allowed to, I didn't hug him. Instead, I picked up the still-warm coffee and handed it to him. He smiled as he took it. In a very cheesy moment, his hand brushed mine around the cup.

"Hey, Al," he said as he sipped.

I sat and he followed. The picnic table was old and splintery, bowing and cracking with age and stained around the nails and bolts with rust. Lucas looked around. And I searched my brain for something to say. *This is it, guys, gals, and nonbinary pals, the Gunner has one shot at an opening if he can line this up right—*

"I appreciate the card," Lucas said.

I smiled, surprised. "I'm glad."

He shrugged. "It was corny."

"That's my middle name."

"Can I call you A.C. for short?"

The next words out of my mouth wanted to be a confession about being in love with him. Instead, I closed my mouth.

"I really didn't intend to break up with you," he said quietly.

I let out a long breath. "I know that now. It took a bit of help, but I got there."

"Help?" he asked. I told him about the huddle in my office. He listened, his eyes never leaving my face. I tried not to preen.

"That's a room of people I never would've put together," he said.

"Trust me, I tried to get them all to leave shortly before they started pryin'."

"That doesn't answer the question, though," he said. "How do we do this?"

I snapped a finger gun at him. "Well, I've thought of that too. I think there's some things we—I—can do differently."

He cocked an eyebrow.

"Turns out I had my own expectations about dating that I didn't really think through. You were asking for time, and I want to show you I can do that. I was thinkin' I'd take more time away from the office, a few hours—say from three to five, when you get out of school—and we could do more little things then."

I felt like I was shouting my idea at him. I was excited.

He chewed on it for a few seconds. Eventually he asked, "What would we do?"

"Whatever you wanted," I said. I put my hands in my lap to stop myself from reaching out for him.

He looked at the ice skating rink. "That?"

I watched a chain of children fall on their asses and winced. "Sure, but any other activity would have to be around front, considering how much I'd fall."

He smirked. "My around-front abilities are as good as my around-back abilities, so no hardship there."

That made my pulse jump from sixty to ninety or whatever was fast for pulses.

"We could do the gym."

"Dani might beat both our assess and complain we didn't invite her, but absolutely."

His smirk got even more smirky. "You talk a lot about your ass and beatings."

I snorted. "I think the more important thing is I know what my ass can take."

He laughed.

"Anyway, the point I'm makin' is that we can work out the *how* of bein' together *together*. I want to. I'm mostly just spitballin' ideas."

Lucas raised an eyebrow, and I regretted the phrasing. I pretended to be offended. I put on my best debutante voice and said, "Why, I do declare, you are an indecent fucker, aren't you?"

He smiled, then got very serious. "I appreciate the ideas and am willing to try. I didn't give much thought to the way I'd fit into someone's life in a non-monogamous relationship before I got into one."

"Well, you're in it, so we better work it out. You kept askin' me if I have time to date, and I think we both sort of learned how little time my current routine has in it. But I'm willin' to rearrange it to make it work."

Lucas nodded very seriously.

I figured I should keep talking. "I guess my first reaction to what you were sayin' was break up because I was used to people givin' me ultimatums. It was usually a 'them or me' attitude, but you weren't askin' that."

He looked at me, horrified. "Why would I? I knew what I was signing up for."

I smiled. "Thank you for that. And now I hear that you were askin', genuinely askin', if I could do this. And I can. I have space for you in my life."

"Hmm, that could have been cornier."

"I have space for you in my life, and you already have the space in my heart?"

"Baw," he said, putting his hands to his chest.

"Corny or not, it's true."

His eyebrows went up in surprise. "Your character flaw is that you're fucking charming."

I did preen at that. Then he turned that appraising look on me. I could see he was finally thinking through my words. I watched him answer a bunch of his own questions in his head.

"Would you want to come on a trip with me?" Lucas asked.

"Come again," I said, not fully understanding all his words or the order they were in.

He deflated a little and looked at the cup in his hands. "Too soon?"

"Hold the phone. I'm just not sure what you're talkin' about."

"I met my father's brother this week."

That left me speechless. I stared at him. It took a full minute before I found my voice. "First of all, your father has a brother? Second of all, you met him?"

He nodded. I had no idea how to react.

"What time is it? I'm gonna need another coffee and a whole lot more information. You want another one?"

I bought another two drinks and set his in front of him.

"All right, babe," I said. He looked at me and I realized what I said. I wasn't going to take it back, so I just pressed forward. "Um... maybe you better drive that one by me again."

He spoke with excitement about meeting Chandler Nation. His

face was bright and warm, and as the evening thickened around us, every light source nearby seemed to add to the beauty of him, like a Bedazzler adding rows and rows of jewels. It was truly an amazing story.

"Lucas, that's so fuckin' awesome," I said when he seemed done.

He nodded. "I can't believe it myself."

"I'm really happy for you."

He smiled and shied away. "Chandler and I decided I should go up to Virginia to talk to DeAndrew properly."

"That's great."

"And that's the trip I was thinking you could come with me on."

My brain went completely blank. The idea of a trip, days away with him, days away from my day-to-day was overwhelming enough, but to meet his uncle and his father… The blank space quickly became a monsoon of questions, so I picked the first one I caught and blurted it out. "When?"

"Next weekend," he said, then he listed the specific dates.

"Well, the kids have doctors' appointments," I said, processing out loud the schedule that lived in my head. I closed my eyes. "So does Coach, actually. Paul'll be back in town by Thursday and won't leave again till the week after. Dani—"

"God, Al, if you can't come, just say so. I don't really need a list of why."

I looked at him. He was looking back at the ice skaters.

"Wait, Lucas."

"Just forget it," he said standing. He started walking away. "We should get going to Rose's."

"Christ on a cracker." I sighed and went after him. He was low-key fast. I caught his arm and pulled him to a stop just before we reached the parking lot. I let him go after he stilled, though, knowing I shouldn't touch him without knowing for sure he wanted me to.

"I want to go," I said.

"But?" He crossed his arms over his chest.

"No buts. I was just thinkin' out loud. I want to do this with you. And I'll make sure I'm there, one hundred percent. Just let me know when, like the minute you want to leave. I want it. I want to trade drivers and argue about what music to play and who gets to sleep on what side of the bed in the hotel."

He finally fixed his dark eyes on mine.

"I'm sorry if it sounded like I was makin' excuses. I wasn't, I'm not...I told you I have time for this, but I need you to be willin' to give me time to adjust."

He pursed his lips and took a deep breath. "You get to drive first, we'll listen to a horror novel audiobook—I'll send you some to pick from—and you get your own hotel bed."

I frowned. "Is any of that negotiable?"

He tried not to smile. "You can pick one."

I pretended to think. "Can't we listen to a happy book?"

That got him to laugh. He shoved me a little. "You wouldn't listen to a horror novel for the chance to share a bed with me?"

I laughed as he walked away. I followed him. "I'll have nightmares."

I wanted to ask if this meant we were back together, even though he insisted we hadn't broken up. I didn't ask. It felt too fragile. If something came up and I couldn't make this trip, I knew it would cause irreparable damage to the thin threads holding us together. Well, maybe not fully irreparable. But close. I wasn't a fool. I could feel the weight around this opportunity for him, and for me to tag along, no matter how much he tried to downplay it.

We were in separate trucks, so we parted ways to get to Rose's party. I spent the whole eight-minute drive staring at the taillights of his truck and weighing my obligations. I could swing it. I would have to bribe Teach ten times what I bribed him to stay for the holiday, so he would cover me at work. I would get it done.

❖

Rose Ness lived on the edge of town in a single-story ranch style house. And somehow she had managed to get a solid third of Painted Waters inside. I parked somewhere down the block, near Lucas. I hadn't expected him to wait for me, but he did, leaning against his truck as I pulled in. We went into the house together. I lost track of him physically after that, Ky and Rose calling to him immediately, and Dani waved at me from the corner.

"How'd the talk go?" she asked, handing me Tess so she could help one of the other girls.

"Good enough, I guess. He wants me to take a trip with him."

She gawked at me. "And you call that *good enough*?"

"It's complicated. But can I go?"

"You don't need my permission," she said, handing me the half-eaten cupcake Ursa didn't want.

"I know, but—was this on the floor?"

"No, she put it in Vicky's cup because Vicky didn't want to share her drink, and Ursa wanted it back, so I gave it back to her."

"Ew…anyway…I know I don't need permission, but I do need help makin' it happen."

"Oh, absolutely, I love wingmanning," she said with a grin. I tried to hand her the cupcake back, but she laughed and hauled Ursa toward the bathroom.

"Let's go wash Daddy's hand, Tessy," I said. She demanded to be put down and ran from me as fast as possible.

The party was perfectly festive, but I was only half present. The other half of me was trying to figure out how to make sure I could go on that trip. But since everyone in town who might help me make that happen was in attendance, I figured I could get a head start on my plan. I told Dani the dates and she said she would work out the girls' appointments. Teach was also at the party, wearing the worst Christmas sweater I'd ever seen. He saw me coming from a mile away.

"Two hundred bucks, no questions asked," he said.

"That's pretty steep, and I plan to pay you anyway."

"Fuck, I don't want to work for you anymore," he groaned.

I blinked at him. "How about you work for time and a half, just Friday and Monday is all I'm askin'…and the two hundred for takin' Coach to the doctor."

"Where are you going?" he asked, putting the pieces together.

"I thought you said no questions." He waited, knowing I would answer. "Virginia."

"For what?"

"Long story. Do we have a deal?"

"All that *and* you add my name to all the Christmas presents for your kids, and you have a deal."

"What?"

He threw his hands out. "I have fifteen nieces! And my last job was as a grocery stock boy. I had to open a vein last Christmas just to get all the girls' cards."

"Christ, Teach, are you that broke?"

He rolled his eyes. "I was. But it's different now because we have some sponsor interest. And I have a roommate. Rent in Colorado isn't cheap."

We shook on it. He didn't hesitate to send me a payment request in Cash App. I smiled. With all of that settled, I felt more compelled to engage in the party. I filled in Fin, who had already been filled in by Lucas and Orion. Then I caught up with Rose, who was talking to Ky. Ky, to my surprise, winked at me. At some point, my phone pinged with a list of books from Lucas and a wink face. I scanned it—all horror. I sighed.

Lucas and I crossed paths only one time that night, when we had to pull Lila and Victory off one of Rose's nephews after they all got into a fight over one of Lila's magic tricks. It was really Lila's fight, but Victory had been telling me for weeks that Lila was her best friend and she was pretty ride or die, so I wasn't surprised she was in it. It took a lot to keep from laughing over the whole thing. I could tell Lucas thought it was funny too. And we were a weird, united front in making sure our girls understood why they couldn't fight like that.

At the end of the night, I packed the kids into the van while Dani tried to defrost the windows from the inside and Teach scraped from the outside. Then I walked through the silence to my truck. The spot Lucas's truck had occupied was empty, which was only slightly disappointing. But stuck under my windshield wiper was a note.

I rear-ended you, I read, my own voice disruptive in the darkness. It was signed *Lou*. Surprise and alarm flared in my guts. I marched around the back of the truck to inspect the damage. It didn't feel right being so mad at Lucas, but it also didn't feel right that he hit my truck and didn't even come back in the house to get me. "That fucker! How'd he even manage when he was parked in front—"

Another note was stuck into the bumper. I snatched and read it in the dim light of the moon.

I didn't mean like that. I just wanted to make you think of me. The note was signed with a winky face. I snorted a laugh. My irritation turned quickly into a flush of lust. It did make me think of him, his thick, hard body and thick, hard—

I hurried into my truck, feeling weird about getting a boner standing out in the road. That thought attached itself to the feeling I'd been having all night. In actuality, I didn't feel at all like a weirdo. At that party Dani, my wife, and Lucas, my…whatever Lucas was, were both openly there, and people could see us all. Some of them even knew we all were what we were. Lucas had taped suggestive notes on my truck for anyone to find. I had never been so out in my whole life. I was in two kinds of love, I had beautiful kids, my brothers and sister accepted me, and my relationship with my father had never been better.

"How the fuck did that happen?" I thought about what my dad had said about small changes.

"They really sneak up on ya."

❖

I called Lucas throughout the week, sticking to my own new plan to be more focused on how I parceled out my time. He answered every day. We didn't talk about the trip, though. I wasn't sure how to bring it up, and since it wasn't scheduled for a few days, I figured I could wait and leave the ball in Lucas's court. Not that I didn't dedicate a substantial portion of my time to thinking about it and planning for it. Well, I planned for all the details I did know. I figured out how much money it would take to get from Painted Waters to our destination just outside Richmond.

But when we talked on the phone, the conversation stayed on other things. Some of those things were deep and made me feel like the rift between us was closing. Still, it never went back to the trip or his father. The departure date for the trip was Friday. And the less he talked about it, the more I knew I had to be the one to bring it up. I had resolved to do it during our Thursday phone call.

And, of course, come Thursday evening, I was running late because Xander and Winifred thought it would be no big deal to give Ursa a mud and honey face mask. I watched the clock tick past eight, then eight fifteen, while I tried to de-goo a very squirmy three-year-old. My phone rang and I asked one of the many girls standing in the bathroom to answer it.

"You got Al," I said. "And you're on speaker."

"It's me," Lucas said. My heart leapt.

"Sorry I haven't called yet. Ursa is…or was…covered in honey."

"And mud," Xander said. I looked at her, knowing my expression was stern. She just shrugged and at least looked a little sorry.

"That sounds like a spa day," Lucas said with a laugh.

"It was," Winnie shouted. "We were goin' to paint her nails, but she was too sticky."

"I think next time you should ask your parents to buy spa stuff and not make it on your own," Lucas said.

"Okay," the girls said. I could have kissed him for that.

"Let's dry off the toddler and get ready for bed," I said, lifting her out of the tub.

"Here, Ursa," Ysabel said, holding up a towel. Ursa ran to her sister, and the rest of the girls poured out of the bathroom toward their rooms. I took the phone off speaker and held it to my face.

"Hi—ew," I said, realizing the phone and most of the bathroom was splattered with mud and honey.

"Do you need me to let you go?"

I closed the door most of the way and sat on the toilet lid. I needed to clean the bathroom, but I wanted to talk with him. My kids were pretty good about privacy and I could hear them if they needed. If all else failed, I could call Coach or Teach up to help me.

I relaxed against the toilet tank. "No. As long as the kid is clean, the rest can wait."

"I was wondering what had kept you."

"I like that you called."

"Can't let you do all the work, I guess."

"That's a funny way to say you missed me."

He laughed. "How was your day?" he asked.

"I...good. I, um...well...what time would you want to leave tomorrow?" I asked, not really sure how to just open the conversation.

There was silence on his end for a few seconds. "You're coming?"

I looked around the bathroom, not really seeing it, but hoping for a witness to the strange intensity of the question.

"I said I would."

"You just hadn't said anything since Saturday."

"I get that. It's not like I was avoiding it specifically. I guess I didn't know if you needed space because of all the feelings or whatever. I didn't want to make meeting your father somehow about me."

"Are you coming just to win me over or something?"

I put a slightly soapy, damp hand over my mouth. I considered my words, then I just went for it. "Well, I can't say it didn't occur to me this was a chance to prove myself, but...not so much win you over. I guess even if you'd said on Saturday you didn't want to be with me romantically anymore but still wanted me to go as a friend, I'd be there."

"Why?"

"I care about you," I answered, adjusting from "I love you" at the last second. Not over the phone.

"Do you care enough about me to leave by four?"

"That's a little late," I said.

"Four a.m. is late?"

"A.M.?"

We laughed.

"If you want," I said. "I can figure out four a.m., but McDonald's doesn't open till six."

"McDonald's?"

"What? You don't get two sausage McMuffins with egg and two hash browns at the start of every road trip?"

I could hear him smiling. "No. I stop at the first IHOP I come to when I get hungry."

"Wow, you really treat yourself."

"How about I'll be outside your house by six, we get your McMuffins and see where we end up the next time one of us needs food."

"Deal."

He went quiet. It wasn't awkward anymore, waiting in the stillness for him to think. It was interesting how he could make a silent moment feel productive. Silences around my house usually meant the completion of conversations, but for him, silence meant the continuation of the conversation.

"Al."

"Babe," I said. "Uh…Lou."

"How…Why did you…Sometimes it sounds like Coach wasn't a very good parent. And it's obvious Wynona was a bitch. But how is it that Coach is still in your life? How do you look past the bad that happened?"

"Oh, um, I've never thought about it." That question was straight out of left field to me. I tuned into the fact that I was still in my bathroom. "Can you give me a second? I need to A, think, and B, check on the girls."

"Sure."

"Okay. Don't hang up."

The girls were settling into their respective nighttime routines. They usually read to each other, except Xander, who would walk around the room pretending to guard her sisters like a knight. They were all fine. I picked up Tess from where she was sleeping in her sister's lap and deposited her in bed before I went down to my own room. I closed the door and could hear the gentle murmur of my oldest reading on the baby monitor. I had really never thought about why Coach was still in my life while Wynona was someone I wanted nothing to do with.

"Hey, I'm back," I said into the phone.

"Hey."

"Well, I've not given it much thought, so here it is straight out of my brain. Wynona left the year I turned eighteen, so I only lived a year with Coach alone before I went to school. It was just me and Teach at that point. But Wynona was pretty checked out even before then. She would take these long work trips. They started about a year after I started high school. And she would just up and leave for weeks at a time. But I guess the real difference was that Coach at least put in some effort to be more, even if he was rude or uncomfortable or whatever."

"Is that all it takes?"

"For me, I guess that was all. I can't say much about others. It was like no matter how much he disliked some of the things I did or how much racist, homophobic shit he said, he would stop if I told him to. And it was never about me, which I guess matters. It's weird lookin' back on it. Wynona would say she was worried about how I would turn out, but she stopped comin' to my games or, like, participatin' in my life. Coach never missed one."

"Wasn't he the coach?"

"Sure, but he also never missed a choir concert."

"You were in the choir?"

"Yup, for one year."

"Let me hear you sing."

"I only did one year for a reason. Anyway, the point is, he was there and he was tryin'. He went to every pageant Bets was in, even though he thought she should quit. He learned all the rules for 4-H and Junior City Council when she wanted to do that instead. He didn't coach Gage, but he went to every baseball game, and you wouldn't know it from lookin' at him, but Gage did four plays in high school and Coach was at all of 'em."

"And Teach?"

"It was harder to figure out how Coach supported Teach. When we were cleanin' what was left of the old house after the fire, I found a box of books. Mixed in were a few about skateboarding. They were dog-eared. And whenever Wynona used to demand Teach get a haircut,

Coach would take Teach to the skate park. When they got back, he'd tell Wy he had trouble startin' the truck, so they never made it to the barber. The homophobia and the racism and such were all what he was taught he should be. But as soon as we kids started challenging him, he started to be different. It was like moving a glacier, but what he said or did was with our best interests in mind. When I play his highlight and failure reels against Wy's, it becomes clear why we stuck with him and not her.

"She used to say *she* had our best interests in mind, but she only ever tried to take things away from us and demand we change. She never *gave* anythin'. When I started hangin' out with Fin, she pretty much washed her hands of me 'cause she said not to. Betsy was about fourteen when she quit pageants because a judge wrote on her score card that she needed to lose weight. Wy's reaction was to get Betsy a subscription to a diet program—"

"The fucking audacity."

"Right! Worst of all, Wy had never been to one of Betsy's pageants. Well, that's not true. She was at the first and Bets took fifth of five. But Wy wouldn't let Betsy quit 'em either. Coach let her quit after she wouldn't get out of the car from cryin'." I paused to try and think about my childhood as quickly as I could. Every memory I had that mattered had Coach in it.

"I think it's hard to think about your parents as people and examine how they might treat others. It's hard to think as a kid, full stop. I think for kids it's as simple as this person doesn't make *me* feel like garbage and that person does, even if that first person isn't as good to the rest of the world as he should've been. He wasn't always good to me, but he got better and he tried."

"I get that."

"Lou. I think it's okay to feel exactly how you feel about your parents, all three of them. There's no *supposed to* and you don't have to treat them the way you think a generic parent should be treated."

Lucas didn't say anything for a minute. Then he sighed. "I guess I'm just nervous."

"That makes perfect sense."

"I…thanks for coming with me."

"Always. But I think we need to talk about those conditions."

"Which?"

"The audiobooks you sent are all thirty hours long!" I practically screeched.

"But they're all *a good* thirty hours," he insisted.
I groaned. "Can't it be a nicer, shorter book?"
"Like what?"
"I hear *Hop on Pop* has a decent audiobook."
That made him cackle.

CHAPTER NINETEEN

Lucas

I could barely sit in the truck. DeAndrew Nation. I couldn't stop seeing his letter in my head. It felt weird, unfair maybe. Was I taking advantage of him? He had turned down a visit with me when I was a kid, and now, I was on my way to see him. Could he have turned down this visit if he wanted? Did he have the ability to make the choice to see me? Memory loss was complicated. I had seen plenty of people taken advantage of because they couldn't remember certain details. Did Chandler tell him it was me? Would DeAndrew care? Honestly, if I hadn't been strapped into the truck, I probably would have thrown the door open and bailed.

Every time we stopped driving, I updated Chandler. He was already in Richmond doing an interview with the Richmond Flying Squirrels, a minor league baseball team. Some sort of queer scandal broke, and he was on the case. He had already spoken to the home DeAndrew was staying in and given them mine and Al's information. I had a thousand questions, but I hadn't asked Chandler his thoughts on any of them.

The rest of my nerves came from Al's presence. He kept the drive light and fun, despite my hardly talking to him. He drove like a grandpa, which I had pretty much expected. And he was in a pretty good mood after I agreed to let him skip out on the horror novel in favor of his radio app. The longer he drove, the more my thoughts turned from DeAndrew to him, which made me feel a whole different kind of bad.

He looked good behind the wheel of my truck. I didn't think I was one of those guys. I wasn't possessive about my things. He had one of my shirts, after all, and that was even before sleeping with me. Then again, I really did like him in that shirt. I wished more than once I'd saved the photo he'd sent. But him driving somehow topped that. It was comforting and sexy and... I needed to think more G-rated.

He had been the only one to drive so far, getting us out of Georgia into South Carolina before I even realized it. I spent a lot of that time watching him drive, trying to focus. I considered his hands, the animated way he spoke. I wanted to hold them again. I wanted to be touched by him in some way. I knew he was waiting on me, but he respected this trip enough to not make it about us. And part of me felt like a hypocrite because this wasn't a date, and we weren't the focus of our time and I had been up Al's ass for emergencies and interruptions, but here I was doing it back. Why was it so hard? By the time we reached the North Carolina border, I was flat out exhausted from thinking.

"Well, I'd agree on killing Kirk, but I think I'd marry Captain Sisko," he said. He carried on with the conversation despite my constant spacing out.

"Over Picard?" I asked half-heartedly.

"Yeah, Picard would be a boring husband." Al laughed.

"At least he'd be around. Sisko abandoned everyone to be a light god."

Al just nodded. "Fair enough."

"All right, fine, um...Blanche, Rose, Dorothy?" I offered, saying the first trio I could think of.

"I'd fuck Blanche," he said.

I gawked at him. "No hesitation at all."

"No, I believe her reputation speaks for itself."

The ding of the gas light on the truck derailed any follow-up questions.

"There's a stop up there," he said, pointing into the cloudy, gray forest surrounding the highway.

"Would you want to trade? I can drive."

He flashed his beautiful smile. "I like driving, so if you want."

"Al."

"Yeah," he asked, glancing at me, his brown eyes almost like a forest in the cool morning. It was still barely ten a.m. There hadn't been much traffic, even through Atlanta. It felt like we were alone. His phone hadn't even rung.

"Do you think this is a good idea?" I asked.

He glanced at me again, longer, as if looking for a sign or hint on my face.

"Which part?"

"Meeting him?"

He didn't answer until he pulled off the highway onto a short exit into a gas station. "Why wouldn't it be?"

"Chandler said DeAndrew is disabled and has short-term memory loss."

His eyebrows raised. "That don't explain why it's a bad idea."

"Maybe I'm just taking advantage of that. Chandler says he won't remember me, and maybe that's safer because…well, when he *did* know who I was, he didn't want anything to do with me."

Al turned off the truck but didn't get out. So I didn't either. He turned in the seat to look at me and crossed his arms. I mirrored him just for something to do.

"Well, babe—"

Fuck, I loved it when he called me that. I shook away the thought.

"I won't yank your chain by pretending to know what your father might want or not. But here's how I figure it. You trust Chandler, right?"

"I do."

He absently rubbed his head with his hand, messing up the beanie he was wearing. The hair underneath was flat but bright, a shock of blond, backdropped by the dense yet vacant mountain landscape.

"Me too. Now, if you thought he was aimin' to get someone hurt, then we might reconsider. It's been twenty years since that letter—"

"Like fifteen."

"And the whole equation is different, so the sum must be too."

"Orion was right about you."

He squinted. "What'd he say?"

"He said your accent gets thicker when you're giving advice."

"How's this for advice, you both can fuck off. Now, do you want anythin' from inside there?" He smiled and tossed a thumb over his shoulder to the gas station.

I chuckled as he started to get out of the truck. "Naw, I'm gonna get gas and call Ky."

He winked at me and left. I did call Ky and she said pretty much what Al had, even going so far as to also use a math reference. Al came back to the truck with even more snacks. I didn't mind since he was willing to share. I drove the rest of the way to the hotel in Richmond. We checked in since we weren't going to meet Chandler until tomorrow for breakfast.

Al's and Ky's words had helped a little. It made sense to trust

Chandler's intentions. I wasn't feeling one hundred percent about things, though. Being in the city felt like a lot. I had never been to Virginia despite having lived in at least ten states and visited three times that. Al was his usual pillar of responsibility. He collected the keys from the concierge and even asked about places to eat dinner. Then he led the way to the room and let us in.

"Ah...two beds...but the single hotel room bed trope is my favorite," he joked.

I tried to laugh, but it was hard to get around my worry. *Was I supposed to get just one bed? I could have, but it's not like I know what we are. I want to sleep with him, sure...Oh shit, this is our first overnight, isn't it?* I placed my bag on a bed and paced to the window.

"This is a nice room, mini-fridge and microwave, classy. Well, it's seven, so we could get dinner," Al said from somewhere behind me.

"Yeah?"

"Or we could go find some tourist trap."

"Do people still do that?" I asked, not really giving a fuck.

"I guess. Brochure says there's...well, a lot of plantations—"

"What?" I turned to look at him. He just waved the booklet. "How about *not* that?"

"This hotel has a gym," he said.

That annoyed me enough to say something. "Why do you keep suggesting things?"

He didn't flinch under my tone. He even smirked. "You said once your nerves give you energy, I'm just offerin' things to do with that energy."

"Why?"

"Why what?"

"Why bother? Why not just let me be nervous?"

He put out his hands. "If that's what you want to do. I was only makin' suggestions."

I glared at him. So polite, with his face and his tight jeans, and his healthy, fatherly relationships.

"If I'm annoying you, you can go do any of those things by yourself," I said.

"Who's annoyed?" He crossed his arms and grinned.

I mocked him a little, making a face and a less than polite sound. It only made him smile, though.

"I have seven daughters. If I couldn't handle a little poutin', they would've burnt my toast years ago."

"I'm not pouting, fuck off."

"I'd rather fuck on," he said, flopping onto his bed with a wink.

Fuck him. Though that was kind of charming, and I didn't want to admit that it was also helping. "You flirt like a grandpa."

"What's it say about you that it works?"

I had to admit, that was a good one. The only thing I could think to do was flip him off, which just sent him into a fit of laughter. His deep belly laughing made me smile. He stood and came closer. He didn't stop at a casual safe distance but came all the way into my space instead. It took me by surprise. I didn't step back, I just let him come. He put a big hand on each shoulder. It was like being submerged, to have him so close. I met his eyes.

"You're goin' to be okay, no matter what happens. You've gained a lot from this trip already, so even if it doesn't go any further, you've done great."

"Don't be so nice," I grumbled.

He looked around the room, his hands slipping away. "We could always trash the place like an eighties rock band."

"Says the guy in a polo," I teased.

He looked at his shirt, some fashionable collared sweater thing. "Is this a polo?"

I chuckled. He looked at me, his face expressing something I couldn't place. Then to my absolute disappointment, he stepped back and put at least half the room between us. *Come on, guy, really. You get in my space and then nothing? All this time and all I get is a card?*

My brain was doing a fairly decent job of turning that card into a cousin of the letter my father had sent. Or worse, its twin. I stared at Al, who was looking back at the brochures he had been handed by the hotel staff. He had apologized, had said he wanted to try. But it felt too distant. Maybe it wasn't love. Maybe the thing he couldn't say in a card was *goodbye* or *we're just friends*. The longer I thought about it, the more DeAndrew's letter tainted Al's card. It was so hard to trust Al's intention. The only difference was that Al was here and DeAndrew never had been. I had to hold on to that. Still though, I was doing a really good job of hurting my own feelings.

Shit. That thought went a long way to shift my mood from anxious to plain old sad. I sat on the bed and did my best to answer Al's questions about dinner. He ordered for us and had it delivered. We just sat on our separate beds watching TV. Al did try to make conversation, I'll give him that. I just ate and fell asleep to the sound of *Catfish* on MTV.

❖

It was even harder the next morning. The restaurant we met Chandler at was some Virginia chain around the block from the assisted living complex. We were going to leave the truck in the parking lot behind the restaurant, then ride over with Chandler.

Al chatted, while I don't think I said more than five words. He was nice enough to Chandler, and they seemed to get along, so I let them carry the conversation. Not that I didn't notice Chandler staring at me. He watched me all through the meal, but I didn't look at him. Finally, we were in the car on the way to the facility.

Pulling up to it was like driving into a memory. It reminded me vaguely of the boys' correctional facility I'd worked at. It had looked more like a tiny college than a prison, with separate dorms and a schoolhouse. The walls around it were high chain-link topped with razor wire, while the walls around Walnut Meadows Assisted Living Campus were tall semi-ornamental iron. Chandler had to show paperwork at the gate, then we drove through the assorted rows of townhouse-style apartments to the parking lot at the back. It was the same off-white as the correctional facility, but this place had more trees and was neatly landscaped. There were also a surprising number of people walking around, nurses and patients and families.

"This place is always nicest around the holidays," Chandler said quietly, as if he was trying to talk to just me.

"I forgot it was the holidays," I said, noticing the cheery wreaths and fake candles in each window.

"This place seems nice," Al said from the back seat.

Chandler pulled into a spot and parked. "Al, would you mind waiting for us outside? I want to talk to Lou."

"No problem," Al said, exiting.

I looked at Chandler. He stared at me from under yet another ball cap. *I don't know what it is with some men and ball caps.* Al was a ball-cap guy too, even though he hadn't brought one on the trip.

"Ya good?" he asked.

"Good enough."

"Try again," Chandler said.

"Look, I'm all right. My anxiety isn't about being here, at least not all the way."

"Is it maybe Kronk out there?"

I looked at Al and thought of Kronk from the cartoon, except with a Georgia accent. It was kind of accurate. I smiled, then I noticed Chandler watching me smile, and I forced a frown.

"Want to talk about it?"

"No, he's not why I'm here."

"Perhaps, but *you're* why *he's* here. So, you can't really separate the two now."

I stared at him. "What does that even mean?"

"Life will always give us something to go through, but sometimes it's kind and will give us some people to go through it with. You seem like you can handle your own shit most of the time. And even if someone can't fix things, sometimes it helps just to say it all out loud."

"Okay." I heard him. And I recognized it as something I maybe even needed to hear. I just didn't have the bandwidth to think about that right then. Chandler's eyes narrowed but he didn't say anything. He just nodded and started out of the car.

I followed. Al was standing on the sidewalk looking at the land as if he was appraising it. And maybe he was. We followed Chandler to a house in the center of a row near the front of the campus. Chandler took one last look at Al and me, then knocked. A woman with a bright face and wavy black hair opened the door.

"Mr. Nation," she said.

"I've told you a million times, Carmen—"

She put her hands up and laughed. "Fine, Chandler, sir. Come on in. I've been reminding D all morning of your visit."

He introduced her to me and Al, and she shook our hands politely. She let Chandler lead the way. The entry led down a long hall that shared a wall with the next townhouse. It stretched all the way to the back door, and entryways opened along the right side only. I followed my uncle into a neat living room. A man hunched over a table turned at the sound of our walking up.

"Chandler," DeAndrew said, putting down a puzzle piece.

In my head, I had the image of the thin, tall college graduate student standing in the bright sun of campus where my mother had taken his photo. Then there were flashes of the man I had known, holding my hand as we went to McDonald's, pushing a swing, his eyes in the rearview mirror as he drove. Standing there, he looked like himself, but also exactly like a stranger with a shaved head and a healthy belly. He sidestepped a card table to hug Chandler.

"Hey, D." Chandler laughed, hugging back.

"You're letting your beard grow out?" DeAndrew asked.

Chandler nodded and answered in a voice that suggested he had answered that question a thousand times. When his brother let him go, both turned and looked at me. I stepped back on instinct, but Al and the nurse were behind me, so I had nowhere to go.

"D, this is Lucas and Al, friends of mine."

"Morning," he said. Then he looked at the nurse. "And you are?"

"Carmen, DeAndrew. I'm your helper," she said in a practiced tone. "Don't worry, I won't mess up your visit. I have stuff to do."

And with that, she was down the hall.

"Lucas and Al, please come in. What brings y'all here? I didn't expect visitors." DeAndrew pointed out three spots in the room for us to sit. I sat across from him in an armchair.

"Well, I wanted you to get the chance to meet Lucas," Chandler said.

"Oh?" DeAndrew said, looking straight at me.

God, what the fuck am I supposed to say?

"Do you remember Lucas Laverty?"

"Sure, that's the name of Jojo and Silvy's boy," he said cheerfully. "I haven't heard from them in a minute."

I sucked in a breath as quietly as I could. I hadn't told my parents about DeAndrew's condition. I don't know why. Maybe because they had been so supportive of this trip. Or maybe it was because there was a small amount of hope for their friend. Maybe I hadn't believed it until just now.

"Right, that's who *this* Lucas is," Chandler said. "This is that same Lucas."

DeAndrew stared, his eyes surprised and welcoming. "Wow, you're a whole man."

To my surprise, I snorted a laugh. "Yes, sir."

He stood and leaned forward, offering me his hand. "Wow."

"I didn't mean to just show up," I said, taking his hand.

"No, no, I just can't believe," he said. His eyes went narrow and a little dark. "Has it been that long?"

"It was long overdue," Chandler said.

We stared at each other for a little while. I watched him take in who I was. I knew he would likely remember all that had happened before the accident. There were at least twenty years of my life within his field of memory.

"I bet you have some questions," he said finally.

I sure as fucking hell thought I did. But sitting across from him, my mind was an absolute blank. I said the first thing I could think of. "What do you want for Father's Day?"

It felt like ice breaking when DeAndrew tossed his head back and laughed.

CHAPTER TWENTY

Alexander

The meeting between Lucas and his father went surprisingly well. Chandler didn't seem like an uptight person, just a careful one, but even he relaxed. DeAndrew Nation ended up asking Lucas more questions than I think Lucas was ready to answer. He asked me a few too, but I told him simply that I was there to support Lucas. I knew DeAndrew himself was gay, but that wasn't reason enough to out his son to him.

I listened to them share memories about the college they both had attended. DeAndrew was fairly interested in Lucas's career, asking about his degree. When DeAndrew told us he'd done the paintings on the walls, the conversation turned to those. Forty minutes or so passed in easy company. Then there was a natural dip in the conversation. Lucas looked more uncomfortable in that small silence than he had since we had arrived.

DeAndrew broke the quiet, his voice wistful. "It's so interesting. I haven't been back to Albany since 2010 maybe. Guess not much would change in five years."

"It's been eleven," Chandler said gently.

"Anyway, thanks for coming and listening to an old man relive his glory days," DeAndrew said to Lucas.

"I'm happy to listen," Lucas said with a grin.

DeAndrew nodded. He stared at Lucas and a small crease formed on his forehead. "I can't…I'm sorry, what was your name again?"

A feeling descended in the room like dropping from the top of a Tower of Doom ride. Lucas looked at his uncle. I watched him. On his face was a look that would have been familiar to any parent, I think. It was that look of suspense, of panicked waiting. It was the look a parent had in that moment after their kid falls, hitting the ground with undeterminable force, waiting as the kid decides what their reaction is. It was a lofty, weightless sense of dread.

"Lucas," he answered slowly.

"Lucas," DeAndrew said.

"Your son?" Lucas added.

A flash of realization went off behind DeAndrew's eyes. "That's right, come up from Georgia."

Lucas smiled, only a little relieved. "Right."

"Wow, you look just like Jojo."

"Thank you."

DeAndrew looked hard at him. "Did I ask you to come?"

Lucas's smile tightened. "N-no."

I got the sense of something on the brink of happening. It was like smelling the rain.

DeAndrew squinted at him. "It's not like you're here for child support or something, so is there a reason you came?"

Lucas looked for a moment like someone had slapped him. Then he clenched his jaw and turned on his nurse's face. He looked suddenly like he was talking to *my* dad instead of his own.

"D," Chandler said.

"It's okay, Chandler. I don't mind the question." Lucas put up a hand to show his uncle that nothing was amiss, then he turned back to DeAndrew. "Nothing like that. I just wanted to know you. I live near Valdosta."

DeAndrew's expression shifted back to something more like when we first came in. "Valdosta, now that's country. You live near there? Where?"

"Painted Waters," Lucas said.

And just like that, they were back on track, not that it was the same train. Lucas never lost the professionally polite look he had adopted after his father's memory started to slip the first time. In the two and a half hours we stayed, he had to remind DeAndrew of his name and who he was one more time. But he handled it with more grace than I probably could have.

If Chandler caught on to Lucas's mood shift, he didn't give any sign. I felt for Lucas, though. I could see the directionless sorrow behind his eyes. I had been staring at his handsome, warm face for long enough to know his practiced tone and facial expressions were holding back a floodgate of some negative feelings. Sadness, maybe. Rage? Both?

The meeting ended amiably, and we loaded back into Chandler's car. They talked pleasantly, but Chandler seemed to know enough to not ask what Lucas thought about the reunion. I kept quiet and listened to the false lightness in Lucas's tone. Chandler offered to take us to dinner. It was only one in the afternoon, but Lucas flat out lied and said we'd planned some sightseeing. I don't think I'd ever heard him lie before, at least not recognizably. We did settle on a small, fast lunch and made plans for a brunch or lunch the next day before Lucas and I left for home. After the meal, we changed cars and drove to the hotel in silence.

I followed Lucas into the room. He said he was going to shower, then he quickly grabbed some stuff out of his suitcase and shut himself in the bathroom. I watched him, surprised. I certainly wasn't going to follow him. I turned in a circle, then sat on the bed and pulled off my shoes. My phone beeped. It was a message from Coach.

There's news...call when you can...

That sounded ominous, but if it was anything really bad, he would have called. I responded with an emoji. I tossed the phone somewhere. A guilt settled. There was a time where I wouldn't have responded at all to that text. Not like Coach texted often. But after he got sick, I started to appreciate those cryptic messages. And after meeting DeAndrew, whose fatherhood was almost totally lost, I wanted to call my dad, to speak for hours with each of my kids. I didn't. My guilt wouldn't change how much time I still logically had with them. I could appreciate it more, though. Especially after these last few months, I knew I was a good father and a good son. I caught myself looking toward the bathroom wondering what Lucas was thinking about.

I didn't expect him to spend forty minutes in there. It was long enough that I got sucked into a local news story about a neighborhood bear. I shut off the news and shifted around to look at him when I heard the door to the bathroom finally open. He dumped himself on his bed and sighed. I crossed the room and twisted the cap off one of the waters we had brought in from the truck. I offered it to him. He shook his head. I chugged it and watched him. He didn't move.

"How are you feelin'?" I asked.

He glared at me.

"Do you want to talk about it?"

"No."

"Do you want space to reflect?"

He sat up. "What?"

I twisted the cap back on the water. "I'm just seein' what you might need. There's probably a lot to process."

"So, what would you do if I said yes?" he asked. "Would you leave?"

That was a surprising question. "If you wanted me to."

"You want me to tell you to leave?"

"No."

"So, you want to stay?"

"Yes?"

The progression of his questions was starting to get confusing. *All right, folks, it's showtime for our MVP. If his recent coaching is going to account for anything, it's going to be right now. The question was just a question. Keep your eye on the ball.* Even though my brain was starting to shout that this was a trap, I took a breath and tried to focus. I had to try to give him the benefit of the doubt in this.

"So, you'd just, what, stand there while I *reflected* or whatever?"

"I could lie down and watch TV," I said, trying to sound casual.

He rolled his eyes.

"Lucas, I have to admit I'm not sure what you're wantin' to know."

He stood and looked at me. He was standing like a cowboy in a western who had resolved to let himself be shot. *Does he think I'm gonna hurt him?*

"Al, why did you come here?"

"I…to support you."

"Why?"

"Why what?"

"Did you come because you care about me or because you thought I'd need someone?"

My first response to that was a long "uh" that made me feel a little stupid. Finally, my brain concluded, "Both."

"How can it be both?"

"How can it *not* be both?" I asked, feeling steadily more confused.

He put his hand on his hips like an old man who was fed up. "So, you're here because you pity me?"

If that had been a snake it would've bit ya. "Who said anythin' about pity?"

"You just did. You said you thought I needed someone."

"Yeah, but that's not because I pity you."

"What is it if not pity?"

"It's because I care about you. And this is a hard situation. Anyone would need someone if they were doin' what you're doin'."

That seemed to slow him down. He froze for a moment, and I thought maybe I was finally making sense to the guy, but his eyes narrowed.

"You care about me?" His tone was as hard as stone.

"Yes?"

"What does that mean?"

"What?"

He turned in a frustrated circle. "Al, what do you mean you care about me? I can't tell."

"You can't tell?" That comment sent off a flare in my brain. How could he not tell? I had to force my mouth closed. If I could just think about what he might mean.

"No, Al. I get that you're a good guy."

"Lucas," I said as a second flare let me know that "You're a good guy" was a problematic sentence too.

"And I know you'd do anything anyone asked of you. But I just don't get how you caring about me is different from you caring about anyone else—"

"It's different because I don't fuckin' love everyone else. I love *you*." It was out of my mouth so fast both Lucas and I were stunned silent. My own heart clenched, irritated at myself. "Shit, Lucas, I'm sorry."

"For?"

I let my arms fall to my sides. I hadn't even noticed I'd crossed them. I looked at the floor. "I been feelin' that way for a while, but I shouldn't've said it like that. I'm not angry. I just have no idea what you're tryin' to figure out."

"Do you mean it?"

"'Course I mean it. I wouldn't say it if I didn't mean it, even if I didn't mean to say it like that."

"You love me?"

"Yes."

"Are you *in* love with me?" he asked.

"Yes."

He sat on the bed completely defeated. "Fuck, I'm sorry, Al."

I sat on my bed across from his. There was a small aisle between us. He was on the foot of his bed, so our bodies formed sort of a right angle. He was within arm's reach but I didn't reach out. I didn't know if he wanted it, and it seemed like a weird time to ask.

"What for?"

He looked at me. "I don't know, everything. Dragging you up here, wasting your time."

"First of all, no time I get with you is a waste of time. Second of all, do you feel like you wasted your time?"

"If that wasn't a waste of time, I don't know what it was."

That was another shocker. "I thought it went well."

"Went well? Went well for what?"

"What do you mean?"

He stood again and paced a few steps away. "I mean…What was the point? Nothing's different."

"Did you think somethin' would be?"

He flapped his arms helplessly. "Shouldn't it be? God damn it, I'm such a fucking fool. I should've known better."

He blinked a few times, looking over my head at a photograph of the Virginia mountains on the wall behind me. He stared at it like the answers he was looking for would come rolling out of there like the fog.

"It's not like I expected him to change his mind about wanting to be in my life, but there isn't anything left for that anyway."

"Anything left? You mean because of his memory loss?"

"Yeah."

"But he can't help that," I said as gently as I could.

That made him laugh. "I know, I know he can't, which makes me an even bigger asshole. Al, I can't help thinking that he *more* than didn't want me. For years he chose to stay out of my life, and I didn't get a say in it. I wanted him around and he chose not to be. Now I still don't get a choice, but neither does he."

He had practically shouted, his eyes still on the void somewhat behind me.

"Oh, I think I get it," I said. He looked at me. I took a breath and stood too. "Lucas, it's fair to feel cheated out of a relationship."

"No, it's not. Like you said, he can't help it."

"All right," I said, getting my water and handing it to him. "It's fair, then, to feel cheated out of the *chance* to have a relationship with him."

"What?" He drank without seeming to know he was doing it.

I looked out the window for a minute. "I think about that with Wynona sometimes. I think about how I don't want a relationship with her, sure, but even if I wanted one—hell, even if *she* wanted one, there won't ever be a chance for it. The circumstances are all wrong, and there's no changin' that sometimes."

"Yeah, is there a name for that? I feel like he'll never get to be the father I wanted—if I wanted one—and *now* he can't be even if *he* wanted. He might not be able to be a grandfather, either. I didn't tell him about Lila, and he probably didn't even know to ask. Lila is four. The accident was a year before her. Would it have been cruel to him if I had said anything about her and he had wanted to know? And when he forgot? Fuck, how can so much be gone?"

"I think it's just how grief works, babe."

"Can you grieve what isn't dead?" he asked. Then he laughed and answered his own question. "Sure you can. I've seen people do it all the time. I've seen cancer patients grieve birthdays they'd miss, and I've seen grandkids' faces fall when their grandparents start calling them by their father's or mother's names. Sure, I've seen it, but at least they had time before the illness."

"Good point."

"Fuck, Al. I don't know what to do with that."

"I guess...*don't* pay it forward," I said.

"The fuck did you just say to me?" His expression was more cute confusion than anything else, and I had to work really hard to not smile at him.

"I think sometimes the only way you can process what you missed out on in life is to make sure someone else doesn't miss out on the same thing. You're a good father to Lila, and she won't ever have to wonder if her parents love her, if they'd choose her. Maybe focus on that."

He groaned and flopped backward onto his bed, closed water bottle still in hand. "Fuck."

I didn't say anything. I just watched him.

"I knew I had daddy issues, but this seems a bit cliché," he said. I laughed despite myself. He didn't look over. "I feel so fucking unwanted."

"It's a fair enough feelin'. You've been waitin' on this guy for years and today learned that it'll never be. But that's not a reflection on you as a person."

"No?"

"No way. The reality is a lot of people want you in their lives."

"I know, but it feels different coming from him. Just like it feels different coming from Ky compared to coming from you."

"That makes sense."

"How? Shouldn't love be love or some shit? It shouldn't matter, should it? Like, the differences are so fucking arbitrary between father and mother. I have two parents. Isn't that how many you're supposed to have? What's it matter that both are mothers?"

I thought about that. I could see how the lines blurred with parents or lovers, and things like gender shouldn't make a difference. Changing a diaper was changing a diaper. And yet distinctions exist, and those are hard to unlearn sometimes. There was only one way I knew to talk about it.

"My grandmother was known for her famous apple crumble when her and my grandfather lived up north. Then they moved down to Georgia about a year after they were married. And Georgia being Georgia, anytime Gran would make that crumble, people would call it a cobbler. She would get so mad. She'd correct everyone, shouting, 'You wouldn't call a limo a hearse, but your casket would fit either way.' One day she even bounced a wood spoon off my head when I said it was a delicious cobbler. I asked her what the difference was once, and she said she didn't know but they had different names for a reason."

There was a heartbeat of silence before Lucas sat up and blinked at me in general surprise. "I think that's the most country fucking thing I've ever heard."

That sent us both off, rolling on our respective beds with laughter. "God, I wish I were jokin'."

Lucas practically giggled. The sound of him laughing was nice. His quietness in some ways was the most surprising thing about him. His laughing was mostly short, wheezing breaths. It sounded like a cartoon cat. I loved it. Unfortunately, after a few seconds, it dissolved into quiet crying.

"Lucas?"

He waved me off before I could do anything and sat up, pulling his shirt up to wipe his face. "Yeah, Chandler might've said something similar to me a few days ago. I guess that's a lesson I really need to learn. I was thinking maybe I *do* want to go sightseeing."

"Really?"

He shrugged. "Why not? I don't know what there is to see here."

I would have gone anywhere in that moment to keep him smiling. "I'm down. You sure?"

He nodded and stood too. We stared at each other for an instant, then I turned to start collecting our stuff. He grabbed my arm, stopping me from turning away. There was instant intensity in his expression, heat in his touch.

"Al," he said.

He had a shadow of a beard growing in. I could see the slight dent where his lip used to be pierced. My brain relived every experience I had ever had with those lips all at once. I tried to answer, but I couldn't get my own mouth to work. I forced myself to look him in the eyes.

"I'm in love with you too."

Well, friends and family, we've had a pause in game play, a power outage at the stadium...

"What?" I asked. Since my whole brain was dedicated to rebooting, I wasn't really sure what my face was doing. I might have been smiling or drooling. *Did he really say what I think he said?*

A soft grin creased his face and turned up the intensity of the moment. "I broke you, didn't I?"

"Naw...just had to let that one sink in."

His grip on my arm was strong and bruising, but I was elated. Slowly my mind powered up and started sending rapid-fire signals to the rest of my body. I became aware of his foot against mine, the warmth of his thigh on the outer edge of my hip, his big hand on my arm, his breath. He was close and present and in love with me.

That last awareness shook something loose, and I practically fell into him, my mouth on his. *You can thank Heart Co. for the fireworks display, friends, a great way to celebrate. And remember: Steady or racing, Heart Co. is on the beat.* My heart was like machine gun fire against my ribs. His mouth was so welcoming, open and soft and responsive. It had been so long that I felt an urgency to get as much of him as I could, which was automatically a cue for me to pull back a little.

I tried to take a step back, but he came with me, stepping into my space while also pulling me hard to him. Welp, that signal was obvious enough. My hands quickly found their way to my favorite places, like the hard edge of his jaw and the rise and fall of muscle down his arms. And he reciprocated it all, lips and tongue against mine. He slid one hand up my back, leaving a warm, tingling path. The other was on my hip, half under my shirt. His skin on mine under my clothes was apparently my trigger for an instant boner.

"Fuck," I gasped.

"Tickles?" he asked in a way that let me know he wasn't stopping even if it did. His mouth, free now, traveled down my cheek, my neck. He worked both hands under my shirt.

"I…no, but if you keep that up, we aren't going anywhere."

He snickered. "Oh, I can keep it up."

I hummed, excited. Then it hit me. *Holy hell.* We were in a hotel room together. Out of state. I didn't even know where my phone was. I told Dani I would call her when we were done. But there was no time limit to that. We could do anything we wanted. We could fuck on a bed! That was novel still since we didn't even make it to the bed last time.

I must have gone still because Lucas pulled back and looked at me. "Right, I had the same thought. No interruptions."

"We should put the little Do Not Disturb sign out," I mumbled, my mind still racing through options.

"What? Are you expecting room service?"

"Naw, but I did promise a maid a good time."

"I think I've seen that one. Look, I'm game for whatever, but I didn't pack protection." He laughed. "I didn't think we'd get to this point."

I almost collapsed with laughter.

"What?" he asked, coolly watching me giggle.

"I'm just startin' to think I'm easy."

He grinned and maybe even looked relieved. "You packed stuff?"

"Packed and packin'," I said with a wink. I crossed the room and pulled generally the same sort of supplies I had brought on the date. The lube was better and in a bottle, and there were a few more condoms. I remembered packing a whole lot of hope into that bag.

"You're like an Eagle Scout for sex."

I tossed the stuff on the bed and went back to him. How could I make the most of the situation? We wouldn't get time like this again for a while, and even then, we wouldn't get space like this for an even longer while. Which meant I had to figure out the position that would maximize my ability to see and touch and taste whatever I wanted. My brain briefly wondered if there was a way to watch him and fuck him at the same time. Not that I knew he wanted to be on the receiving end of that invitation.

"Dude," he said, nudging me. "What are you thinking about?"

"Voyeurism," I answered quickly. "Never mind that, I want to… would you want to switch this round?"

He laughed like it was no big deal. His expression was eager enough. I nodded and kissed him. I stepped forward until he had no more room and had to sit on the edge of the bed. I only halfway followed, my mouth unwilling to give his up. But I knew it would have to, to get him naked. I stood to my full height and made an effort to pull his shirt over his head, but he was in the way, trying to get at my pants.

"Wait," I said.

"You wait." He tried to shove my hands out of his way, but I won by pulling his shirt over his head from the back. Not a particularly sexy moment, but I could tell we were beyond that. There had been jokes when we first got shirtless together, touched each other, even when we fucked, but now there was just the drive to be together.

He was back at my pants as soon as I got rid of his shirt. I pulled off my own shirt as he finished what he was trying to do. He slowed down once he realized I was staying out of his way. His face was a perfect blend of embarrassment because I was watching him and focus because he knew what he wanted.

"Lucas," I said, holding on to his shoulders as he practically ripped me out of my pants. He just hummed so I kept talking. "Scoot more on the bed."

He did, pulling off his sweatpants as he went. I watched and was practically scandalized to see he wasn't wearing underpants. I took that as permission to stare. Really stare. Even though we had been alone at his parents', we hadn't had all night. There in the hotel room I didn't feel that pressure at all. So I traced over every dip of muscle, every tattoo. I visually followed every trail of hair to its conclusion. He hadn't been all the way hard when he took off his pants, but the longer I stared, the harder he got.

"I didn't think you were really serious about the voyeur thing," he said. The way he looped his big hand around his dick, however, was a dead giveaway that he didn't mind.

"That's just because you can't see yourself like this." I crawled onto the bed.

"How do you want to do this?" he asked.

I had one idea, but I didn't know how to say it without sounding like a dingus. It's not an easy position to get into. Not like being on top, which you can do just by kissing. *Now we see Jefferson hesitate—can he pick a play that will get his team into a better position on the field?*

"I have an idea."

Lucas glanced at the door. "The maid?"

"Just move your gigantic ass over, you take up like three-fourths of the bed."

I tried to swat his leg, but he grabbed my arm, pulling me down. We grappled for a second. I ended up on my back.

"Your plan sounds great, but first..." he said with a grin.

"You don't even know my plan," I grumbled, only half meaning it. I was a little alarmed at how easy it was for him to get me on my back. I lost my train of thought when he gripped my dick and traced his tongue across the top.

"Fucking geez," I groaned.

His lips closed around my dick and I lost track of a few seconds, focusing on his mouth and his hand. The rest of his body warmed my legs, and he rubbed my torso with his free hand. It was all-encompassing and exactly distracting. I ran my hands over the soft curls on his head, still damp from his shower, and his broad shoulders, thick with muscle.

But I remembered my plan. I really wanted the chance to explore him. I didn't stop him right away, though. I wasn't a fool. I did open my eyes and I watched him. He was fucking beautiful, the bright colors alive on his skin as he moved.

"Fuck, that feels amazing," I said.

I could feel his smile. He intensified his sucking and licking, and I almost couldn't stop myself from jerking, trying to go deeper. There was a line, though, a narrow decision-making channel that turned *I want to fuck him* into *I want to come in his mouth*. I was approaching that line fast, but I wasn't going to cross it.

"God, Lucas," I moaned.

"Don't worry," he said, his breath creating a chill over my spit slick cock. "I'm not going to let you come like this."

"Could've fooled me."

"Naw, I just wanted a taste," he said.

Free of his mouth, I was able to think a little better and gestured for him to come back up the bed. He did, settling himself over me. I kissed him, finding a different way to get lost and distracted by his mouth. His dick was hard against mine. I reached between us and stroked the length of it with the tips of my fingers. He gasped against my lips. Somehow, he was too close but not close enough. No, maybe *I* was too close and yet not close enough.

"Can you reach the condom?" I asked.

He looked at me through one eye and then scanned the room. He snagged it and the lube and handed them to me.

"On your side?" I asked, trying to make it sound as much like a question as not.

"Facing which way?" he asked.

I looked around. "Window...wall?"

"No, who are you, Lil John? I mean facing you or away?"

I snorted. "Oh. Away."

He smiled, exasperated, and rolled. The bed was smaller than it looked. They probably weren't the queen beds we'd been told they were. Or maybe I was just used to my king back at the house.

"Oh, man," he said, snuggling against me ass to dick. "Maybe I should just go to sleep."

"I'd love to see you try."

I felt happier than a penguin in a snow pile. There he was spread out before me, against me, without me being in the way. His back was a warm, long stretch of strength and movement. I pressed against him, trying to find the warmest parts. I propped on one arm so I could see around him too, his sides and his arms and his legs.

I kissed his neck, biting and sucking because I had space and time enough to fill up on him. I ran my hands down his side and around to the front of his body. This side of his body was a jungle of flowers and butterflies and hummingbirds. Mixed in were dark lines and shading, jagged by design, turning the skin under the bright flowers and animals into wood, like a freshly cut tree. I followed those lines down to where they met up with a grim reaper on his thigh that pointed down to a nurse near his calf in some creepy *Creation of Adam* image.

Looking him over, he seemed more tattoo than skin. I loved it. I had only gotten glimpses of these lower tattoos the last time we had sex. It was him, all of his feelings and hurts and growth processed out on his body in carefully chosen images. I wanted to run my hands over every line, though one place was untouched by ink. I traced a path toward his dick. All this time he had simply, quietly lain there, not still but not demanding, watching me explore him.

"You're fuckin' beautiful," I said.

He was going to say something, but I gripped his cock and that stopped his words. I stroked and he rocked back against me, echoing my movement. He rotated slightly so he could kiss me. I kissed him, then I let him have my mouth as I focused on his dick. I opted for slow, massaging strokes. I wanted to make him come with me inside him but that didn't mean I couldn't get him closer. His breathing became short and quick, and the kissing became less complete, more open mouthed and airy. I liked the way he jerked into my fist and back, his ass rubbing against my dick.

There was a second of peace, me looking down at him, his mouth open, eyes closed, whole body reacting to me. He opened his eyes briefly as I watched him, and he smiled at me. I half expected him to say something loving or blubber the way people can during sex.

Instead, he warned, "You have about three seconds to get whatever else you had in mind together before I fucking have my way with your hand."

"Don't threaten me with a good time."

I rolled and he sat up to watch me. I felt like a goof, but I knew his observation was just a product of his impatience. I almost laughed as he watched me fumble with the plastic seal on the new bottle of lube.

"Hey," he said after a minute.

"What?"

"I'd like to have sex before we have to check out tomorrow."

I got it a half second later and he took the bottle. I was more than happy to sit back as he poured some on my cock. He gave the bottle back and held out his fingers for some. I obliged. He rolled his hips, exposing his ass to me. I watched as he applied the lube, working his fingers against his hole. He topped the whole display off with a wink. I grinned.

When he was ready, I put myself back into place behind him. He kept his mouth toward me, so I kissed him. The alignment of our bodies, his hard muscular ass pressing against my groin, one thick leg hooking over mine, was almost perfect enough that I could have entered him without using my hand. But I adjusted myself anyway, holding in place so the slow way he rolled his hips pushed me deeper inside him.

"Fuck, I...God," I heard myself moan.

"You don't have to be gentle," he said, breathing shallowly against my mouth.

I was ready for a rough sort of gentle. I shifted enough to pour the lube on my palm and tossed the bottle somewhere. I put the arm I had been leaning on under his neck and around one shoulder, giving me perfect access to his chest and neck and face, then turned him back toward me, demanding more of his mouth and tongue. Stroking his dick with the other hand, I spread the lube as he thrust for more.

"Fuck," he whispered, "harder."

I obliged. I closed my hand tighter around his dick and fucked deeper, banging my hips against him. That completed everything: mouths and dicks and bodies, connected and in use. It was impressive how much of a person you could hold, be in and around, from that position. He was exposed and completely under my control and absolutely in control, setting the pace. His mouth fell away after a few perfectly linked seconds, and all of his attention became the tempo of his body working.

"Shit, you're so hot like this," I said.

It was weird hearing my voice and getting nothing but a sharp exhale and a clench around my cock to show he was listening. I watched his perfect face. His eyes were closed and a sheen of sweat had broken out on both our bodies. I loved watching the cords of his neck tighten, the abs and thighs contract with the effort of working on my dick.

"I love this," I said in his ear.

I shifted slightly, creating an angle that would give him the last half inch or so of my dick. He moaned. His hand came around mine, around his own dick. It wasn't to direct me or to change what I was doing. He maybe just needed something to hold on to. The change of angle inspired him to pick up speed. I added small, equal movements of my own. It meant shortening my own ability to hold out by about half, but he didn't seem far off. I wanted to see it. I wanted to watch him melt with pleasure. I used the arm around his chest to pull him closer.

Heat piled in my body, wanting to explode from me. All of me wanted to give up on holding out and dive in. He beat me to it. His whole body tensed around me and he inhaled, holding his breath, squeezing my hand against his dick, and thrusting two or three more times. Cum oozed over our hands. He started to relax, panting and unclenching.

"Keep going," he managed to say before recapturing my mouth.

I lost anything that looked like focus. His mouth, hot and wet, reconnected that circle from my dick inside him to my tongue inside him. I was aware of thrusting and squeezing his body to me. I let go of his cock and held on with both hands, using him. Those last thrusts turned my orgasm into a missile, and I came hard and fast. He held me as best he could from that angle. There were a few moments of relative quiet. His breathing was long and lulling. We adjusted only so far as to ditch the condom and haphazardly wipe up. Then we were back together in bed. I held on to him and tried to calculate how long a nap I could get before dinner.

"Al."

"Babe," I said mostly into his shoulder.

"Are you disappointed we didn't go sightseeing?"

I snorted. "A little. I might cry later."

He laughed. There was a stretch of silence. I thought maybe he had gone to sleep. I thought maybe I had.

"Al."

I grunted.

"Do you want to be my partner?" he asked.

"Yeah, I do, but I get to plan the next vacation. This one kinda sucks."

His response was to shove me off the bed into the gap between it and the wall.

CHAPTER TWENTY-ONE

Lucas

"Probably not until after midnight," I told Ky when she asked when we expected to get home. I was sitting on the edge of the bed tying my shoes. Al came out of the bathroom, a billow of steam following him. He had the smallest towel around his waist.

Are you on the phone? he mouthed at me.

"Yeah, it's a video call." I laughed, turning the phone so Ky and Al could see each other.

Al glared at me but waved at Ky. "Hey."

"Hello, Khaki Daddy," Ky said, pantomiming looking over the rims of glasses for a better view.

"Ky," I warned.

"Khaki Daddy, that's funny." Dani howled.

Al looked at me. "How many wives are on that call?"

I turned the phone back on me and held up my hands. "They called me."

"I wanted to know when you were getting home, but he said you were in the shower. Lucas, turn the camera back so I can get a screen shot," Dani said with a laugh.

"Can you do that?" Al asked.

"Duh, shouldn't you know?" I said, confused.

He put his underwear on without removing his towel. I didn't turn the phone back.

"What?" he said.

"You take screenshots in this app all the time."

He actually blushed. "How do you know?"

I laughed harder. "It tells me every time you do it."

"It tells people?"

"Damn it, Lucas, Teach and I have a bet every year about who gets more screenshot alerts," Dani said.

The three of us cackled at Al's expense. He just frowned and dressed. When he was totally covered, he crossed to me and held out his hand. I gave him the phone.

"Bye, wives," he said and hung up the call. That sent me into another round of cackling.

"Are you ready to go?" he asked. The corners of his mouth turned up. He was trying to look annoyed, but it wasn't working.

"Baw, I think it's cute," I said, trying to pull him toward me. A semi-gentle wrestling match progressed, and I ended up on my belly face-down on the bed with one arm behind my back. I was laughing so hard I couldn't even say uncle.

"You're a dingus," he huffed, letting me up. He kissed me as freely and as easily as if he'd been doing it for years. I followed him out to the truck, kicking the underside of his feet half trying to trip him.

Both that morning and the night before, we had taken full advantage of having the room to ourselves, using all four condoms he'd brought. We'd also slept together, in the "non-sex bed," as Al called it. It felt exact and casual in the way true compatibility can sometimes. I honestly could have been on vacation.

We had a conversation over dinner about what it would take to be partners. It amazed us both how differently we thought about the title. Even when I got frustrated, he didn't back down, insisting I explain what I wanted and needed from him. I wasn't really used to starting with myself. By the end of the conversation, I was elated and terrified. We were really going to give this a shot.

Packing up and checking out didn't take long. I had gotten a text from Chandler confirming our brunch plans, and I had confirmed for us. I wasn't as sad or angry or confused or bereaved as I had been the afternoon before. It was all there, but some of it had receded into the past. Enough good had come from the trip that it was worth it even if nothing deep or fatherly grew from my relationship with DeAndrew. I had pretty much decided I was going to keep talking to him. Maybe I'd call. Or maybe I'd write so he had something tangible.

"You know, if Chekhov gave directions like you, the *Enterprise* would've been lost in space," Al said.

I blinked back to the reality of being in the truck with him. "Ask Google, grandpa. Sorry I couldn't print you out the MapQuest directions."

"Penny for your thoughts?" he asked.

I shrugged and told him I was thinking about how to stay in contact with DeAndrew. I also gave better directions to the restaurant. This time it was a ritzy-looking pub-style place with mostly elderly white people in yacht shoes and pearls. Chandler waved at us from a table by the front windows. He was dressed in a suit, so the only identifying thing about him was his bright, tropical blue Miami Dolphins snap-back.

"Damn, I'd say I'm underdressed, but I did bring a white guy, so that's got to count for something." I laughed, shaking Chandler's hand.

"This seems like a nice place," Al said, looking around like he had never been anywhere that had actual tablecloths.

"Look, don't let it fool you, in about twenty minutes a Judy or a Carol is going to get into a full-on fist fight with a Martha or a June. This might be a nice place, but it's still the South, and the mimosas are bottomless. Besides, your grandmother owns this place."

I looked around, floored. Then my anger flared. "If she owns something like this, why does DeAndrew Junior walk around starving?"

Chandler put his hands up. "I know...I know, but you're walking in on the fifth inning, nephew. Welcome to the team."

I took a breath. Al patted my back and asked, "Is she here, your mother?"

Chandler sighed. "Ma Nation? She's not my mother. She's DeAndrew's, but she's gotten used to me over the years. That's also why things with Latisha are the way they are. Latisha is Ma Nation's youngest and her hellraiser, but she felt like Ma left her to clean up after our father. Ma really has tried with Latisha. Anyway, Ma is on a culinary journey in Europe right now. But I wanted you to see the place. Besides, do you think you could've handled a grandmother too? I thought you were going to melt like a wax figure in hell the way you left the nursing home."

"I wouldn't have melted," I grumbled. Al made a face as if to disagree. I just kneed his leg under the table. He laughed.

Chandler smirked at us. Then he reached down and pulled a photo album out of the bag he had set near his chair. He handed it to me.

"What's this?" I asked, taking the black book. It said *Memories* on the front.

"It's DeAndrew's. I asked him if I could borrow it."

I opened it. Inside were pictures of absolute strangers whose faces were almost familiar.

"I...I guess I wanted you to see how he was...how we were. I used to go to a support group for people who had family with memory loss. It was a lot of dementia and Alzheimer's families, but it was nice. The only thing was I couldn't decide who had it better. They talked about their loved ones losing their memories slowly. A little, then a little more. That part I couldn't relate to. Then I was surprised by how many of them would finish their stories with 'then all of a sudden, they didn't know me anymore.'"

"The speed of slow changes," Al said softly.

Chandler smiled at him. "Right. But for me, it was all at once. DeAndrew was fine one day and then the accident. To him I'll always be twenty-one. Or at least that's what we thought."

"What do you mean?" Al asked.

I wanted to ask, but I was too engrossed in the photos. Him behind the wheel of a car holding the keys. A woman and a man holding a puppy, DeAndrew laughing beside them. Him in profile looking out a window. A woman, his mother probably, cutting the ribbon in front of this very restaurant. Painted Waters, Albany. Me—

I froze. In the back few pages of the book were my senior photo and, next to that, the letter I wrote when I was a kid. I looked up at Chandler, and he shrugged, already looking at me.

"I went over there this morning and I asked him if I could borrow his book. He said sure. Then for no reason at all he opened to that photo and said, 'The kid at the back is named Lucas, he's got my genes.'"

I lost sight of Chandler through the tears suddenly in my eyes.

"He remembered?" Al gasped.

Chandler shook his head. "Who knows? Years ago after he told me about you, Lucas, he let me look through the book. Whenever I've looked through it with him, he says certain things at each photo, even now the same thing every time. But at your photo, he'd only look at that picture with pride, then move on. He said that exact sentence once and never again until this morning."

"What's it mean?" I asked, wiping my face on my unknown grandmother's fancy napkin.

"I'm not really sure. Maybe nothing. Maybe you mattered to him even when you thought you didn't."

Al put a hand on my knee. I looked at him in a way that I hoped was reassuring.

"Sirs, what can I—oh, do you need a minute?" the waiter asked.

"Naw...wait, I mean yes, we haven't looked at the menu," I said, closing the photo album. I would have to sit with that for a while. I didn't know how to feel about my father keeping my photo, my letter. Mostly I realized, sitting across from my uncle and next to my partner, that I missed my mothers.

❖

Al and I started the drive home right from the restaurant. Chandler said he'd call as soon as he was back in Georgia. He had some news to follow up on in California. I texted Ky and Dani that we were on the road. To my surprise, Al put on one of the audiobooks I suggested. It was my favorite horror novel. I fell deeper in love, watching him grimace and groan as the tension in the novel progressed. He made it three hours.

"I can't," he shouted, pausing the book when the killer stepped into the nursery.

"He doesn't kill the baby," I said. Al looked at me. All right, maybe he was looking a little green. "Okay, okay…thank you for trying."

I took his phone to turn on his radio app for him.

"Is it weird that book reminds me of Wynona?" He half laughed.

"Who? The killer?"

"No, the parents. They don't even believe their kids!"

"Al, do you want me to tell you how it ends? I'm worried you're taking this personally," I said, taking his hand.

"It's *your* favorite book," he snapped, teasing.

"Trust me, my high school therapist was worried."

His phone rang. He pressed answer on the steering wheel. "You got Al."

"What's up with Coach?" Teach said.

"Uh, I left him with you, so…" Al said tiredly.

"Is he okay? Seizures?" I asked.

"Naw, not health. I know he texted you, but he's being a cryptic weirdo."

"Oh, that. No, he said he had news, but that's all he told me," Al said.

"That's all he told me and Bets too. I thought he'd tell you more. Fuck, I wanna know," Teach shouted. "Okay, bye."

And he hung up.

"News?" I asked.

"News," Al confirmed.

❖

A month of holidays and joy passed before we found out what Jeffery Jefferson's news was. That year's Christmas was one of the best I'd had in the last few years. It took a week of trial and error to get Al's new shorter work schedule to work for us, but it felt amazing to have that time together. I had been feeling relatively lonely for the past year, without patients and with my friends being far away and Ky traveling. But Al filled those spaces for me. He came with a whole world, his kids and wife and father and siblings, all passing through my days. And of course, there was Chandler and DeAndrew Junior and my mothers. Come the new year, I felt as if I had stepped into a new life. It was scarily beautiful.

I was reflecting on this when Ky, Lila, my mothers, and I arrived at Grace's the third weekend in January. Ky got out of the truck first to get Lila's seat buckle, then Jojo hopped out and Silvy went to help Ky. But I paused behind the steering wheel and watched people going into the restaurant. Betsy Ross and her husband were holding the door for Paul, Al's business partner, someone who I had yet to meet formally but felt like I already knew. Al's van pulled in right after us, and children were already pouring from it.

"What a crowd," Ky said when I finally exited the car.

"Right?"

"What's this for again?" Jojo asked.

"All Al said was Coach had something he wanted to celebrate." That reminded me to grab the sparkling cider from the back seat.

"Lucas, Ky," I heard.

"Hi, Rose," I said, rushing out of the truck and taking her into my arms. She was radiant in her blue winter coat and furry boots. Her blond bangs peeked out from under her hat. "You remember my parents?"

"Of course, Silvy, Jojo—you look great. Lucas, you look well. How was your trip?" she asked.

"Who told you about that?"

She winked at me. "Word gets around in a small town."

"Al told us," Fin said, trailing behind her. His fiancé trailed behind him. I hugged them both.

"Al told who what?" Al asked, coming up behind me.

As a group we moved toward the restaurant, talking over each other, absorbing Ky and Lila as we went. Lila loved Rose more than anyone, so she ditched us in favor of her as fast as she could.

The inside of Grace's was alive with people, feeling more like a family reunion than I would have expected. Coach had rented out Grace's for a private party in order to announce his mysterious news. I did my best to talk to everyone as we waited on Coach and Teach to arrive. At some point, I ended up at the bar talking with Ms. Wilhelmina.

"I know Chandler's mother," she was saying.

"Excuse me, sorry. Can I get a beer?" a very tired voice asked.

Both Ms. Wilhelmina and I looked over. It was John Adams. I didn't say anything, I just looked back at Ms. Wilhelmina.

"What're ya having, Gage?" she asked.

He told her. Then he looked at me.

"Hello," he practically mumbled.

"Hey, John Adams," I said.

"Gage," he said. Ms. Wilhelmina brought him his drink, and I expected him to take it and walk away. Instead, he turned to me. "Thanks, by the way."

"For?"

He hunched, looking more uncomfortable than I had ever seen him. "Helpin' Al out when the girls were sick."

I tipped my glass to him. "I got you."

He made a face that looked like a mix of pain and annoyance. Or at least it would have on anyone else. He was a grimy-looking man most of the time, but for this event he had cleaned up and even had his sandy blond hair combed back in a TV show drug dealer sort of way that, for all his faults, wasn't unattractive. I realized his weird expression was him making a decision.

He put out his hand, thick and empty. I looked at it. Then, more by instinct than anything else, I took it. For the first time in the months we had known each other, Gage Jefferson and I shook hands. He nodded once and looked as if he were going to say something, but the room erupted in a deafening cheer. We both turned toward the sound.

Coach and Teach came into the restaurant. Teach dipped out of the path of the attention fairly quickly and Coach waved his hands to try and silence the crowd. He looked well, his face bright from the cold. He had a manila envelope in his hands. The room finally fell silent.

"I bet you all are wondering what this is about?" he said softly.

I met Ky's eyes across the room, and she shrugged and squinted suspiciously at Jeffery Jefferson. They had met over an impromptu Christmas gathering at Al's house when she, Lila, and I went over there to drop off a gift for their household. I waved at her and moved into the crowd to try to hear him better over the sound of the giggling children. That brought me shoulder to shoulder with Al. Al felt me step up beside him, because without hesitation his hand came around mine. Everyone here knew, and if my handshake with Gage said anything, no one here cared that Al and I were together, no one cared that we were married and dating, queer and interracial—none of it.

"Well, most of the time people get together to celebrate happy things," Coach said.

A small murmur went around the room.

"Nothing happier than a finalized divorce, I guess," Coach said, grinning.

There was a moment of confused silence. We all looked at each other. I wasn't quite sure how to put two and two together. Coach stared back at us, his shit-eating grin more pronounced than I had ever seen it.

"You mean from Wynona?" Al asked.

"No, son, my other wife," Coach said before doubling over with heaving laughter.

The room erupted as his news sank in. Everyone cheered wildly, and his oldest sons lifted him onto their shoulders like he had just won a sporting event.

"I've never celebrated a divorce," I said to Dani, laughing. We had been pushed around in the swarming crowd and ended up shoved into a booth out of the way of the parade of Coach and his children.

She whistled with two fingers, high-fived Coach as he passed, then leaned back into me and said behind her hand, "I hope it gave Wynona a heart attack."

On principle, I didn't usually wish ill health on people. Looking at the Jefferson family and the distance they had come to undo the damage she had done, I figured I could make an exception.

About the Author

Sander completed his master of science from Purdue University in 2017 and has been published in scientific journals, is a speaker for Ignite Talks, and is a published poet. Wanting to see more of himself in fiction, his works feature LGBT characters and characters of color. He lives in South Florida with his partner, his best friend, and their many pets. As a Colorado native, he spends too much time telling Floridians how great the mountains are.

Books Available From Bold Strokes Books

The Speed of Slow Changes by Sander Santiago. As Al and Lucas navigate the ups and downs of their polyamorous relationship, only one thing is certain: romance has never been so crowded. (978-1-63679-329-0)

Felix Navidad by Nathan Burgoine. After the wedding of a good friend, instead of Felix's Hawaii Christmas treat to himself, ice rain strands him in Ontario with fellow wedding guest—and handsome ex of said friend—Kevin in a small cabin for the holiday Felix definitely didn't plan on. (978-1-63679-411-2)

Manny Porter and The Yuletide Murder by D.C. Robeline. Manny only has the holiday season to discover who killed prominent research scientist Phillip Nikolaidis before the judicial system condemns an innocent man to lethal injection. (978-1-63679-313-9)

Corpus Calvin by David Swatling. Cloverkist Inn may be haunted, but a ghost materializes from Jason Dekker's past and Calvin's canine instinct kicks in to protect a young boy from mortal danger. (978-1-62639-428-5)

Murder at Union Station by David S. Pederson. Private Detective Mason Adler struggles to determine who killed a woman found in a trunk without getting himself killed in the process. (978-1-63679-269-9)

A Champion for Tinker Creek by D.C. Robeline. Lyle James has rescued his dad's auto repair business, but when city hall condemns his neighborhood, Lyle learns only trusting will save his life and help him find love. (978-1-63679-213-2)

Heckin' Lewd: Trans and Nonbinary Erotica, edited by Mx. Nillin Lore. If you want smutty, fearless, gender diverse erotica written by affirming own-voices folks who get it, then this is the book you've been looking for! (978-1-63679-240-8)

Inherit the Lightning by Bud Gundy. Darcy O'Brien and his sisters learn they are about to inherit an immense fortune, but a family mystery about to unravel after seventy years threatens to destroy everything. (978-1-63679-199-9)

Pursued: Lillian's Story by Felice Picano. Fleeing a disastrous marriage to the Lord Exchequer of England, Lillian of Ravenglass reveals an incident-filled, often bizarre, tale of great wealth and power, perfidy, and betrayal. (978-1-63679-197-5)

Murder on Monte Vista by David S. Pederson. Private Detective Mason Adler's angst at turning fifty is forgotten when his "birthday present," the handsome, young Henry Bowtrickle, turns up dead, and it's up to Mason to figure out who did it, and why. (978-1-63679-124-1)

Three Left Turns to Nowhere by Jeffrey Ricker, J. Marshall Freeman & 'Nathan Burgoine. Three strangers heading to a convention in Toronto are stranded in rural Ontario, where a small town with a subtle kind of magic leads each to discover what he's been searching for. (978-1-63679-050-3)

One Verse Multi by Sander Santiago. Life was good: promotion, friends, falling in love, discovering that the multi-verse is on a fast track to collision—wait, what? Good thing Martin King works for a company that can fix the problem, right…um…right? (978-1-63679-069-5)

Fresh Grave in Grand Canyon by Lee Patton. The age-old Grand Canyon becomes more and more ominous as a group of volunteers fight to survive alone in nature and uncover a murderer among them. (978-1-63679-047-3)

Loyalty, Love & Vermouth by Eric Peterson. A comic valentine to a gay man's family of choice, including the ones with cold noses and four paws. (978-1-63555-997-2)

Bury Me in Shadows by Greg Herren. College student Jake Chapman is forced to spend the summer at his dying grandmother's home and soon finds danger from long-buried family secrets. (978-1-63555-993-4)

Best of the Wrong Reasons by Sander Santiago. For Fin Ness and Orion Starr, it takes a funeral to remind them that love is worth living for. (978-1-63555-867-8)

A Different Man by Andrew L. Huerta. This diverse collection of stories chronicling the challenges of gay life at various ages shines a light on the progress made and the progress still to come. (978-1-63555-977-4)